A DEPARTMENT
FO.R. FULL DISCl
THAT LED T
WILLIAMS AF'.

Carla Williams, a mother of three and popular high school teacher, undergoes a routine surgery which does not go as planned. Department Chair, Harold Thompson, becomes an unlikely ally when he vows to find and share the truth about what happened to Carla. Thompson reassures Carla's distraught physician as he becomes convinced that the surgeon did nothing wrong. Despite the hospital's pledge of transparency, once the requisite investigation is completed, Thompson's efforts to keep his word collide with the institution's traditions of secrecy and finger-pointing. The Department Chair's quest to reveal the truth results in accusations of unprofessional conduct, and he is targeted by the hospital's power brokers who move to revoke his hospital privileges and fire him. What began as a fight for full disclosure also becomes a fight for Thompson's career and his reputation.

Excerpt

Warren struggled, "If this isn't a true emergency, I don't know what the hell..."

He looked at Carla and then quickly up at Sue. They both realized Carla wasn't breathing. Warren ignored whatever authority Pauline had. He moved toward the door ahead of him. The group followed his instructions and pushed the gurney through the door marked "O.R. 3."

"Call a code now!" he yelled, while letting down the gurney's side rail. With the first two fingers of his right hand, Warren felt the weak, thready pulse in Carla's neck. He fought the tsunami of anxiety and raw fear that was poised to overwhelm him. Instead, without hesitation, he started mouth-to-mouth resuscitation. Sue located a hand held resuscitation balloon bag and handed it to Warren. He formed a tight seal over Carla's mouth and nose with the face cover portion of the device, and rhythmically squeezed air into her lungs with his right hand. Janie connected an oxygen line to the bag's side port.

A FIGHT FO.R. FULL DISCLOSURE

Stanley M. Berry

Moonshine Cove Publishing, LLC

Abbeville, South Carolina U.S.A.

First Moonshine Cove Edition
September 2021

ISBN: 9781952439162

Library of Congress LCCN: 2021916262

© Copyright 2021 by Stanley M. Berry

This book is a work of fiction. Names, characters, businesses, places, events, conversations, opinions, and incidents are either products of the author's imagination or are used fictitiously. Any resemblance to actual events, locales, conversations, opinions, business establishments, or persons, living or dead, is entirely coincidental and unintended.

All rights reserved. No part of this book may be reproduced in whole or in part without written permission from the publisher except by reviewers who may quote brief excerpts in connection with a review in a newspaper, magazine or electronic publication; nor may any part of this book be reproduced, stored in a retrieval system or transmitted in any form or by any means electronic, mechanical, photocopying, recording or any other means, without written permission from the publisher.

Front cover courtesy of the author; back cover image public domain, interior design by Moonshine Cove staff

This novel is dedicated to the memory of my parents Pauline S. and Stanley M. Berry, to the memories of my sisters Alyce, Robin and Sharon, and to my remaining sister Holly A. Berry and to my wife Shelley Carthen Watson.

About the Author

Stanley M. Berry is a Maternal-Fetal Medicine physician who has provided care to women with high risk pregnancies for 37 years. Although Dr. Berry has authored or co-authored a large number of medical publications, *A Fight For Full Disclosure* is his debut novel. He was born and raised in Minnesota, and from age eight, lived in a working class north Minneapolis neighborhood. His professional musician and music teacher father, along with his social worker and university faculty member mother, passed to him a love of music, reading, and a respect for hard work. These values were reinforced by his public school education which he received through the 9th grade. The author received a full scholarship to a Vermont boy's boarding school where he finished grades 10 through 12. A major in English literature was his goal as an undergraduate freshman, but after floundering and dropping in and out of college over a four-year period, he read Ernest Hemingway's *A Farewell To Arms*, and like the novel's protagonist, the author joined an ambulance service in Minneapolis and was trained as an emergency paramedic. He found his calling and was eventually admitted to medical school where he graduated in 1984. He completed an Obstetrics and Gynecology Residency followed by a Maternal-Fetal Medicine Fellowship. Although he refers to himself as a, "failed English major," Dr. Berry never lost his passion for creative writing or his goal of communicating his ideas about the world of medicine and medical research through the medium of fiction.

stanleymberry.com

Thank You

This is a list of some friends who taught me, encouraged me, and helped me create this story. This list is by no means all inclusive. Please forgive me for my omissions. Thank you to all of you.

Dr. Hallie Hendrieth-Smith	Kovida Rao	Kypros Nicolaides
Jack W. Moskowitz	Ann Massion	Rupinder Bhatia
Nida Williams	Kathy McKendry	Kathy Parsons
Brian Mason	Devi Lashkar	Roger Blakeley
Shery Cotton	Theresa and John Uckele	Sung Kyu Kim
David Cotton	Jonathan Sisler	Gerrit Roelofs
Honor Wolfe	Sonia Hassan	Theodofs Vlachos
Elsa and Marianne Brown	Ted Bermingham	Harold Brake
Marc Clark	Mahmoud El-Kati	Laura Moody
Timothy Clark	Mitch Dombrowski	Christine Wade
Betram Days	Sidney Bottoms	Kathleen and Richard Garrett
Stacy and Harold Henry	Lenora Smith	Richard Longfellow
Owens and Robbie Franklin	Angela Musey	Andrea Coleman
Richard Woldorsky	Daniel Becker	Sean Blackwell
Earl Schwartz	Alyce Hamilton	Ralph Valitutti
Napoleon Knight	Maureen Dumphy	Nate Paul
Joseph Wartts	John Dalton	Sherry Griffin
Kwaku Wartts	Ton Jenks	Tia Ramsey
	Roberto Romero	

Principal Characters

Carla Bethany Williams – Mother of three and popular high school teacher who has an unexpected outcome after a routine surgery

Sylvia Williams – Carla's mother

Warren Chambers - Carla's surgeon

Harold Thompson – Winslow's Ob/Gyn Department Chair who gets involved in Carla's case

Henry Davidson – Winslow's Chief Safety Officer

Victor Sedaris – Senior Ob/Gyn Appointed to the Sentinel Event Committee

Dr. Sam Reinhardt – Former Chair of Winslow's Ob/Gyn Department

Dr. Michael Isaacs – Chief Medical Officer who replaced Dr. Richard Caruthers

Dr. Martin Octavio – An old medical school friend of Thompson's

Dr. Celia Green – Chair of the Professional Conduct Committee

Marshall Cummings – A Winslow Administrator and Ron Blazer's Brother-in-Law

Dr. Michael Stewart – Vascular Surgeon and Member of the Professional Conduct Committee

A Fight For Full Disclosure

Chapter One

Carla Williams was gripped by the high-speed traffic of her nonstop thoughts and memories. She lay on the living room couch of her modest bungalow half watching a video with her oldest son Christopher. It was almost 10 p.m., and she was exhausted from a demanding week of high school teaching and coaching, along with the attendant counseling and mentoring. Her current state of mind was also dragging on her emotions. She was a single mother with 3 youngsters who, as she would tell friends, "...drain the love and energy right outta me."

Christopher sprang to his knees from the pillowed position on the carpet he had taken just beneath his mother and shouted,

"Momma did you see that?"

She shifted her eyes to see a freshly born Beluga Whale trailing its mother.

"That little whale just came out of its mother."

His excitement, for a moment, took Carla's attention off the mental race track she was cruising.

"Sweetheart," she said, doing what she believed was an excellent job of masking her inner terror, "that's how baby whales are born."

He turned quickly back to the screen. The nine-year-old loved nature videos, and he frequently recited the facts he learned from them to almost anyone he spoke with. Carla returned to her rush of ideas and memories. She had a surgery coming up in 3 days, and the unease in the pit of her stomach grew each day over the last week. She was convinced she did not have cancer — none of her tests showed that, and she invested many hours online over the previous month reading about "band aid surgery" hysterectomies as well as the traditional methods. She convinced herself the procedure she was going to have was safe, yet...

"Momma are you sick?"

"Why are you asking me that sweetheart?"

"Because, you're goin' to the hospital on Monday."

"But, Chris, didn't mama tell you that the doctors had to do some fixin' on me?"

"Yeah, but hospitals are where sick people go. Are you sick?"

"No baby, momma's not sick."

"Then why, why do you have to go to the hospital on Monday?"

"Chris, if you were out playing basketball and you fell and broke your wrist, would you be sick?"

"No, I'd just have a broken bone."

"Then tell mamma what you think sick is."

"Sick is like, like — hmm... It's like when you have a cold, or... like Davy Sawyer whose blood turned against him, and he had to go to the hospital and he lost all his hair and got real skinny."

"That's right honey, and mama's not sick, she has like a broken part in her tummy, and the doctors are gonna look inside me with a special microscope and fix it, and then everything's gonna be fine. I won't be bald, but too bad, I'll still be fat, just like you like me."

Christopher giggled at his mom's joke, and his worry seemed to fade. Although Carla no longer had her athletic physique of sixteen years earlier when she was a star college varsity basketball player, she was at most 10 pounds heavier.

"It's time for bed young man. Tomorrow's not gonna be a sleepin'-in Saturday. We're all gettin' up early to go grocery shoppin' and then we're goin' to see that new cartoon movie you and your brother have been pesterin' me about."

"*Yes*," he said emphatically while jerking both outstretched index fingers downward, "*The Space Crawlers*!"

"That's right. Now it's time for you to join Xavier and Elise in dreamland."

They shared their delighted smiles.

"Come here and give your mama a hug and a kiss, and then it's off to bed."

Carla's embrace enveloped her son who was the product of a friendly union gone awry. His father did not want a child, but stayed involved through the first weeks of Christopher's life until emotions, the genesis of which neither he or Carla understood, motivated him to walk out. He rationalized his abandonment, never returning. And now, with moistened eyes, but a calm, steady voice Carla whispered into Christopher's ear,

"While mama's away, you're the man of the house. You look after your brother and your little sister — always, you hear me?"

"I will mama."

"No teasing, 'cause you know it upsets Big Mama."

"Okay, mama, I won't."

"And, you do what big mama tells you, no arguing — you hear me?"

"Yes, mama."

"Chris, you know how much I love you and your brother and sister don't you?"

He broke away and stretched his arms as wide as he could, and with a broad smile said,

"This much."

"That's right, baby, this much."

Both had outstretched arms now. They came close, clapped one another's hands and embraced again, laughing.

"Shhh, Shhh, you'll wake them up." she told him through his giggles. The outstretched arms and clapping hands were a year's long ritual for them.

"Now it's off to bed brother."

Carla lay back on the couch, alone. Her last conscious thoughts were about her children, "what if...," and her students, especially the girls who she knew looked up to her.

***

Three days later, at 5:30 a.m., Carla stood with her mother Sylvia at Winslow Medical Center's pre-op sign-in desk on the second floor. The hospital's main operating rooms were housed there. Carla was directed to the third of seven consecutive small partitioned areas located along the twenty-five-foot length of a slightly curved piece of mahogany that served as a desk top. She took a seat and fidgeted with the pen in front of her while answering questions for the registration clerk.

"Name please?"

"Carla Bethany Williams."

"Date of Birth?"

"January 20th, 1965"

"Name of the surgery you're having?"

"They call it a laparoscopic hysterectomy."

The clerk checked off Carla's answers on her intake sheet, confirming that the nervous appearing woman sitting before her was the correct patient listed for the correct surgery. In five minute**s,** they were finished.

"Ms. Williams, here's a pamphlet that outlines your surgery and describes the risks and benefits of the procedure. I'm sure you've read this before, but please, take a few minutes and go through it now, before the folks upstairs give you the final consent form to sign. It's short and very basic. If you have questions about it, you need to ask your doctor when you see him just before the surgery."

"I will."

"Now, Ms. Williams, if you'll have a seat right here in the waiting area," the clerk motioned with her left hand, "I'll be back with your ID bracelets in just a few minutes."

Carla took the seat next to Sylvia, and handed the pamphlet to her mother. Sylvia read while Carla looked up at the 45-foot-high ceiling with a rush of zooming thoughts. *The risk is, I will never see my kids again, never breathe or feel or have thoughts again. Those are the damn risks, and none of them are spelled out in that little pamphlet.* The pit of her stomach was roiling her fears and anxiety. She felt a sharp sudden urge to jump up and run. Her grip on the arm rests of her chair tightened enough that her hands became numb. In her head she was thrashing and fighting for control, and her life. And, then, in an instant, her logic and rational self took primacy. Sylvia was lost in the pamphlet, never aware of her daughter's moment.

"Ms. Williams," the clerk motioned Carla to the desk. "This red wrist band is for you, and the blue one is for your mother." She invited Sylvia over and attached the bands to both women while explaining that Sylvia's would allow her to visit with her daughter in both the pre- and postop areas. The clerk told them Carla's surgery would be performed in an operating room on the 6th floor in the Labor and Delivery suite, and she directed them there.

Carla and Sylvia got off the elevator four floors up. There were five colored lines on the hospital floors near the walls. As instructed, they followed the pink line and walked the equivalent of a medium length city block across the hospital to the Labor and Delivery suite. They went directly to the sign-in desk they were directed to. The recently redecorated area was comforting and joyous with its pink and blue theme colors.

"Hi, Ms. Williams, I was expecting you," the sign-in clerk greeted. She was a tall, slender dark-skinned woman with a broad smile and beautiful teeth. "You must be Ms. Williamses' mother," she said shaking Sylvia's hand. "Are you Ms. Williams too?"

"Yes I am."

"If you'll wait here, Ms. Williams, I'll take your daughter back to the pre-op area where she'll change clothes and get a quick physical exam. That'll take about a half hour. When they're finished up with the exam, someone will come out to take you back so you can wait with her until it's time for her surgery."

"Thank you so much." I'll be in this front row of seats right here in the middle."

Carla was taken to a cubicle with a chair, a mattressed gurney, and a movable step. Once inside with the curtains drawn, she undressed and put on the white hospital smock, with its pattern of tiny green diamonds. She placed her clothes in the big see-through purple plastic bag she was given and covered her flaming mass of straightened reddish orange hair with a sheer light blue bouffant cap. Her hair inspired the nick name she was given by a guy she briefly dated in college — "Sun." Close friends and old classmates still called Carla Sun or Sunny. She used the single moveable step, with its hand rail, to climb up and sit on the gurney's four-inch thick sheeted mattress. Her caramel colored African American complexion, along with her hair color, still visible through the thin blue head cover, posed against her green speckled gown and the white sheets formed a tangle of discordant colors. She waited — chin and cheek resting in her right palm, with the elbow planted on her thigh. She looked at the floor and concentrated on her memories of Sam Brooks. He was the father of her youngest child, three-year-old Elise, and the only one of the 3 fathers of her children that she loved. *Thank God I realized that before he got sick.* She married Sam in the midst of his terminal illness, but she did not take his name. *If he were still here, he would take care of my babies like they were all his. Mama can do it if she has to, but it'll be hard for her at her age with those young babies.* Her emotions were welling up when she heard,

"Ms. Williams?" A voice called from the other side of the front cubical curtain.

"That's me. Come on in."

"Hi, Ms. Williams, I'm Amirah Hassan. I'm one of the nurse anesthetists, and I'm here to do a quick exam."

Listening to Carla's heart and lungs, examining her mouth for sores or loose teeth, along with palpating her neck for its shape while noting any abnormalities took Nurse Hassan less than ten minutes. She also got in several questions. Carla was alone again. Her impending loss was on her mind. *I know I don't want any more kids, but that's different than not being able to have more. I'm being silly but, still... Will sex be the same? Not like that's been an issue for way too long, Most of the stuff I read said yes, but you know you've heard some women say it ain't as good afterwards, course some say it's better, hell, I don't know...I don't know...*

Carla looked up to see Sylvia being ushered in by one of the nursing assistants.

"They sure are efficient around here," Sylvia said. She lowered herself into the single chair in the cubicle. "They said it would take about a half hour before I could come back, and that was 25 minutes ago."

"Well, I just wanna get this show on the road."

"Are you nervous?"

"A little. I'm just ready for all this to be over."

They sat in silence for a moment. Sylvia got up and took the two steps to Carla's gurney. Her only child was on her back with her upper body propped up by the 45-degree angle of the gurney's adjustable mattress. Standing by Carla's side, her mother reached over the gurney's rail and grasped her daughter's left hand.

"Let's pray, baby."

Sylvia said a short prayer asking God to "... guide the hands of Dr. Chambers and all his helpers. Please dear God, keep my baby safe." Carla was silent.

"The Lord is my shepherd, I shall not want..."

"Yea though I walk through the valley of the shadow of death...," Carla joined her mother, and they finished the prayer in unison.

"Do you feel better now?"

"Yeah, I do." Carla said this without conviction.

* * *

Warren Chambers concentrated on his reflection in the mirror while he finished shaving. He wiped off the excess lather with a warm moist washcloth and thought about how seldom the face he stared at smiled now days. *How did I ever get here?* There was just enough pre-sunrise March light for him to see the backyard Silver Maple through the bathroom window. Its branches were covered with buds that had not yet burst.

As was his habit before a major operation, Warren went over the step-by-step-progression of the hysterectomy he was to perform later that morning. The resident doctors would do most of the surgery, and his role would be more proctor than surgeon. His pre-operation mental walk through the case helped sharpen his attention to detail once the procedure started.

Warren's guilt over leaving his two young children gnawed at him while he prepared for his drive to the hospital. He often felt these emotions after a long, heated argument with Gina. They were in their ninth year of marriage, and for the last two years, screaming at one another was their primary medium for conveying marital passion. The themes of their verbal battles almost never varied.

"*Gina, you're spending over four hundred dollars a month on Lattes let alone the two grand on the rest of the frivolous crap you buy 'cause you can't keep your god damn credit card in your purse.*"

"*Fuck you, Warren! If you'd done what you should've done and stayed in private practice you could support your family like a man, instead of whining like a baby about a few bills.*"

Warren peeked in on his sleeping children. *I'd be completely miserable without you guys.* Neither six-year-old Chelsea nor four-year old Jason was awakened by their father's gentle opening and closing of their bedroom door.

He arrived at Winslow Medical Center and met Dr. Sally Woodson on the eighth floor Gynecology Ward. Sally was in the fourth and last year of her Obstetrics and Gynecology Residency. Warren looked forward to doing surgeries with this bright, enthusiastic young physician. She was the Chief Resident on the service and was, therefore, responsible for the two junior residents and the three medical students assigned to the gynecology rotation.

"Hi, Dr. Chambers," the medium height, natural blond doctor greeted Warren. Her hint of make-up accentuated her features and contributed to her air of pleasant confidence and professionalism.

"Good morning, Sally. You guys ready to round?"

"We are."

Rounds lasted 45 minutes. Five years earlier, walking around to each room, talking with each patient, doing a quick exam, discussing the patient's condition, and writing a short note would have taken the entire allotted time. But, with the advent of Minimally Invasive Gynecologic Surgery, there were usually only two or three patients to round on because most, even those undergoing major operations, went home less than 24 hours after their procedures. Warren made use of the remainder of their time by giving the residents and students "chalk talks" in one of the unit's conference rooms, or listening to one of the trainees present a topic to the group that either he or Sally assigned. The students and residents appreciated Warren's efforts, and during his time on staff at Winslow, he was the recipient of several teaching awards from them.

After the group finished seeing two postop patients and listening to a medical student presentation on pelvic inflammatory disease, Warren said, "Sally, I'm on my way to change, I'll meet you in pre-op in 10 minutes, we've got a 7:30 start-time right?"

"Yep, and her pre-op note is already done."

"Great, I'll see you in a few."

Just after seven o'clock, Warren announced himself, Sally, and a third person who inspired a look of vague remembrance from Carla after she invited them into her cubicle.

"Hi, Carla."

"Hey, Doc."

"Hi, Ms. Williams." Sally repeated Warren's greeting.

"Carla this is Tara Jenkins. I don't think you've met her, but Tara's a second year Ob/Gyn resident, and she'll be assisting us," Warren said. Tara was a short, somewhat overweight medium brown skinned African American woman who wore her hair in long colorfully beaded braids.

"I've seen you in the clinic a couple times," Carla said to Tara. "Doc, is there any hope for this young duckling," Carla asked with a smile. Tara smiled too. She had experienced Carla's teasing before, and she liked her.

"Hope springs eternal." Warren sighed facetiously.

Carla chuckled.

"I'm taking personal responsibility for her training."

"Then honey, you've got it made, 'cause you're gonna be *well* trained."

Carla and Warren first met almost twelve years earlier when, as she put it, they were both "young ducklings." She reminded him of this many times. Then, she was a newly minted teacher, without health insurance, who was trying to establish herself as a substitute at Detroit's Phyllis Wheatley High School, and Warren was nearing the end of his first year of residency. He didn't know what to make of the shapely black woman, with a pretty face, clad in tight black jeans, a screaming blue blouse, and enough ankle and wrist bracelets to jangle awake the dead — all of which was topped by a flaming mop of straightened orange-reddish hair. He was put off by her near ghetto like speech pattern, and shocked when he later learned of her education and occupation.

"So how do you feel," Warren asked.

"I'm a little nervy, but I'm holdin' up."

"Nervy huh?" He appeared to ponder for a moment. "Well teacher, you taught me a new word today." They all got a laugh from Warren's mockery. "Carla, everything's gonna be just fine. Any questions?"

"How much longer 'til we get going," she asked through her laughter.

"About fifteen minutes, and they'll come wheel you into the O.R. Dr. Woodson and I will be there just before you go to sleep. Any more questions," he asked in a friendly tone.

"I don't have any, do you mama?"

"Dr. Chambers, about how long do you think the surgery will take?"

"We should be done in about two to two and a half hours. When they come for Carla, they'll show you back to the waiting room Ms. Williams. I'll come talk to you right after we finish up. Sound good?"

"Yes, it does, I'll be waiting for you!"

Fifteen minutes after the doctors left, Carla was wheeled into O.R. 1, one of the two Labor and Delivery operating rooms used primarily for Gyn surgery.

Several years earlier, in an effort to improve efficiency and safety in the Labor and Delivery area, operating room use on the unit was reorganized. All scheduled cesarean sections, as well as some gynecologic procedures, were now performed on L&D but staffed by personnel from the main operating room department four floors below. Instead of having to staff both scheduled and emergency cesareans, the L&D staff could now concentrate on the emergency cesareans and the non-emergency unplanned surgical deliveries done for women in labor when, for instance, they were not able to deliver naturally because the baby was too big or the mother was too exhausted to continue pushing. After the changes, scheduled cesareans were rarely delayed by emergencies or unplanned cesareans. And, moving some of the gynecologic surgeries to this area allowed busy Ob/Gyn doctors to do Gyn surgeries while being close to their laboring patients, rather than four floors away.

Warren, Sally, and Ann Penny, the 3rd year medical student who was assigned to Carla's case, walked into the cold O.R. minutes after Carla arrived. She was covered with a white woven cotton blanket which came out of the linen warmer.

Nurse Hassan, after speaking quietly into the wall phone, hung it up behind her. "That was Dr. Mithicari," she said, "and he apologizes for being late. He got pulled into an emergency, but he will be here very shortly." Her soft Egyptian accent pleasantly seasoned her perfect English.

Warren placed his hand on the blanket where it covered Carla's right forearm.

"Are you doing all right," he asked thru his blue disposable surgical mask. He and Sally were dressed in drab green scrub suits with masks and blue bouffant hats to cover their hair.

"Just a little chilly," Carla said through a shiver.

Warren walked out, and quickly returned with another blanket he grabbed from the warmer.

"This should help," he said while he and Sally spread the blanket over their patient.

"Ah, that feels good, doc."

"We'll stay 'til you're asleep, you're gonna be fine." He reached under the covers and held her hand.

"I'm so sorry," Dr. Vishnu Mithicari said as he strode into the room. He was a man of medium height and pleasant demeanor. His dark brown eyes twinkled above the top of his light blue surgical mask with its thin white border and white tie strings. His tardiness was very uncharacteristic.

"We had a cardiac emergency that came in at seven. I went in to help, and they kidnapped me. Can you believe it?" His Hindi accent spiced and enlivened his words. "You all saw Amirah on her phone. Thanks to God for her and her good credit. She paid my ransom with her Visa Card and finally, here I am." They all laughed including Carla.

Earlier, Amirah placed Carla's intravenous line which was running perfectly. Dr. Mithicari pushed a mixture of drugs through her IV line, and Carla was asleep in less than two minutes. With Amirah's assistance, he placed an endotracheal tube that enabled the passage of anesthetic gas, which would keep Carla unconscious, and it would convey the oxygen which would keep her alive. If Carla vomited or her secretions accumulated at the back of her throat, the tube would prevent her from breathing these fluids into her lungs.

Once Carla was asleep, Warren and Sally placed her feet in the stirrups and prepped the intended surgical areas with bactericidal solution. After the cleansing, Sally used her left hand to open Carla's vagina and place an instrument called a uterine manipulator thru Carla's cervical opening and into the uterus. The device had clamps which grasped the cervix to prevent it from slipping off. This manipulator was used to move the uterus during the surgery. The two doctors then left the room and joined Jenkins and Penny for their antiseptic scrub. The quartet finished and pushed thru the O.R. doors without using their hands or arms to receive their sterile surgical gowns and gloves from the scrub tech who was already outfitted in sterile attire.

Chapter Two

"You can go ahead," Mithicari said to the four gowned, gloved, and masked surgeons positioned around Carla.

"She's under," Warren announced as he released the small steel clamp from Carla's skin. He had pinched hard enough to cause pain, but not hard enough to leave a mark, and there was no reaction from Carla.

"Sally, go ahead and make your incision." Warren's voice did not betray his thoughts. *I hate this. I hope to God she gets the god damn Verees in without killing Carla. I hate this shit!...Dave Sobel, when I was an intern...Dr. Offerlay let him start one of these and he buried the fuckin' trocar in the woman's aorta and we had to bury her!...She bled to death before we could open her and get the surgeons to help us...Why am I lettin' her do this?...Breathe...just breathe...99.99 percent of these don't wind up bad, and Sally's very good...*

The Chief Resident made a tiny 5 mm vertical incision that extended down starting from inside the lower end of Carla's navel.

"Verees needle please."

"Here you are Dr. Woodson," Iona Morris, the short, plump, very dark complexioned, African American surgical tech said from behind her mask, while handing the instrument across the table.

The device is a blunt tipped, spring loaded stylet, housed within a sharp, beveled and pointed metal sleeve. It has a diameter of two millimeters. Sally grasped as much of Carla's abdominal surface as she could with her left hand and pulled up. She pushed the fourteen-centimeter long instrument through the tiny incision, directing the tip toward Carla's feet, while keeping the shaft parallel with, and close to, Carla's inner abdominal wall. Pushing in this direction helped ensure that no organs or vessels would be accidently punctured.

"I'm in," Sally told Warren after a final hard thrust. "I felt it pop into the cavity."

"Are you sure?"

"I'm sure."

"All right go ahead."

"Line please."

Iona handed Sally a thin opaque hose tipped with a small shiny circular metal collar.

"It's tight," Sally announced after attaching the hose to the top of the Verees with a half turn which locked it in place.

"Gas please."

The CO_2 tank was opened by the circulating nurse who was not sterilely gowned.

"We're good Dr. Chambers," Sally said. Their eyes met across the table.

"I agree."

Carla's abdomen was adequately inflated after several minutes. Sally removed the Verees needle and lengthened the incision about two millimeters.

"Trocar please."

She griped the instrument in her right hand. It looked like a shiny steel railroad spike housed within a metal sleeve. The small mushroom shaped top of the device rested in her palm, and her stiffened middle finger lay along the shaft to act as a stop against pushing too far. Again, Sally grabbed Carla's abdomen, pulled up, and pushed the trocar through the incision.

"I'm in."

Thank you, God, for no Sobel/Offerlay action!

A soft *whoosh* sound was heard when Sally briefly broke the inner air seal while removing the spike portion from its sleeve, and some of the CO_2 escaped. Although the abdominal tissue formed a good seal around the trocar sleeve, small amounts of the gas leaked, especially when the sleeve was moved. To maintain the inflation that pushed

Carla's abdominal wall up and away from her organs, Sally connected the CO_2 line to a port on the sleeve and a small, steady amount of gas flowed in. This arrangement allowed optimal visualization once the scope was in, and adequate space was maintained to perform the surgery.

"Scope please," Sally called out.

She inserted the 38 cm laparoscope through the trocar sleeve and a portion of Carla's inner anatomy was clearly displayed on a large video monitor. Sally manipulated the camera containing laparoscope and carefully brought the major structures into view. During Sally's examination of Carla's abdomen and pelvis, Warren described the organs and other anatomy displayed on the monitor to their student protégé.

"First she's turned the tip of the scope toward Ms. Williamses' head and she's bringing the liver into view. See how smooth and glistening it is? There aren't any filmy bands attaching it to the diaphragm or abdominal wall." He asked Penny, "Can you tell me what those filmy bands would be called?"

"Adhesions?"

"Very good, but now for the jackpot question, if she had the adhesions, what would the condition be called?"

"Fitz-Hugh-Curtis Syndrome."

"Outstanding doctor and what causes Fitz-Hugh Curtis?"

"Gonorrhea or Chlamydia."

"Exactly doc, exactly. Dr. Penny, you get a star for the day."

Sally moved the scope into the lower abdomen just above the pelvis.

"The large pulsating structure, covered with peritoneum is the lower portion of the aorta. Now she's moving down toward the pelvic brim. See how the large pulsations kind of end. That's because the vessel divides into the common iliac arteries. These arteries then divide into an internal and an external iliac artery. He paused while Sally methodically continued her exam.

"Dr. Jenkins, what is another name for the internal iliac artery?"

"The hypogastric artery."

"And, it supplies what?"

"The pelvis, and the external iliacs after some dips and turns becomes the common femoral arteries."

"Outstanding Doc, Outstanding."

"Now that little white wormy structure in the center of the screen is what," Warren asked Penny

"The appendix," she answered after a brief pause.

"Right you are," Warren said encouragingly.

"As you can see now, Dr. Woodson is looking at the top of the uterus and moving to the left. She's now over the fallopian tube. Notice the little mass of finger like structures at the end of the tube."

"Fimbriae," Penny answered to the question that wasn't yet asked. "After an egg is released form the ovary, the fimbriae sweep the egg into the tube."

"Very good."

When the laparoscopic exam was over, Tara inserted another smaller trocar through an incision she made, under Warren's direction, on the right side of Carla's lower abdomen. This insertion was much safer because the laparoscope was used to visualize the instrument's sharp tip when it first entered Carla's abdominal cavity. The ability to see the tip throughout the insertion process allowed for a change in direction, if necessary, to avoid vital structures. Once the spike was withdrawn, an operating instrument was placed through the sleeve. Another puncture was made through a similar three-millimeter incision on Carla's left side, and the final instrument was placed. The final two insertions allowed the introduction of instruments for cutting, suturing, stapling, as well as cautery devices.

"Everything looks good, Dr. Woodson," Warren said surveying the instrument placement on the abdominal surface and on the video monitor.

"Go ahead," Warren said. He took over the scope and Sally took the instruments.

"Tara, bring the uterus forward and straight up please," Sally told her first assistant.

"How's that," Tara asked after moving the uterine manipulator. "Perfect."

"What she's doing," Warren explained to Penny, "is tying off the round ligament in two places on the left side and she'll do the same on the right side. These ties will ensure no bleeding when she cuts between sutures to separate each ligament."

Sally's hand-eye coordination made her technique smooth and confident.

"Stop for just a minute please," Warren said to his young surgeon. Sally stopped immediately. "Show me the cut ends of the right round." He looked hard at the monitor for several seconds to make sure there was no bleeding coming from the cut surfaces. "Excellent. Keep going."

A week earlier, Warren and several faculty members discussed the residents they most enjoyed working with. Sally was at or near the top of everyone's list. All agreed that, in addition to being motivated and smart, Sally made them comfortable by following their directions when they operated with her. In this regard, she was unlike some of her fellow trainees. Several of her colleagues, after completing a few procedures in which their attending physicians guided them step-by-step, behaved as if they were now master surgeons. Two residents in particular became slow to follow the directions they were given. One was known to become a little testy when corrected on his technique during cases. Sally's skill and behavior gave her mentors confidence, and put them at ease about allowing her to operate on their patients.

Sally continued working. Her scalpel use was precise, her suture placement was excellent, and her instrument knot tying was deft.

"I want you to move that clamp just a bit lower on the uterine artery," Warren told Sally. She quickly moved the clamp. "Now I'm happy," he said. "Always remember, Doc, in the history of medicine there's never been a clamp placed, an incision made, or a stitch placed by a resident that couldn't be moved at least a quarter of a millimeter." Sally laughed at her proctor's joke.

Just after the final portion of the uterus was removed, Warren and Sally noticed a small steady amount of bleeding in an area just behind the bladder.

"Sally, see how well you can retract the bladder forward away from the bleeding. Good, now use your cautery and see if you can get it stopped."

"It doesn't look like the cautery is stopping it," Sally said after two attempts.

"Okay, try a suture."

She placed a figure-of-eight stitch, but after a moment, the bleeding began again, slowly.

"How are the vitals," Warren called out.

"Pulse is 82, blood pressure is 132/78," Mithicari responded. "Everything is quite good now."

"Sally, let's change places for a minute."

Sally took the end of the scope from Warren, and he took the instruments.

"First I'm going to dissect out the ureter on this side so we can keep it out of the way and safe while we suture down here."

His mastery of technique was evident to everyone in the room who watched him use the micro scissors and a grasping instrument to expose the ureter, the tubular structure that brings urine from the kidney to the bladder and is at high risk of being damaged in all major pelvic surgeries. Sally retracted it out of his field using a probe in the laparoscope's trocar sleeve. Next, Warren found and exposed the end of a very small artery pumping a tiny stream of red into the surrounding area. He tied off the offending vessel and resumed his job as "camera man." The whole process had taken him less than 10 minutes.

"I can see I still have a few tricks to learn," Sally said. She could see Warren's smiling eyes.

"I've still gotta earn my keep around here once in a while, Dr. Woodson."

With removal of the uterus complete, Sally now finished removing the fallopian tubes and suturing.

"Ms. Williams is only 34. She most likely won't start menopause for at least another 17 years, so we're leaving her ovaries in," Sally explained to Tara and Penny.

"But, doesn't that expose her to the risk of ovarian cancer," Warren asked, playing the straight man to Sally's professor role.

"It does, but, because of her negative family history for ovarian or breast cancer, and the fact that she had her first child before she was 26, all make her risk of ovarian cancer lower. So, leaving her ovaries in means that she can still produce the hormones she needs to protect her heart and bones along with her urinary and genital tracts."

"Very good, Doc, very good."

They did a meticulous examination of the pelvis and decided that hemostasis was excellent. After withdrawing the laparoscope and other instruments, Sally and Tara began closing. Warren asked them to close the deep layers of all the incisions before closing the superficial portions of each one. When they had completed the deep closures, Warren thanked everyone in the O.R. for their help.

"You did a great job Sally, and Tara, you are a master manipulator," he winked as he said this and his double entendre drew laughs. "Penny, you ought to seriously consider making this your career. I'll be back in a few," he said. He stripped off his disposable sterile gown and gloves, tossed them into a special receptacle, and walked out of the O.R. He went to the physicians Surgical Lounge. Sally let Tara continue the closures, and they finished in another ten minutes.

Warren returned just as Mithicari and Amirah were awakening Carla. They pulled her breathing tube and Carla coughed and struggled at first to breath. With his hands behind her neck and thumbs on her jaw, Mithicari kept Carla's head bent back and her jaw thrust forward in order to keep her airway open. She was groggy as Warren helped the team slide her off the operating room table and on to a gurney using a roller device. He walked with the group while they wheeled his patient across the hall to the recovery room area. Carla was again placed in a curtained cubicle. She was coughing periodically from the irritation left by the endotracheal tube, but Mithicari no longer held her head because she was breathing on her own, and her vital signs were all normal. Warren stayed with Carla until he was sure she was stable.

"You did really well," he told her. She looked confused. "Everything looked normal inside, but we'll talk more later. I'm gonna find your mother and let her know everything went great."

"Okay," she answered in a soft whisper.

He passed by Sally, Tara and Penny at the long, raised desk. The work space had room for at least six people. Sally was helping Tara as she wrote an operative note. In one paragraph Tara's entry would describe the surgery done, the doctors involved, and other details like the type of anesthesia, the estimated blood loss, and the amount and type of IV fluids given. While Tara worked, Sally coached Penny through writing her first-ever set of postoperative orders.

"I'll dictate the op-note," Sally told Warren. Her dictation would be a much more detailed description of what was done during the procedure.

"That'll be great. I'll read it when the transcription is done, and I'll go over it with you if anything raises an eyebrow."

Warren walked over to find Carla's mother. It was 10:45 when he found Sylvia sitting by herself reading a book in the waiting room which was dominated by people watching a TV talk show.

"Hi, Ms. Williams," he said with a smile.

"Hello, Dr. Chambers, how's my baby?"

"Everything went just fine. The surgery didn't take quite as long as we thought. There was no scar tissue which made things much easier, and we didn't find anything abnormal at all."

"No cancer?"

"No ma'am, none whatsoever that we could see. We do have to wait for the pathologists to look at the uterine lining under the microscope, but I'll be really surprised if they find anything bad."

"How long will I have to wait here?"

"They should come for you in about two hours. They're watching Carla real closely right now because she had a breathing tube in, and because she had major surgery. But, after a couple hours, they'll move her to what we call the post-op observation unit. You'll be able to stay with her there. They'll watch her four to six hours, and then she'll be discharged home."

* * *

Forty-five minutes after arriving in the recovery room, Carla's nurse, Janie Wallace, noticed her patient thrashing around on her gurney and trying to sit up. She went to Carla's bedside.

"Ms. Williams, are you okay?"

Carla looked at her middle age, red haired nurse with eyes that were vacant. Carla was incoherent, and her nurse had a look of intense concern. A second nurse came to help. She held Carla's hand, helped her sit up, and tried to calm her. Together the nurses were able to take Carla's blood pressure. At eighty over forty, the pressure was alarmingly low. They put in an emergency page to anesthesia, and in three minutes Dr. Jack Arrington arrived. He was in his late fifties and wore a very gray buzz cut which was a holdover from his twenty-year Marine Corps career. Arrington gave Carla an injection of ephedrine, a drug that elevates blood pressure by causing the patient's arteries to constrict. He also increased the rate of her IV fluid bag and instructed the nurses to give Carla a full five hundred cc bolus of the normal saline she was getting in her IV. The additional fluid would expand the circulating volume in her blood vessels which would also help raise her blood pressure.

"Once she's gotten the half liter of fluid, turn the IV down to one hundred seventy-five cc's an hour," Arrington said. "Call me if you need me."

Within five minutes, Carla's blood pressure normalized at one hundred thirty-two over seventy-six. Janie Wallace pulled a high stool next to Carla's gurney. The automated vital sign monitor was now taking Carla's blood pressure and pulse every ten minutes.

Chapter Three

It was a few minutes past 11 o'clock when Janie answered her portable phone.

"Hi, Dr. Arrington, thanks for getting back to me so fast."

"What's up Janie?"

"I'm a little concerned about Ms. Williams again."

"What's goin' on now?"

"Well her pressure is 105 over 60."

"Janie, I know that's a tad low, but between the volume she lost in the case, all the blood pressure meds Mithicari had to give her during the surgery, and the fluids and ephedrine we gave her, she's just equilibrating. I'm sure she'll be fine. Go ahead though, turn up her IV and run in another 500 ccs. Just keep a close eye on her like you're doing, and call me back if you need me."

"Okay, then, I just wanted to keep you up with what's going on."

"I appreciate it," he said as he hung up.

Twenty-five minutes later, Janie had another emergency page sent to Dr. Arrington. He was standing next to her at Carla's bedside in less than 5 minutes.

"What's the problem this time Janie," his tone carried a hint of irritation.

Janie answered by pointing to the digital read-out on the vital sign monitor. The blood pressure display read 86 over 52. Janie had already increased the IV rate to wide open, and she had just hung a new thousand cc bag of normal saline. Arrington looked at the blood pressure read-out, and his voice betrayed his alarm.

"Draw up two syringes with twenty milligrams of ephedrine in each." He pushed one of the syringes into Carla's IV line. Ten minutes later he gave another dose because Carla's pressure hadn't responded. Carla was thrashing and barely coherent. Unlike the earlier hypotensive episodes, this time Sally Woodson was paged. She was at Carla's side in minutes.

Arrington asked Sally, "Is this gal usually all there?" He tapped the side of his forehead with his index finger.

"Yes, Dr. Arrington. Ms. Williams is a high school teacher who's working on her Master's Degree."

"I think you better get your boss down here real fast."

Warren was in the emergency room proctoring a resident when he received Sally's page. He raced from the ER and joined the group in post-op.

"Carla, Carla." Warren restrained one of her arms to stop its aimless flailing. "What's the matter?" He tried to talk with his patient, but she was incoherent. He attempted to examine her abdomen with his hand. If her belly was rigid, that would be a sign of possible internal bleeding. But, Carla's depressed cognition, and her almost violent movements, prevented Warren from doing a meaningful exam. Carla tried several times to remove her high flow oxygen mask, and Janie had to forcibly hold it over her nose and mouth.

Warren was at a loss to explain what was happening to Carla. He thought about internal bleeding, but her pulse was not elevated. Usually if a person is hemorrhaging, their pulse quickly elevates. The faster heart beat helps to keep the diminishing supply of blood moving through the system at the highest pressure possible. The low blood pressure/normal pulse "disconnect," and his knowledge that there was no bleeding when they finished the surgery, pushed Warren's thinking away from internal bleeding as the cause of Carla's condition. He was beginning to fear that maybe she had a pulmonary embolism, a blood clot in her lungs. Or, God forbid, maybe she had suffered a stroke. A stroke would certainly explain her incoherence. Warren was stuck. He couldn't figure out what was going on or what he should do.

Years earlier, during the first year of his Gyn-Oncology Fellowship, he was on-call at night covering the Obstetrical Unit with the residents. This was a periodic obligation for all Fellows regardless of their subspecialty training area. A pregnant patient who was having a sickle cell anemia crisis was admitted to the Labor & Delivery unit writhing in pain. She was in her 25th week of pregnancy which meant her fetus was very premature. The patient's red blood cells were being deformed in large numbers, and these "sickled" cells were not able to carry enough oxygen for her or her fetus. The abnormally shaped cells also clogged the tiniest blood vessels which hampered circulation and further decreased oxygen delivery.

Warren treated the woman aggressively with IV fluids, oxygen, blood transfusion and pain medicine, none of which relieved the mother's pain or significantly raised her oxygen levels. He could tell from the fetal heart rate monitor that the condition of the unborn baby was deteriorating. Although he made phone calls to two senior Maternal-Fetal Medicine attendings, neither gave helpful or definitive advice and neither offered to come to the hospital and help. Warren was incarcerated by his dilemma. Should he deliver the extremely premature baby, knowing the high risks of mental retardation and death the newborn would face, or should he try to buy time and hope the mom responded to the treatments.

Finally, after several hours of agonizing indecision, Warren did an emergency cesarean section. The mom died before the surgery was finished — just after they got the baby out, and her newborn son died several hours later. Warren was devastated. He immediately became the object of a torrent of criticism from other attendings and trainees. The behind-the-back chatter from these retrospective "masters of management" eventually motivated him to quit his fellowship before he finished his first year.

Now, eight years later, and he was again at that place of life or death indecision.

"Sally, can you go to Labor & Delivery and bring over one of the ultrasound machines please?"

Carla began to calm down, and Warren attributed this to more oxygen reaching her brain as the treatments started to work. Several minutes later, he looked up, while listening to Carla's heart and lungs, to see Sally had returned with the laptop-computer-sized ultrasound machine and Dr. Susan Stone. He took the stethoscope buds out of his ears.

"Hey, Warren, Sally told me what was goin' on. I'm covering L&D, but I thought I'd come over and see if you could use a hand."

"Thanks a bunch, Sue."

He was thankful and relieved to have her at Carla's bedside, and he explained his diagnostic impasse. Dr. Stone was a Maternal-Fetal Medicine specialist who was an expert hands-on ultrasonographer. Though she was only in her very late thirties, visually, she was reminiscent of the hippie era with her light brown hair in two long braids that fell forward over her shoulders. Her laid back air added to her nineteen sixties persona. She wore green scrubs and a calf length white lab coat which partially covered her five-foot, eleven-inch generous figure.

"Sue, go ahead, if you wouldn't mind, and take a look," Warren said.

After squirting a glob of light blue gel on Carla's abdomen, Stone spread it around with the ultrasound transducer. The gel eliminates the air interface between the transducer and the skin of the patient. This allows the ultrasound waves to better propagate which makes for a clearer image.

Stone explained what she was seeing as she looked inside Carla's abdomen with the ultrasound.

"See, these are loops of bowel." She pointed out structures on the screen with her left hand while moving the transducer over Carla's belly with her right hand. "You see that large dark area right here?" She froze the image and measured it with the video calipers that were part of the machine's software. "That's a fluid pocket, and it measures twelve by nine centimeters. Warren, for sure she's doin' quite a bit of bleeding in there." She removed the transducer from Carla's belly. Sally took it and placed it back in its holder on the machine's cart after wiping it off.

"Thanks, Suz."

"Warren, please, anytime."

"We've gotta move gang." Warren did an excellent job of masking his fear. He made a phone call while the team made preparations to move Carla back to the operating room.

"Main O.R., Kelley Hibler speaking."

"Kelley this is Dr. Warren Chambers. I'm in the L&D recovery room, and I have a critical patient that I need to take back. She had a lap hyst this morning. Can you get a crew up here A-S-A-P?"

"How bad is she?"

"Her pressure is 76/48. Can you get a crew up here *now*?"

"Dr. Chambers, you know those O.R.'s up there close at 1 o'clock. I'm not saying I won't send a crew, but if your patient is really bad off, get her down here, and we'll have an O.R. all set up and staffed by the time you arrive."

Warren reluctantly agreed.

"Everything will be in place for us, you guarantee?"

"Yes, I do."

"We're on our way — and Kelley, please notify Blood Bank. Let them know we're gonna be using the Massive Transfusion Protocol."

"Patient's name?"

"Carla Williams. Her blood bank labs from this morning are still good." The conversation took less than two minutes.

"We're goin' to the main O.R.," Warren told the group. The vital sign monitor was already unplugged, removed from its bedside stand and placed on the gurney. It weighed about three pounds and operated on batteries when needed. The two I.V. flow regulators also had battery capability. They were unplugged from their wall sockets but stayed on their rolling floor stands and were wheeled alongside the gurney. Janie placed a portable oxygen tank between Carla's legs and connected the mask to it. They began the bulky, necessarily slow, move to the elevators as fast as they could. When the team arrived on the second floor, they had to travel to the other side of the hospital. Their movement was deliberate, but running was out of the question – it was far too unsafe for Carla and her caregivers.

Thirteen minutes after leaving L&D they were standing at the receiving desk inside the Main O.R. suite. A young woman, with ear lobe length coal black hair, and clad in a green scrub suit, met them as they entered the suite.

"I'm Pauline, one of the techs here. I'll take you to the holding area, while we wait for a crew."

"Wait for a crew? Are you out of your mind?"

Pauline was visibly startled.

"Kelly promised me a room would be ready and staffed when we got here," Warren said tersely through clenched teeth.

"Her secretary paged me, but that's not the message I got. She told me they were calling in a crew." Her voice cracked.

"You don't have people here?"

"Yes, we do for true emergencies."

Warren struggled, "If this isn't a true emergency, I don't know what the hell…"

He looked at Carla and then quickly up at Sue. They both realized Carla wasn't breathing. Warren ignored whatever authority Pauline had. He moved toward the door ahead of him. The group followed his instructions and pushed the gurney through the door marked "O.R.3."

"Call a code now!" he yelled, while letting down the gurney's side rail. With the first two fingers of his right hand, Warren felt the weak, thready pulse in Carla's neck. He fought the tsunami of anxiety and raw fear that was poised to overwhelm him. Instead, without hesitation, he started mouth-to-mouth resuscitation. Sue located a hand held resuscitation balloon bag and handed it to Warren. He formed a tight seal over Carla's mouth and nose with the face cover portion of the device, and rhythmically squeezed air into her lungs with his right hand. Janie connected an oxygen line to the bag's side port.

"We'll take over, Dr. Chambers, you can go scrub," Mithicari told Warren from the head of Carla's gurney. He arrived seconds earlier with a nurse anesthetist and the three-member code team. They attached electrocardiogram leads to Carla's chest and moved her to the operating table while continuing to breathe for her with the balloon bag.

"She's in V-fib," Mithicari called out from the head of the table where he was looking at the cardiac monitor screen. Ventricular fibrillation is an abnormality in which the heart's electrical conduction pathways initiate an unsynchronized contraction pattern. The heart muscle quivers like a "bag of worms." This uncoordinated activity is dysfunctional and doesn't allow the chambers to fill with blood or the heart muscle to push blood out to supply the body. Carla was in cardiac arrest. The code team began CPR.

"Stop for a second and let me intubate," Mithicari told the team. He had the tube in on his first attempt.

"Stop CPR," the leader of the CPR team said, a minute later. He was responding to a hand signal from Mithicari.

"Continue," Mithicari repeated 3 seconds later after listening to Carla's lungs with his stethoscope, "The tube's in the right place, continue CPR."

"He's pushing Amiodarone, and epinephrine," Mithicari's nurse anesthetist called out while writing down doses and times given. We're also hanging a Magnesium drip."

Three minutes after the last drug was pushed the code team leader commanded loudly, "Stop CPR, everyone stand clear." He positioned the defibrillator paddles on Carla's chest, and, in an effort to restart her heart, he delivered an electric shock powerful enough to cause Carla's entire body to violently convulse. Before resuming CPR, the team waited for Mithicari's assessment.

"We have a pulse," the anesthesiologist yelled.

"We're gonna open her," Warren said from just beyond the foot of the table. He and Sally were dressed in their sterile coverings. He knew Carla's heart stopped because it wasn't getting enough oxygen because she didn't have enough blood. Her bleeding had to be stopped to give the transfusions any chance of working.

"I'm ready Dr. Chambers," the scrub nurse said, in a light Pilipino accent.

"Scalpel," Warren said. He cut through Carla's rust tinged skin — the discoloration caused by the hastily applied sterile prep solution. Despite his almost imperceptible hand tremors, Warren's movements were fast and precise. He tried to portray calm confidence and not succumb to his racing heart and emotional terror. His intensity of focus rendered him nearly oblivious to everything else.

He stared through Carla's open incision. "My God! There must be 2 liters of blood and clot in here."

"Sterile basin," Sally called out.

"Here, Sally, bring it right up to the incision, and nurse, get 3 liters of warm saline ready."

Using both hands, and a frantic pace, Warren scooped out the abdomen's bloody contents, while Sally assisted with the surgical suction tube.

"Liter of saline," he almost shouted just before they finished. "Sally, dump in the whole liter. I'll suction and then we'll pour in another one."

"More saline," she asked — her voice quivered. She poured in the second liter.

"We'll leave it in. It's clear, and we'll look through it for any bleeders. They're sometimes easier to see when they bleed into clear saline."

Carla was receiving a second unit of blood when Mithicari said with exasperation, "She's coded again."

"Okay, step back," Warren said to his operating team. The code team, now sterilely clad, started CPR.

"We're pushing an amp each of epinephrine and bicarb," the CRNA announced.

"Everyone stand clear."

Carla's body jerked again as the electricity coursed through her.

"We're pushing another amp of epi."

The CPR resumed.

"I think we need to open her," Dr. Erin Meyers said quietly to Mithicari. She was the Chief of Surgical Trauma who arrived 4 minutes earlier with 2 members of her team. She was sterilely masked gowned and gloved. Her long dish water blond hair was stuffed under her surgical cap. With her height of six feet, she towered above Mithicari at the head of the table.

"I don't disagree," Mithicari responded with resignation.

"Dr. Chambers, we're gonna open her chest," Meyers said.

"I'm gonna keep looking," Warren said. He motioned his team back to the table.

"Splash her chest," Meyers ordered.

Carla's chest was doused with sterile prep solution in an instant, and Meyers was in her chest cavity in what seemed like another instant. From her position just across the short curtain between them that divided the crowded operating table, the chief trauma surgeon looked directly into Mithicari's eyes when she said,

"Got my hands on her heart and I'm squeezing."

Meyers compressed the heart about once every second to force blood flow through Carla's body. This technique was more effective than CPR, and it was the last option.

After 15 minutes of more drugs and 4 direct shocks to the heart, Meyers held up her right hand.

"We're done. That's it gang." She looked at the clock high up on the wall opposite Mithicari. "I'm pronouncing her at 3:02 p.m."

Warren was engrossed in trying to find the bleeding source. He was intent on saving Carla's life and Meyers' words hadn't registered.

"Dr. Chambers," Meyers said in a calm clear voice.

Warren's head did not rise from the operative field.

"Warren!" Meyer's tone was sharp and commanding.

Warren's head and body jerked up. He looked straight ahead.

"She's gone, Warren. I stopped the code."

He glanced at Meyer's for a second and then stared ahead again as he backed away from the table. He appeared to be disoriented. Warren was shocked, and numb, and frightened, and anxious, and depressed. He lost Carla's life. She was gone, and he knew he was responsible. His eyes darted between Susan and Sally. He wanted to run and not stop, ever. No one had words for long seconds. Finally, Warren said,

"I've gotta go find her mother." He looked down at the two gapping incisions and her eyes which stared straight up from her stillness. Several seconds passed before he cleared his illusion that Carla was having slight breathing movements. He knew his mind was tricking him. He tore off his surgical coverings, tossed them on the floor, and exited slowly in silence.

Chapter Four

Warren found Sylvia sitting in the family waiting area. His bearing was stiff and distant.

"What is it, Dr. Chambers?"

"Let's find a consult room."

When Sylvia stood, Warren, at five eleven, was a little more than a head taller. Sylvia's complexion, which was normally a rich café au lait, was beginning to look ashen. Her hair was straight, mostly black, and close cropped. She was dressed in a light reddish-brown pants suit with a white collared blouse and black low heeled shoes. She folded her light weight, brown leather coat over her left arm and began her walk with Warren. They crossed the large waiting area and reached a line of small rooms. Each had a single large window facing the waiting area. The thin white venetian blinds, embedded in the windows, were closed. Once inside, Warren closed the door he had held for Carla's mother. Four chairs were positioned around a small Maplewood circular table. Warren pulled a chair out for Sylvia, and he took a seat next to her.

"She's dead, Ms. Williams." Warren's voice cracked as he spoke. "I'm so sorry." He fought to contain his tears.

"What happened, Dr. Chambers," she asked, seconds later, through the lace bordered hanky that now covered her nose and mouth. Sylvia's eyes watered, but tears did not spill. There was wonderment in her voice, and she placed her right hand on Warren's left forearm.

Warren said nothing. He was struggling to maintain composure.

"What happened, Dr. Chambers," Sylvia asked again. This time her voice was a bit muffled by the wadded cloth, now damp from dabbing at her eyes. This time her question sounded like she was also asking herself. Her tone was gentle and sympathetic, the warmth made Warren uncomfortable about the tenuous grip he had on his emotions, but this moment of awkwardness pushed him to focus.

"She started having trouble maintaining her blood pressure. I didn't realize she was bleeding internally. When I did, I took her back to the operating room, and just as I was getting ready to open her tummy, her heart stopped. We were able to get it started after several tries, and I went back in and started looking for the source of the bleeding and her heart stopped again. We tried everything, but we couldn't restart it."

Sylvia was quiet. Her arms were crossed in front of her in a near self-embrace. She rocked, front to back, almost imperceptibly. Warren uttered soft repetitive apologies. He was full of guilt, discomfort, and had no other words or thoughts of what else he should do. After several moments Sylvia asked,

"What happens now Dr. Chambers?"

"Carla's death was completely unexpected, Ms. Williams, and the Medical Examiner will insist on performing an autopsy."

Thirty-three years earlier, a Medical Examiner's mandated autopsy of her husband, Sterling, roiled Sylvia's emotions. Sterling had been a hard-working auto plant electrician with a vision of building a large real estate holding to provide wealth and security for his family. He bought dilapidated properties which he refurbished into clean, safe, affordable housing, often with Sylvia's help. Sterling's background as a combat United States Marine, who had been to war, was not enough to save him from one of his tenants, who, in a rage of alcohol sodden paranoid schizophrenia, without warning, buried a butcher knife in Sterling's chest while he was trying to collect rent from the man. Sylvia told her sister Janice Mae at the time, "My poor darling has been cut on enough. I don't want him desecrated anymore."

"No, no, no, I don't want that, Sylvia said."

"I understand, Ms. Williams, but the Medical Examiner has the authority to override all protests."

There was another long pause. Warren was puzzled by Sylvia's stoicism. He had no idea about Sterling's death.

"All right," she said. I need to call more family. My oldest sister, Janice Mae, is on her way." Her sentences were spoken after long pauses.

"Who's going to take care of those babies," Sylvia said, her words were almost inaudible. Warren wasn't sure what she said, and he decided not to ask. "And who's gonna teach her classes?" Her speech had a distant resonance. Warren remained at a loss about what to say or do.

There was a soft knock at the door, Warren responded, and the door opened. A man about two inches shorter than Warren walked in. Although his appearance suggested he could stand to lose ten ponds, he was well dressed in a tan sports coat, with tan dress slacks and an open collar light blue dress shirt. He was a good-looking man, clean shaven with a head of thick, dark brown, and neatly trimmed hair. His aura was warm and kind — exactly what Sylvia and Warren needed.

"Hello, Ms. Williams, Dr. Chambers. I'm Rabbi Ethan Cantor, one of the hospital Chaplains. I'm here to help in any way I can."

He took Sylvia's right hand in his and covered it with his left hand. The Rabbi's hands were warm and dry.

"I'm so very sorry for your loss," he looked directly into Sylvia's eyes.

Warren did not know the Rabbi.

"How can I help you and your family?"

"My sister is on her way. Dr. Chambers told me there would be an autopsy ordered by the Medical Examiner. How long will it be, Rabbi, before they let me have my baby?"

Rabbi Cantor explained the process as best he could. He was careful to emphasize that no time lines were one hundred percent in cases such as this.

"Ms. Williams, do you have a faith?"

"I'm a Christian."

"Do you have a church Ms. Williams?"

"Yes, I'm a member of Sumner A.M.E. Our pastor—"

"I know Reverend Majors very well. We've worked closely together on the Metro Interfaith Council. I'm happy to call him for you if you'd like."

"Thank you so much, Rabbi, that would be very helpful."

Rabbi Cantor assured Warren he would stay with Sylvia until her family arrived. Warren shook Sylvia's hand after giving her his card.

"I put my cell phone number on the back," he said. He turned the card to show her. "Please, Ms. Williams, you call me anytime if there's anything I can do for you or you have any questions. I don't care if it's two in the afternoon or two in the morning — please call me." Sylvia's expression was grateful and she nodded.

Warren went back upstairs to the L&D doctors lounge. The two residents in the lounge abruptly stopped talking when he walked in. *Damn, bad news travels fast around here!* He picked up a phone and paged Sally. When she answered, he asked her to meet him. Her crying made it a little difficult to understand her words. She agreed to meet him, but not in the L&D lounge.

"I'm in the coffee shop in one of the back booths. Could you please come down? They closed a few minutes ago, there's no one else here, and the way I feel, I don't want to face a bunch of nosey gossipy residents and attendings."

"I'll be right down."

It was 4:12 p.m. when Warren took a seat across from Sally. A screen of spaced horizontal aluminum bars connected by metal mesh enclosed the display coolers, the counters, with their cash registers, and the space behind them. The seating area, however, remained open. Sally's face was red, and her eyes were blood shot, but she wasn't actively crying. Warren knew she would shed more tears and felt guilty about all of it.

"I killed Ms. Williams, Dr. Chambers." Sally's tears flowed again. Her voice was quaking and had a pleading quality. The uncontrolled, hiccup-like breathing that frequently accompanies crying also distorted her words.

"No, you did not. I was the Captain of the ship and everything that went on, or didn't go on, is my responsibility and mine alone. You're a very bright, hardworking great doc, and the attendings around here love operating with you *because* you follow directions in surgery. You do exactly what we ask, and that's what happened in there today. If there's any fault here it's mine, not yours."

Warren's attempt to sooth had the opposite effect. Sally began shaking with her tears. She dabbed at her eyes with a growing wad of damp white paper napkins she was collecting from the dispenser on the booth's table.

"I'll never be able to operate again, Dr. Chambers. I took a patient's life."

"Even if that were true, which it isn't, you can't quit. When we take on the mantle of physician, we sometimes latch onto a God complex. But, we're not God, we're just little mistake prone humans, and the best we can hope to do is learn from our mistakes and try real hard not to repeat 'em."

"But, how do I know this won't happen again?"

"You don't. We get so blinded by our successes in medicine these days. Incidents like this are very rare, but they happen, they happen sometimes to excellent docs, and none of us can quit. Carla is teaching us something and we're obligated to learn the lesson — then we've gotta use the knowledge to take better care of future patients, and teach others what we've gained. We have to muster all our reserves and push on." He hoped everything he was saying was true.

No words passed for several seconds. Sally regained some composure. Her breathing was occasionally hicuppy, but her tears and sobs were stilled.

"When I was a fellow at Creason, I lost a mother and her baby. The circumstances were very different, but I was devastated. The criticism I caught both to my face and behind my back was hellacious. Even though deep down I was sure I hadn't done anything wrong, I doubted myself, and felt terrible. And, yeah, I wanted to quit medicine. If Dr. Thompson hadn't pulled me aside and reassured me, I might have."

"Why didn't you," Sally asked quietly.

"Because Thompson helped me understand that these things happen, and even if it was my fault, I needed to learn from it and try to help people with my enlarged experience."

"How did you deal with all the back stabbing and gossip?"

"You know, in high school we had to study the civil rights movement in the 60s which I knew almost nothing about. I remembered there was a song the marchers used to sing sometimes when they were facing the dogs and Billy clubs. It was called *Ain't Gonna Let Nobody Turn Me Around*. I thought about that song after my patient died, and I decided to live that song and go on."

As they continued talking, Warren could tell Sally felt a little better. Her eyes were still very red, but they were dry. The rhythm of her breathing was almost normal, and her normally white complexion was no longer flushed.

"I've got to go make rounds, Dr. Chambers."

They rose, and Warren hugged Sally. This was very unlike him. Sally hugged him back.

"Be tough, Dr. Woodson, be tougher than a football player," he said softly while they hugged, and then Sally turned and walked toward the elevators.

Warren sat by himself. He thought about his Creason days which seemed to be an eternity ago. Not all of his recollections were painful. He was in a swirl of memories when it dawned on him, he should be the first to tell his Department Chair about Carla's death. He used his cell phone to call Thompson's office.

"Hello, Dr. Harold Thompson's office, Chair of the Department of Obstetrics and Gynecology, Cathy Weaver speaking."

"Hi, Cathy, this is Warren. Is Dr. Thompson in?"

"No, Dr. Chambers, he's actually in Dallas attending an Ob/Gyn Board meeting."

"I really need to speak with him today as soon as I can."

"I can try getting a hold of him right now, and asking him to call you, or, he calls in twice a day for messages. It's 20 to 5 now, he usually calls in about 10 minutes before 5:00, just before I leave. Do you want me to wait for his call?"

"Yeah, wait for his call if you would, but please tell him it's important."

Warren gave Cathy his cell phone number.

"Is that all?'

"Yeah, that's all. Thanks."

"You're very welcome."

Warren's brief silence was broken by a familiar beeping. His pager read, *Please return to your surgery consult room.*

Rabbi Cantor was waiting when Warren reached the surgery waiting area. The chaplain took him into a larger counseling room down the hall from where they previously met. Sylvia's sister, Janis Mae Sipple, and their brother, Johnny Tate, were waiting. Patti Kramer, a member of the hospital's grief counseling team, was also there. Sylvia introduced Warren to her sister and brother. Janis Mae's height disguised the considerable weight she carried. Her reddish brown straightened hair was medium length and it stopped just above her shoulders. She had a warm trusting look. Her brother did not. Tate's look was suspicious and unfriendly. He looked to be in his early fifties, and his voice was deep and possessed a definitive no nonsense quality. He was a large man, and his size contributed greatly to his imposing presence. He was dressed in a very dark blue suit and white shirt with a deep maroon tie.

"Dr. Chambers, my sisters told me this was gonna be a routine procedure..."

"That's right, it was—"

"Then, what happened to my niece?"

"It was supposed to be. The surgery went—"

"It was *supposed* to be? Then what the hell happened?" The anger in Tate's voice was over flowing as was the sarcasm of his question.

"Let Dr. Chambers tell you, Johnny," Sylvia said with quiet firmness. She looked straight into her younger brother's eyes, and his demeanor cooled.

Warren told the group again what happened. His explanation was substantively the same account he gave Sylvia earlier.

"I want all of you to know, as I told Ms. Williams before, in a case like this, the hospital always does an investigation. We will get to the bottom of what happened."

"How do we know y'all will tell us what you really find," Tate asked.

Warren was stunned by the challenge. It was like a stinging slap. His face, ears, and neck reddened. It took him a few seconds to regroup before he responded.

"I can't promise what the hospital will do, but I expect they'll tell you what they find."

"*You expect?* We don't want some expect, we want answers."

"Now, Johnny, Dr. Chambers told us what he knows," Sylvia said, "and we're gonna trust his word, and that's what we're goin' with."

There was no room for debate in her tone. Janis Mae slowly nodded her head in agreement.

Warren knew Tate didn't believe him, but he didn't try with him again. He answered a few more questions from Sylvia, and then reminded her to call him for any reason. He left after shaking hands with Sylvia and Janis Mae. Both were gracious. Tate ignored Warren's proffered hand, and as he left the room, he felt his ears, flush and warm with embarrassment. He found an empty call room on the 6th floor, went in, turned off the lights, and lay in the bed, on his back, in the windowless dark. Sylvia's comment about trust humbled him and inspired his anxiety. It was a heavy obligation, and he knew he would have to fulfill it. After twenty minutes, he got up and walked to his office, loaded up his briefcase for the trip home and went to his car.

* * *

When Thompson got his messages, they included Warren's request.

"Between you and me, Dr. Thompson, a friend of mine in the O.R. told me Dr. Chambers lost a patient this afternoon."

"Really? Do you know what happened?"

"No, she didn't say, but she did say the patient had a hysterectomy and had to be taken back to surgery about 3 hours later, and she died while Dr. Chambers was operating on her."

"Wow, that's bad."

"And, Dr. Thompson, you can't tell Dr. Chambers I told you."

"I do realize that if I reveal my sources, soon I won't have any, but, thanks for the reminder. Anything else?"

Cathy gave him updates on some situations he had asked her to look into.

"Thanks. Take care, and I'll talk to you in the morning."

"Sounds good, and have some fun while you're down there, God knows you deserve it. Bye-bye."

Thompson called Warren soon after he disconnected with Cathy. It was 5:15 and Warren was driving home when he answered Thompson's call.

"Hi, Warren, it's Harold. Cathy told me you called."

"I did. I've got bad news. I lost a patient on the table this afternoon."

Warren explained the situation to his boss.

"You've been through this bad dream once before. Hang in there. Are you all right?"

"Yeah, I'm depressed, but I'll live."

"Were there any other docs or med students involved?"

"Sally Woodson and Tara Jenkins. Tara wasn't actually there when we took the patient back and she died, neither were the students. I had a long talk with Sally. She's shaken up, but I think she'll be okay."

"And, Tara?"

"I didn't even think to check on her. I'll find out where she is. If she's still in the hospital I'll go back."

"That sounds good, also, call nursing and make sure someone from grief counseling met with the nurses and O.R. techs involved."

"Will do. And, Sue Stone was there at the end too."

"How did she get involved?"

"She came over from L&D and scanned the patient's belly for me, and found the bleeding."

"Is she okay?"

"I don't know, but I'll call her too."

"All right good. One last thing — this wasn't that Williams woman was it? I can't think of her first name."

"Carla, and yes, it was her."

Thompson was silent before he said,

"I'm so sorry Warren. I won't be back in the office until Wednesday. You've got my cell number now. Call me if you need anything.

* * *

Tales of Carla's demise, many of them tall, began circulating almost before her soul had departed. Predictably, Winslow's "masters of management" became quite animated, and Warren's competence was questioned in the stories that were passed. Much of the word trafficking revolved around the surgical ineptitude of Ob/Gyns, and their repetitive need for general surgeons to bail them out of their messes. The role of the Anesthesia group was not questioned. Some of this gossip was the epitome of the Supreme Court's definition of libel, "...a reckless disregard for the truth."

Chapter Five

His first morning after returning from Dallas, Thompson opened the door to his office and was greeted by his ringing telephone.

"Thompson."

"Hi, Harold, its Henry."

It was Henry Davidson, Winslow's Chief Safety Officer. Thompson forgot that this call was coming, and he felt a twinge of dread. He began thinking about this conversation from the moment Warren told him about Carla's death. It was Davidson's task to conduct root cause analyses on all negative occurrences he deemed to be Sentinel Events.

"Hi, Henry, I was actually expecting your call."

"Then you've already heard about the intra-operative death we had while you were out?"

"Yeah, I did," Thompson answered with a sigh. "Warren Chambers called me a couple hours after it happened."

"Well, this was certainly, 'An unexpected occurrence involving death or serious physical or psychological injury, or the risk thereof.'" Davidson quoted verbatim from the *Manual of Guidelines* published by the American Board of Hospital Accreditation, usually referred to as ABHA. The *Manual* refers to these events as "Sentinel" "...because they signal the need for immediate investigation and response."

"Do you want to serve on the committee that will do the root cause analysis, and work on the action plan, along with someone else from your department, or do you want to assign two members?"

"I think for this one, I'll designate two people. I think it's good for full-time clinicians to serve on these committees. They can many times be more insightful than department Chairs."

"You know, I support your view on that. Can you let me know soon?"

"Can you give me 'til the end of the day?"

"No problem Harold. Thanks."

Although Thompson came to admire Davidson's work, he realized the Chief Safety Officer inspired disgust and a sense of intimidation in many at Winslow. Davidsons's feigned ignorance of the emotions he provoked contributed to the disdain held for him by the majority of the staff who knew him. His short stature, and occasional imperious tone of voice, gave Davidson a Napoleonic air which further divided him from most of the staff he had to work with.

An effective Chief of Safety in a healthcare organization is analogous to the Chief of Internal Affairs in a police department. Each investigates employees who suspect the primary goals of these inquiries are the protection of the organization's image and leadership. The potential targets believe the mindset of these Chiefs and their subordinates is, 'If the reputations of individuals are unjustly sullied during the investigative process, so be it.' At Winslow, the belief of the overwhelming majority of doctors, nurses and other caregivers was that Davidson was out to absolve the hospital, in these situations, of any failures in staffing or equipment procurement or maintenance. The belief was widespread that the Chief Safety Officer and his committees were not in pursuit of truth, rather, they sought to affix blame. Too often, this belief held, Davidson steered his committees to their familiar conclusion which was that the mishaps they studied were due to "human factors."

After finishing his conversation with Davidson, Thompson turned to sifting through the pile of documents Weaver left in the inbox on his desk. He was very familiar with some of the papers requiring his signature. To these, he added his quick scribble and put them in his "done" pile. Other papers, he skimmed and tossed into his recycle waste basket, or if they demanded a closer look, he put them back into his inbox for a later read. When he got to his email, he scanned the subject lines and deleted most of the messages without opening them. The unread portion of his inbox was small because he was diligent about keeping up with the endless torrent of mostly irrelevant messages, even when he was out of the office.

While he worked, Thompson thought about possible choices for the Sentinel Event Committee. His first choice came without much effort. He would ask Dr. Victor Sedaris to serve. Sedaris was an excellent, well rounded clinician who, not infrequently, was asked by other physicians for his help in difficult gyn surgery cases. These requests were often made urgently when his colleagues found themselves in trouble in the operating room. His surgical mastery and ego strength gave him the ability to provide lifesaving aid without belittling those who asked for his help.

Before Thompson could think much about his second choice, he answered the knock on his door.

"Come in."

"Welcome back, Dr. Thompson."

It was Cathy Weaver, and Thompson smiled when he greeted her.

"Good Morning, Cathy, how are you?"

"Well, the shit's about to hit the fan again isn't it?"

Weaver was white and in her mid-30s, with just-below-the-earlobe length auburn hair that framed her twenty-year-old looking face. Her mischievousness peaked through her clear dark brown eyes which were fitting windows on her gregarious spirit. At 5 feet six inches, she was slightly plump and very attractive.

"What makes you say that?"

"When you've been around here as long as I have, you can smell the blame game before it even starts."

"Why, whatever do you mean," Thompson asked, facetiously. He was quoting one of his favorite cowboy movie lines that Weaver knew well.

"Oh Dr. Thompson, whenever something goes wrong with a patient around here, Dr. Davidson and administration do back flips to blame the doctors and nurses and anyone else they can as long as the hospital gets totally off the hook."

"In the two years I've been here, I've seen some real positive changes come from this Sentinel Event process."

"Yeah, but how many of the reviews you've seen were about patients who died?"

"None, you know that."

"You'll see. And, just remember, once again, your lowly little secretary told you so."

He smiled. "Secretary huh, I thought last week when I was filling out your evaluation for a raise you told me, 'I'm not just a secretary you know, I'm an administrative assistant to the Chair,' what changed?"

She threw her head back in mock exasperation, "You'll see," she repeated in a high-pitched joking but serious tone.

Thompson smiled and rolled his eyes at her playful cockiness, but he also knew that even though he had been Chair for 2 years, Weaver's 19 years of Winslow experience gave her an insight he had grown to respect.

"Let me get up and go start my day, Boss."

"Can you get a hold of Warren for me please, and ask him if he can come over."

"Sure thing."

Twenty minutes later, Weaver called Thompson to let him know Warren was at her desk. Thompson opened the door for his beleaguered faculty member and invited him in.

"How are you feeling," was Thompson's greeting. Warren spoke while slumping into a chair facing his Chairman's desk. Thompson retook his seat across from Warren.

"I feel lousy. I'm not sleepin' very well, but I'm gettin' by."

"Do you think you need to see someone, you know, get some help?"

"I think I'll be okay."

"Let me know if that changes."

"I will."

"I know that after what you just told me, my timing here isn't very good, but I want you to tell me again, in as much detail as you can muster, what happened."

Warren went through a detailed recitation of the medical part of the story. He also included his encounters with Sylvia, and Rabbi Cantor, as well as his interactions with Sylvia's two siblings. He even described his few words with Patti Kramer.

"After going through it again, how do you think she died?"

Warren cleared his throat several times while shifting around in his seat. Thompson waited. At least 40 long seconds passed.

"She bled to death," Warren finally said, and then he stopped. He drew his right hand up until the palm covered most of his face, while he pinched his closed eyes together with the tip of his thumb and the side of his index finger. His torso leaned far forward and his head was bent down. It took a moment until he slowly sat up and took a very deep breath through his nose.

"She died because I didn't tie off all the vessels that were bleeding before we closed her." His voice cracked several times.

"Did Sally do much of the case?"

"She did, but I was scrubbed and at her side the whole time. I took over just that once like I told you. She wasn't the issue, I was, and am."

"What do you think happened to make you miss bleeders, if you did miss any, before you closed?"

"I'll probably never know and that's what scares me the most. I mean, some of the sutures we put on vessels during the case could have loosened or slipped off, but then we should have seen bleeders when we went back in and we didn't. It means an operative field can look completely dry, you close, and then have a disaster."

"If her blood pressure was really low by the time you went back, you probably wouldn't have seen bleeders."

"The thing that I really can't figure out, post-op, is why, with the amount of blood she was losing internally, her pulse never went up? I mean with hemorrhage and impending shock, the pulse essentially always goes up to try and maintain blood pressure before the pressure finally drops from lack of blood volume in the vessels, right? I just don't get it. It doesn't make sense."

"I agree with your physiology, and no, it doesn't make sense. The whole thing is bizarre."

"I'm worried, and I'm sick about this."

"What are you worried about?"

"I'm worried that I did something really wrong, and that I'm in big trouble, and that I'm never going to be able to practice again." He was dry mouthed and rapidly bouncing his right leg on the balls of his foot. Thompson tried to console him.

"This is not the end of your career. You've faced this before."

"Yeah, but that's the point. I hurt someone again."

"Warren, despite our best efforts, patients sometimes die, but we have to learn and go on."

They were both silent for what seemed like a long time.

"So where do we go from here?"

"Henry Davidson called to let me know he's designated this as a Sentinel Event — no surprise. He's putting together a committee to do a review, and I'm going to ask Sedaris to represent the department along with one of the residents."

"I hope they find something besides 'physician error.' I'm hearing that's Davidson's favorite conclusion."

"Well, from what you've told me, it sounds like there are some system deficiencies, such as emergency O.R. capability, that need looking into. Let's hope for the best."

Thompson stood up and Warren did the same. Thompson walked around his desk and the two shook hands.

"All I can tell you, is to hang in there. It's probably gonna get a lot worse before it gets any better. I'll tell you what a tow truck driver told me after an accident I had when I visited Scotland, 'These are what we call the joys of motorin'.'" Thompson's Scottish brogue was very convincing, and Warren cracked a genuine smile at his boss's tangential humor.

"The funeral is this Saturday, and I'm going. It's the least I can do."

"I'll go with you. We can drive together. I feel terrible about this too. I only saw Carla Williams two or three times in the clinic, but obviously she was special, to say the least, and this is a tragedy for everyone."

Warren left and Thompson stared out his office window into the courtyard four floors below. A robin flew off one of the lower branches of the large American Elm in the corner of the enclosure. The bird landed on a grass patch and walked with a slow strut as it felt for the shifting of earth beneath its feet, the tactile signature of crawling worms, a part of its warmer weather sustenance.

Could that bird, with its flamboyant coloring, be Carla? Do the Hindus have it right — an eternal cycle of birth, life and death?...if I knew the soul never dies, it sure would make death easier to accept...Two years after I meet her and she's gone..."Hello Ms. Williams, I'm Dr. Thompson, pleased to meet you." "And you."...a shake of hands...medium brown skinned black woman wearing numerous bracelets and necklaces...facial features, collectively beautiful, and a smile with radiance...loud electric blue blouse, slightly baggy fit, and high neckline, play down generous breasts...butt hugging black jeans betray a shapely and fit figure...gold bracelet adorns the left ankle...golden thin straps and golden foot bed on open black bottomed sandals, display painted toenails, colors match blouse...a mass of flamingly orange-reddish hair crowns her five feet nine inches...Dr. Bauman, first year resident, also in the exam room... "Dr. Bauman tells me you're here because you've had intense vaginal itching." "Yes, that's exactly right. I've been itching so badly I thought I was about to lose my mind."...slang free, obviously educated diction...she looks like the hood but sounds like the university... "Do you have a discharge?" "I sure do; it's thick, white, and there's a lot."...Dr. Bauman calls...a medical assistant enters...gyn exam completed... "It's a yeast infection for sure," Dr. Bauman says, "You can go ahead and get dressed. We'll be back in to talk with you in a couple minutes."...back in the room and going over the treatment plan...intrigued and wanting to know more about her... "Ms. Williams what do you do for a living." "I'm a high school teacher at Phyllis Wheatley in Detroit." "Are you from Detroit all your life" "Yes sir, I am." "Where did you go to college?" "I graduated from Whitmore in Pennsylvania." "Well, make sure you use the medicine every night for seven days. If things don't clear up completely, get back in here right away so we can take care of you, and best of luck to you."...Dr. Bauman says, "Any questions?" "No ma'am; nice meeting both of you."... "Amanda, why is Carla Williams in our clinic if she's a full-time teacher?" "When she was hired full-time, and got benefits, she told me she liked the care, and it was fun for her to help teach the residents and students. In my 15 years as clinic manager, she's the only patient who stayed when she didn't have to."

Chapter Six

Thompson emerged from his intense memories of Carla, and his attention focused on present matters. He was grateful that the remainder of his schedule for the day was free of meetings. People complicate every task imaginable he thought. The simple goals of Sentinel Event reviews are to discover what happened and formulate action plans to eliminate the identified root causes — keep the damn bad thing from happening again. It really was that simple. But, then humans, with their quirks of personality and task execution, get into the mix. Thompson's thoughts centered on Davidson — meticulous and passionate to a fault about patient safety, but his obsession with being on time with report completion fueled a management style that turned so many people off.

Thompson recalled the first review he participated in shortly after he started as Chair. Davidson's attitude became asinine when he realized the committee was in danger of missing the 60-day deadline for report completion mandated by the Board of Directors. It was widely known among Winslow's department Chairs that the Board often did not look at Sentinel Event reports for sometimes six months after they were completed. There was no history at Winslow of negative fallout because a report took a few weeks longer to complete, particularly if the reasons for the delay involved unavailable personnel or holiday or vacation interruptions. At the time, Thompson doubted he could work with the Chief Safety Officer in the future because he refused or was incapable of realizing that his unpleasant and dictatorial demeanor only compounded his difficulties. Some of his subordinates viscerally resented the kind of pressure he exerted, and Thompson believed Davidson's behavior made the process move slower. He behaved as if even potential tardiness was a personal affront.

His behavior moved Thompson to speculate on the man's psyche. He believed somewhere in Davidson's psychology there was an element of inferiority that weighed significantly on him. To Thompson's way of thinking, it was too simplistic to attribute the man's personality quirks to a Napoleonic complex. He did realize his attempts at psychoanalysis were amateurish, and he didn't push them too far, but he often found value in his forays into trying to more deeply understand what motivated people's behavior.

What Thompson didn't know was that Henry's entire life was a fight. His parents never married, and his father abandoned the boy and his mother when Henry was three. His mother's alcoholism ended in a psychotic break and confinement in a state hospital. Her decade of estrangement from her family resulted in five-year-old Henry being consigned to the foster care system. He was small for his age and spoke with a lateral lisp — his "s's" came from the sides of his tongue thru his lateral teeth. The encumbrance of his speaking disability lessened with time but never disappeared. His stature and speech made him a frequent target of relentless teasing and physical bullying. Four foster home reassignments landed him with the Johnsons. The couple had no children of their own, and Henry was the ninth addition to their foster family. They would have gladly taken in more children if the state permitted — the family was their only source of income. The Johnsons were no more of a shield from Henry's peer abuse than his previous foster parents. Despite the negatives, the new home offered the boy a degree of stability — he stayed for five years until Mrs. Johnson's stroke forced the couple out of the business.

The other major part of Henry's life, academics, was a disaster. Social promotions enabled his transitions from 1st thru 3rd grade. "He's not defiant or disruptive," his third grade teacher told a colleague, "and I don't think he's stupid, I just couldn't get him to do much of anything." To that point in time, his teachers didn't understand, or they chose to ignore that the bullying, combined with the lack of anyone to provide constant ego support and affection, left the child emotionally famished. It was a near miracle that he was in class almost every day, although much of his class time was lost to day dreaming. His thoughts flipped from the universal orphan fantasies of his parents returning to rescue him with loving arms or that he would be adopted by the nicest parents "...in the whole world." Henry vividly imagined living on his own, with his own room, with his own stuff, and his own life.

These dreams didn't come true for the young Mr. Davidson but, Mrs. Thelma Hendrickson did. Unlike his previous teachers, Mrs. Hendrickson was intolerant of missed assignments, passive behavior, and social promotion. An African American, his new teacher was in her early 40s and grew up in rural Alabama. Her two life devotions were her husband, who was a Baptist minister, and teaching, which for her was a vocation. Her students were her children, as she had none of her own. Henry started fourth grade a year-and-a-half behind in math and two years behind in reading.

The young white boy had never interacted with a black adult before, and this could have been part of the explanation for his visible intimidation in the presence of his new teacher. When Henry did not complete assignments, Mrs. Hendrickson stayed after school to help him complete them. On the rare occasions that his in-class behavior earned him stay-after-school-time, his punishment was writing sentences 100 times on the black board like, "I am much smarter than I think I am." Or, "I can be anything in the world I want to be if I work hard." When he finished these character-building-by-repetition exercises, he had to wash all the black boards in the class. While he worked, Mrs. Hendrickson got him to talk — sometimes about himself, other times about nothing in particular.

Henry, at times, appeared disoriented when these encounters first began, but his teacher finally figured out that his bewildered mien derived from unfamiliarity with anyone showing such sustained interest in him. By midyear, Henry's missed assignments drastically diminished. Mrs. Hendrickson started to suspect that Henry's, now rare, incomplete home work was his excuse to spend one-on-one time with her. By the end of fourth grade, the small kid with the speech impediment was speaking more clearly and was reading and doing arithmetic at a sixth-grade level. Henry's progression through the grades strengthened his relationship with Mrs. Hendrickson, and this enabled a relationship with her husband. They were his anchor and refuge. He confronted his challenges of ridicule and social awkwardness, as well as several more foster home changes, with a degree of confidence born from the security of knowing there were people who cared very much about him.

High School graduation came for Henry two months after his 18th birthday, and he aged out of the foster care system. He graduated third out of his class of 671, and unlike so many foster kids who find themselves suddenly emancipated at age 18, Henry's future was bright. With encouragement, and sometimes prodding, from the Hendricksons, Henry applied and was accepted to the University of Michigan. He was awarded an all-inclusive scholarship which he took full advantage of. This was remarkable given the large number of his foster peers who were turned out into the world without high school diplomas, jobs, or a place to live. He attended college and the Hendricksons attended parent weekends, took him in during school holidays, and in general, became his non-foster "nicest parents in the whole world."

* * *

Between thoughts, Thompson tended to phone calls, emails, and several of the other distractions that accompanied his position. It was almost 4:30 in the afternoon when he paged Victor Sedaris, who answered promptly and was sitting across from Thompson fifteen minutes later.

"Victor, you probably know why I asked to speak with you."

"Actually, I haven't the slightest idea." Sedaris' words bore the audible imprint of his Greek birth place, although, his speech was tempered by 20 years of hearing and speaking American English. At six, one, the 46-year-old gynecologic surgeon and obstetrician had a considerable height advantage over most of his former countrymen. His good looks, calm aura, and frequent smiles gave reassurance to his patients while belying the fierce drive that served him well during his four years as a squadron leader in the Greek Air Force.

"Obviously you've heard about the patient of Warren Chambers who died in the O.R.?"

"Of course. It was a tragedy — a woman, not even forty, comes in for an elective surgery and, gone." The ex-pilot's palms were up, with the tips of his thumb and fingers gathered together in each hand. He suddenly thrust all of his digits out to emphasize his point. "I understand she was a single mother and left three very young kids behind."

"Do you know what happened?"

"I was told they took her back to surgery for bleeding, so I assume...but no, I really don't know what happened."

"As you might expect, Henry Davidson has designated the case as a Sentinel Event, and you know what that means."

"Yes, a review committee so they can conclude "human factors" was the cause."

"Well, after serving on several of these reviews, I can tell you for sure, the conclusions *are not* preordained."

"If you really believe that, then I'll push my preconceived thoughts to the side, because I have tremendous respect for you."

"I don't know what I did to earn that, but I'll take it. Thanks. So, as you know, I've started asking private and fulltime faculty docs to serve on these committees and you'd be perfect for this one which is why I'm asking you to serve. Will you do it?"

"Yes, of course, but I must tell you, I know nothing about these committees or the process they follow other than what I hear from the gossip columnists who work here fulltime."

"With your background, you know that a lot of the patient safety changes we've made around here were based on safety principles and practices that come from the airline industry."

"Right."

"The process Davidson uses is very similar to what the National Transportation Safety Board uses when they investigate plane crashes."

"I'm sure they don't act like the donkey Davidson seems to always be."

"Maybe worse."

"I can't imagine."

"Yes. The overarching motivation for the NTSB, and presumably Davidson, is to prevent future catastrophes and save lives. I know he can be a bear to deal with, but I believe his dedication to saving lives and preventing patient injuries is sincere. It's his dedication that motivates him to make his Sentinel Event inquiries meticulous and comprehensive even when it drives everyone working with him nuts."

"What kind of time commitment is there?"

"One thing I'll give ole Henry — he runs a very time efficient process. I think he realizes that if he doesn't, it'll be even harder to get doctors to participate."

"So, he's not so deaf and blind to things around him as he acts sometimes — good to know."

"No, he's aware, and he enforces a business-like process that keeps the number of meetings to a minimum. He directs his folks to get a bunch of the ground work completed before the first meeting. His staff interviews people with direct involvement in the incident being studied along with hospital members who have special knowledge about specific aspects of the case, but hospital guidelines bar the process from involving anyone who's not a member of the

Winslow organization. But, to answer your question, the time commitment — meetings-wise, is probably 4 hours and maybe another 3 to 4 hours reviewing charts, some medical literature, and timelines put together by the staff."

"This is so different, what you're telling me about Davidson, that now I'm actually looking forward to being part of this committee."

"I'm glad to hear that. I think you'll find it worthwhile, and you'll learn a lot — I sure did."

"Anything else about the process?"

"Lots, but how much do you wanna hear?"

"You've really spirited my interest, so please." Sedaris held out his right hand, palm up, inviting Thompson to continue.

"Okay, the information the staff brings in is used to construct a factual description and timeline of the occurrence. I have to say this part of the process gets a little tricky sometimes when the recollections the staff collects from people involved in the case are contradictory. But, to Davidson and his department's credit, their meticulous review of the medical records usually resolves any inconsistencies."

"But, what happens if a contradiction absolutely cannot be reconciled?"

"That doesn't happen very often, but when it does, the committee notes the discrepancy and concentrates its problem solving on what appears to be the most likely root causes of the event. If the discrepancy is crucial, they develop alternative solutions for each possible root cause. The staff 'event narratives' are sent to the participants before the first meeting with the understanding that anyone can challenge any aspect of this 'fact description,' if you will."

"And, are they ever challenged by anyone?"

"Yeah, once in a while someone does, but these narratives are dependably tight and objective, so a successful challenge means producing supportive facts. That's a high hurdle because Henry's staff is known for its dead-on accuracy. The bottom-line, though, is that, yes, a few successful challenges have been made."

"The reason I ask is because I want to know if I'm being recruited to be a rubber stamp for Davidson." Thompson was a little put off by this comment, but he tried not to show it.

"I promise you, that's not gonna happen — for two reasons. First off, the process really does accommodate dissenting views. And, second, the one thing I know about you is that you're nobody's 'Yes Man.'"

"I'm quite sorry you noticed that," Sedaris said with a stern expression, and within an instant they both were having a good hard laugh.

"Have you had enough yet?"

"Not a' tall, I enjoy learning about myself." They laughed again, briefly this time. "But, seriously, please go on."

"One of the classic publications in the safety field is the book *Airplanes Crashes: Why They Happen and Why They Don't*. The authors include a pretty lengthy illustration of how the NTSB conducts its investigations. They dig into how their crash probes are constantly pressured by constituencies that feign objectivity to try and appear legitimately eager to uncover root causes. In truth, though, the ultimate ambition of these groups is to be in a position to highjack the proceedings, pun intended, to protect themselves if facts surface that jeopardize their interests."

"And who are these constituencies?'"

"Airline companies, the pilots union, and aircraft manufacturers."

"That's too obvious, I should've been able to figure that one out."

"The visible constituents in our world are doctors, nurses, pharmacists, then of course there's the allied professionals like from respiratory and physical therapy and the others. They can all be at the table and all of 'em potentially have their interests to protect."

"With all that, how does it still work?"

"By empowering one arbiter to make difficult, sometimes unpopular, decisions that keep the party moving toward the goal of an unbiased meaningful conclusion. Henry takes grief from a lot of people, but overall, in my opinion, he's done a damn good job in making this place safer."

"You're the first person I've ever heard say anything good about him, and I'm kind of amazed."

Yeah, I know. He definitely has a fire hydrant job, and too often, his personality doesn't help."

"What do you mean by fire hydrant job?"

"He has to put out lots of fires, and you know what dogs love to do to fire hydrants." Sedaris chuckled.

"Agreed. So, back to what you were saying, are there invisible constituencies?"

"The hospital — the CEO and his people and the Board of Directors. I think of the hospital as being the most visible invisible constituency."

"I'm not sure I'm following you."

"Well, the hospital, the CEO, the Board, none of those folks has a seat at the table, but their bidding gets done at different times by different stakeholders and, yes, on occasion by Henry, although he's not the total kiss ass a lotta folks make him out to be."

"That *is* what many, many people around here think of him. They believe his only concern is to protect Winslow, and they believe he's completely deaf to hospital politics."

"The Board's given Henry some big hammers to use when he needs them. But, all that aside, he's very aware of Winslow's politics, and he maneuvers around them. I have to tell you, I was surprised at the quiet aplomb he can bring to the table to keep the politics and petty rivalries from stopping his process from dissecting out the truth he's after."

"And, you've actually seen him do this?"

"Yes, I have, and I know it's hard to believe given some of his other behavior. But, I'll tell you, one of the ways he pulls off his balancing act is by inviting all stakeholders, even those with very little involvement, to have a seat on the committee. This blunts a bunch of potential criticisms that points of view contrary to his, or the hospital's, are being shut out."

"Then, you believe he's a master juggler to keep his goals, the politics and the constituencies all up in the air at the same time?"

"That's a pretty good analogy, but I guess I've come to think of him more as a deft maestro who massages his egocentric soloists toward orchestration while he masterfully substitutes harmony for dissonance."

"So, the rumors about you are true."

"Some of them maybe, which ones are you talking about?"

"That you're a music lover."

"Yeah, mostly straight ahead jazz, but I've got big ears 'cause I love some classical, blues, rock — all of it really."

"It shows."

"It's like John Lennon said, "Whatever gets you through the night." That's music for me."

"So that's it for the committee stuff?"

"One last prep point, I've gotta say, the vast majority of the docs around here are honest brokers and they own up to their screw ups, but dependably, there are those others."

"Of course," Sedaris nodded.

"So be prepared for anything, like blaming nurses and residents, 'They never told me', 'The staffing is terrible', 'The equipment's from the 1920s and doesn't work', and 'The staff has no training'. Be ready for all of it.

"Be ready? I hear all of it in the surgery lounge and over breakfast in the doctor's cafeteria every day.

* * *

It was after six-thirty when Sedaris left. Thompson reared back in his swivel chair, stretched out his six-foot-four-inch frame, scratched at his full salt and pepper beard, and stared out his window at the skyward splendor of the setting sun imprinting its reddish orange inscription on the southwestern horizon. In contrast to the emotions inspired by the beautiful natural vista he was enjoying, when the Ob/Gyn Chair took a very deep breath, he began to feel his angst while he contemplated what he believed was shaping up to be a tough and ugly confrontation he did not want, and it would be one hundred percent man-made.

Whenever Thompson faced extreme adversity, he drew on his experiences as a teenager attending boarding school in northern Vermont. His time there presented him with the most arduous mental and physical challenges of his life.

Between 9th and 10th grades in early August, Thompson was awarded a full scholarship to attend Bermingham Preparatory School in Wrightsbury Common, Vermont. The opportunity, which his parents would never have been able to afford, could not have been more-timely. Thompson and his father, Jessie, were constantly enveloped in heated disputes, and Jessie often succumbed to his violent temper which resulted in harsh physical punishment for his only son. Thompson's mother, Clara, confided to her sister, Vera, "I dread the thought that one day I'll get a phone call that either Harold has killed Jessie, or Jessie has killed Harold. If Jessie dies, I'll survive, but if he takes my son," she paused, "my life is over."

Thompson was apprehensive about the idea that he would not be attending high school with kids he knew, some since grade school. But, he said his farewells, became a prolific letter writer, and made good on his promises to keep in touch.

In the beginning, Bermingham was difficult for the fourteen-year-old city kid. Despite his three or four 2-week stints at summer camps over the years, Thompson fought not to let his homesickness overcome him. He grew up in a neighborhood transitioning from a

Jewish enclave to a predominantly black community with a sprinkling of white gentiles. Thompson had friends who called him "brother," friends who affectionately called him "Thompsonovich," and others who called him Harold. He was comfortable, and accustomed, to interacting with white kids, although, none that he knew were from affluent families like the majority of Bermingham's students. Thompson's unfortunate difficulty was that almost none of Bermingham's white students had ever interacted in any meaningful way with black kids before Thompson and the other four black students arrived. However, over a few short weeks, unfamiliarity and racial ignorance mostly gave way, at least on the surface, to adolescent camaraderie and commonality around sports and car talk, tall tales about exploits with girls, and the need for team work that was demanded by their school activities.

Bermingham used the challenge of soccer, along with rugby and other outdoor activities like hiking, and whitewater canoeing as physical inroads to mental development, but the school's major challenge occurred in December of each year. The entire student body, along with all able-bodied faculty, embarked on a four-day wilderness experience in the harsh Vermont winter. Training for this, "Outward Bound" or "Bounder" trip began in October and included learning to start a campfire with deep snow on the ground, how to build a lean-to out of branches lashed to trees, as well as what to do in emergencies. And, then there was the physical conditioning. The boys were divided into teams of 8 to 10. They followed a rigorous program of calisthenics and repetitive runs on the school's outdoor obstacle course. Hikes up to 6 miles with 40-pound backpacks, and cross country ski runs of similar distances were included in the training regimen.

In the midst of his high school reminiscences' he was shocked back to the present by a knock on his office door. He shouted out, "Come in." Cathy weaver and Thompson had surprised looks on their faces when the door opened. They almost simultaneously said,

"What are you doing here?"

"I had a late meeting," Thompson answered, "I was just about ready to pack up and leave."

"I walked out and didn't figure out that I left my wallet in my desk until I was standing in line at my drugstore."

They walked out together. Her car was illegally parked right in front of the office door and luckily had no ticket. After saying good-by, he walked to the parking garage.

Chapter Seven

Warren and Thompson entered the ante sanctuary of Sumner African Methodist Episcopal Church to attend Carla's funeral. Thompson noticed the stares they were drawing from several people in the group of mourners waiting to go through the receiving line. He felt a knot in the pit of his stomach. The looks directed at the two physicians were curious and uninviting. He believed they were raising eyebrows because they were both strangers and because Warren was white. Although Thompson was black, it was obvious he and Warren were associates and not members of Sumner.

Thompson admired Warren for the courage he was displaying by attending Carla's funeral. As public interactions in our society have become more detached and impersonal, the doctor patient relationship has trended similarly. The physician behavior, in the face of patient loss or harm, Thompson was most accustomed to involved doctors making themselves as unavailable as possible. Most of the incidents he observed were cases in which women lost their pregnancies during or shortly after a procedure like an amniocentesis in which a needle is inserted through the mother's abdominal wall and into the uterus to get a fluid sample from the bag of waters, or when the same kind of needle is inserted not only into the bag of waters, but also into the fetal umbilical cord to transfuse blood in cases where there is a blood incompatibility between the mother and her unborn baby. In these situations, it was unfortunately not uncommon for doctors to speak with the patient and family in the immediate period following the loss only if they could not avoid the conversation. Future contact was actively minimized. Was this cowardice, a genuine ignorance of better behavior, a form of arrogance, or an inability, or unwillingness, to own their failures?

After years of observation, Thompson reckoned that various permutations of these possible explanations applied to different physicians. He was very impressed that Warren initiated the idea of attending the funeral, and he was there to support him, pay his respects, and make contact with Carla's family. Thompson hoped everything would go smoothly.

While they waited to go through the family receiving line, Thompson thought about the last time he was in a church — it was two years earlier. That occasion was also a funeral, but it was for a friend that he hadn't managed to make time to see during her short illness. He remembered his guilt at the time, and he felt it again now. The memory brought him sadness because he did not afford the time to tell his friend good-bye. At the time he vowed not to repeat his mistake.

The receiving line had formed in front of the center doors leading to the sanctuary. The two physicians began greeting Carla's relatives. Warren was giving condolences and shaking the hand of the first member in the line, when a young thin black man wearing a nice fitting dark suit and tie, with close cropped hair and a thin mustache, confronted him.

"What the hell are you doin' here," he said in a loud angry voice.

The man was about Warren's height and was, at most, in his early twenties. The conversation buzz among other mourners in the area abruptly fell off. Thompson, who was a few steps ahead, walked back and stood next to Warren.

"You heard me," the man yelled.

The fact that Warren was white heightened the tension. A black woman stepped out of the receiving line and injected herself into the standoff.

"Leon," she said in a voice both quiet and uncompromising, "this doctor did everything he could to save Carla's life."

"The hell he did, he killed my cousin."

"No, he did not, and I won't hear another word about it."

She held Leon's attention with a firm demeanor and unyielding eyes. Leon flashed Warren a stony look and walked out of the church.

"Dr. Chambers, you might not remember me, but I was with Sylvia, Carla's mama, when you came and talked to us just after Carla passed. I'm Mae."

"Yes, I remember you Ms. Sipple," Warren said. His voice was quaking slightly.

"Thank you for coming Dr. Chambers. It means a lot to Sylvia and me."

Warren managed to acknowledge Ms. Sipple's gratitude. He looked partially relieved after her intervention. Thompson proffered his hand to her, which she accepted. Mae Sipple's demeanor seemed slightly distant to Thompson, yet she radiated warmth.

"I'm Dr. Harold Thompson, and I'm very sorry for your loss."

"I'm Janis Mae Sipple. I'm Carla's auntie. Her mama, Sylvia, is my sister."

"Ms. Sipple, I'm the Chair of the Ob/Gyn Department at Winslow, and I'd like to meet with your sister, when it's convenient for her. I want to talk about what happened to her daughter."

He handed Ms. Sipple his business card.

"Please give my card to your sister, and ask her to please call me. Actually," he said as he reached out for the card he had just handed her, "let me see that for a minute."

Thompson took out a pen, wrote on the back of the card, and gave it back to Ms. Sipple.

"I put my cell phone number on the back of it. Please, ask Carla's mother to call me whenever she can."

"I'll do that," Ms. Sipple said, "I certainly will."

As she returned to her place in the line, Thompson realized his worst fears about attending the funeral had almost unfolded — in a flash — an angry ugly confrontation with an emotional, grieving family member. It could have erupted in violence. His stomach had the same feeling he used to get when he was much younger — during his grade school and high school days — when he got into big trouble and he would think about the consequences, mostly the ones that would come from his father Jessie — he knew they would be physical, harsh, and inevitable. He was thankful for Ms. Sipple, and he hoped the service would end with no more hostile emotion.

The two physicians walked into the sanctuary through the center doors. They immediately turned right and continued along behind the curved line of rear pews. They both noticed the white casket draped with a white cloth emblazoned with a gold cross and the collection of red and white roses spread atop the cloth. After taking seats on the farthest end of a rear pew closet to the wall, Thompson asked Warren,

"Are you okay?"

"Yeah, I'm doing a whole lot better now." He managed a slight smile and added, "I'll be fine."

This was Thompson's first time at Sumner. The sanctuary reminded him of a symphony or concert hall. The space was enormous — he guessed it seated at least three thousand, and the basic color scheme of light brown, gold, and white suggested joy and optimism. The pews were arranged in a gentle semicircular pattern and faced a large dais that was elevated three steps above the level of the first row of pews and curved outward toward the congregants. From the dais back toward the main sanctuary doors, there was a moderate incline which optimized the view of those in the pews. The floor plan gave the two physicians a clear diagonal sight line to the pulpit which was located near the front left side of the dais.

They sat waiting for the service to begin. Dozens of attendees continued to stream in from behind them. Pieces of conversations, some laughter, from adults and children, along with the occasional cries from infants mixed with the organ music and filled the sanctuary. The notes did not conform to a melody, rather, the collective sound, including the rhythm, evoked in Thompson familiar memories of a black church funeral. As he listened, his mind was not racing, but thoughts came to him one after another on top of another. Some of the ideas swirling around connected directly to others, while some flowed without apparent relationships. *Has Warren ever been in an environment like this?* Thompson was intrigued. *Is Warren doing okay? I hope so. Don't ask again. Is Winslow serious about its new policy of thorough investigation of unexpected "outcomes" like Carla's and disclosing the findings to the family or is this just another of the hospital's many 'initiatives de jour?' Another 'great leap forward,' but nine months from now, if someone mentions it, will anyone know what they're talking about?* Thompson noticed that a huge number of people had gathered in the sanctuary and more continued to file in. *With the way I live, if five people show up for mine, I'll be doin' good.* This thought launched a half grin across his face. When he raised his head, he saw the long queue of mourners in the center aisle slowly moving toward the front. Several minutes earlier, a party of two men and one woman, all clad in black, repositioned the cloth and flowers to the lower end of the casket, and opened the left end for viewing. Either individually, or in small groups, people walked up to the casket in turns. Some silently stared at Carla's remains for a moment before moving on, some cried, and others bowed their heads and said prayers, both silent and aloud, before slowly walking away. Neither Thompson nor Warren joined the procession. Thompson's thoughts kept coming.

There were about twelve hundred people in the sanctuary when the ten-thirty service began just after eleven-fifteen. Reverend Cameron Louis Majors III stepped to the pulpit and opened the service with a prayer and a welcome,

"...to all who have come to celebrate the exemplary life of this Christian Soldier."

The Reverend returned to his seat to the side and just behind where he previously stood. Mrs. Paula Jamerson who was seated next to him rose, walked to the pulpit, and read two resolutions acknowledging Carla's contributions to the church. The first was from the Sunday School Teachers Committee, and the second was from the Deaconess' Committee. Mrs. Jamerson took her seat while Mrs. Joyce Paul took her place and read Carla's obituary over soft non melodic organ music. The reading, of course, acknowledged Carla's parents, her birth, educational and professional milestones as well as the births of her children. The long list of surviving family members ended the reading. But, the obituary did not convey the personal struggles Carla waged and overcame. There was no mention of the painful longing for the father she hardly knew nor the constant cycle of adolescent trouble she generated for herself, both in and out of school. Not even Sylvia knew about her abortion at age sixteen. When the first, and only, boy she ever slept with, to that point in her life, an 18-year-old wanna-be thug, questioned the paternity of their unborn baby, Carla impulsively slapped him with such force he almost went unconscious. She ran, and eventually caught a bus that took her to Belle Isle. After sitting alone on a park bench, lost in a fog of tears and despair for more than 2 hours, she made the hard decision.

Warren struggled to concentrate on the details of Carla's life he was hearing. He learned some of them when he spoke with Carla's mother and aunt in the hospital just after he told them about rushing Carla back to surgery during his effort to save her life. Mrs. Paul finished reading, and the eighty-member choir rose in unison from their seats. All were outfitted in medium blue robes topped with wrap around white collars. They sang *I Shall Wear a Crown Some Day...*

Reverend Majors, wearing his black ministerial robes, again faced the large gathering from the pulpit. He was a tall dark-skinned man, and despite the mid-range pitch of his voice, he exuded authority. The Reverend's physical stature, combined with his appearance of familiarity with his surroundings and comfort with himself, contributed to his commanding presence. His theme for the eulogy was "The Exemplary Life." In shaping his encomium, the Reverend's voice took on the undulating inflection and cadence so unmistakably characteristic of the oration style embraced by many Black American Clergy.

The eulogy wove the story of Carla's mostly fatherless childhood with her teenage struggle against the allure of the streets. Reverend Majors brought these elements together with the saga of how the path of athletics allowed Carla to triumph over her misguided attraction to street life.

"She got her education, and oh yes, least I forget one detail in particular, she bumped into Jesus along her way." The expression drew laughter and many shouts of "Amen."

"Her acceptance of Christ inspired her to earn her teaching degree and go on to witness, *every* day of her life, to young people — not by preaching the gospel to them but by giving them an elbow-to-elbow, hands-gettin'-dirty-with-their-problems, everyday exemplary life of the Lord's teachings." There was much applause and loud affirmations like, "Yes, Lord," "Amen," "Sweet Jesus."

While he listened, the enormity of Carla's death dragged on Warren's emotions. For him, the previous six days were a morass of grief and angst interspersed with periods of horrific second guessing. Now he was experiencing all of it again. The Reverend continued with the details of his patient's life and tears blurred Warren's vision. His thoughts about the care he gave collided with the fullness of the life he had been entrusted with. His jumble of feelings was mixed with terror over the upcoming repercussions he imagined — particularly the embarrassment and loss of esteem from his colleagues and the residents. But, in the midst of his self-doubt and angst, shards of guilt began tearing at him when he realized how self-centered his worries were.

She's dead, I destroyed her family, orphaned her kids, and I'm sitting here doing the poor little me routine. The thought physically nauseated him. He bowed his head close to the pew in front of him and resisted the urge to retch all over the floor he stared at.

Reverend Majors finished his eulogy, and the choir sang Carla's favorite hymn, *Mary Don't You Weep... Oh Mary, don't you weep, don't you mourn...Pharaoh's army got drowned Oh Mary don't you weep...* As the choir performed, many spoke out loudly with "Amen" and "Praise Jesus" while others simply, but emphatically, said "Yes, yes, yes."

Warren did not consciously hear the music or the affirming shouts and quiet words of the mourners. The sounds and motion did not pierce the mental veil that had slowly descended over him. He was adrift in his cerebral stratosphere, and he floated to his emotionally absent mother, Clair, and the rest of his family. She psychologically checked out early in his childhood after years of abuse from Max, her husband, and father of her children. Max was an up-from-poverty hard driving farm boy who had put himself through college and started an automobile dealership from nothing. Max's deep bruising brutality was never physical, rather, his fists were psychological and the battering he meted out was far more devastating. Clair's emotional unavailability ended Max's abusive tirades — instead the family lived in a superficial tranquility for which the children paid dearly.

Two-thirty in the morning... twelve year old Warren...in bed, dreams of walking in the woods and stopping to pee... wakes just before losing any...out of bed to the toilet...a faint thick hissing sound...relief in the bathroom and out...moving down the stairs, ears guide around to the slightly ajar basement door...the hiss is coming from down there...bare footed steps down the stairs are almost silent...at the bottom and a turn to the right gives a clear look into the den...eyes move over the back of the sofa to fix on the television test pattern...a single unintentional clearing of his throat brings gasps that rise over the loud hiss...now closer to the television...startled by Max's abrupt leap off the couch to his feet...hair is matted with sweat...disheveled shirt does not hide his from-the-waist-down nakedness...older sister Cynthia sits up from the couch...grabs a handful of clothes from the pile on the floor and covers bare breasts...sudden silence and stares...then, "This isn't what you think, Warren"...Max, command in his voice — it echoes for long seconds. Warren, for an eternity, looks beyond his sister and father before running back up the stairs...falls into bed...laying to face the wall, pillow covering head, body rocking... moaning and wishing the basement visual would go away...Clair scornfully dismisses his story over breakfast later in the morning. He remembered how close he and his mom were when he was younger, and he craved their lost intimacy. "Put your dishes in the sink and go play. You don't go to work with your dad today." He left early.

With his head still bowed, Warren partially covered his face with his hands, elbows resting on his thighs. He sighed deeply. That memory hadn't been relived in many months, but it was never far away. Intense remembrances of Carla now filled his head, but in this moment, he returned from his oblivion and his overall consciousness was again firmly rooted in the present. The emotions that accompanied his thoughts were a struggle for him. He felt very alone despite his membership in the sea of people around him. The choir finished, and Reverend Majors invited anyone who wished to speak about Carla to come forward and to limit their remarks to two minutes. Many stories were told. The attendees laughed at some of the anecdotes and remained relatively quiet during others. The sounds of crying — both loud and soft — were also heard. The saddest part was when Carla's three young children walked on to the dais and said good-by to their mother. The crying grew louder.

The children were greeted with hugs when they returned to the family pew. Reverend Majors said the benediction. While he finished, the organist began softly playing *Amazing Grace,* and the Reverend walked down from the dais and stood in the center aisle at the pew directly in front of the pulpit. He held out his hand to Sylvia, and helped her up. The remaining family members in her pew rose. The pallbearers steered the casket, on its wheeled stand, up the aisle toward the center doors followed by Reverend Majors with Sylvia and the large contingent of family. They moved through the ante sanctuary and out of the church to the waiting limousines and the hearse that would bear the casket to the cemetery. The remaining attendees left their pews, mostly on cue, when signaled by one of the ushers.

Once outside, Thompson and Warren walked to Thompson's car. They got in and drove back to Winslow where they met before leaving for the funeral. They didn't talk much. When they arrived, just before Warren got out of the car, Thompson encouraged him,

"Warren, don't be hard on yourself. You did everything you could do, and now you've got to carry on as the Brits would say."

"I know that on some level, but I'm still wrestling with it."

"Stay strong, hang in there, and call me for anything anytime, please."

"I will," he said and he opened the door to get out. "Thanks."

"Take care, Warren."

Warren walked toward the hospital parking garage entrance, and Thompson headed home thinking about the mess he was about to be immersed in.

Chapter Eight

Ten days after the funeral, Thompson, having not heard from Sylvia, dialed her number which Amanda Lessum, the Administrative Manager in the resident clinic, gave him after finding it in Carla's chart. He waited through the rings.

"Hello, this is Dr. Harold Thompson. I'm the Chair of the Obstetrics and Gynecology Department at Winslow. I met your sister Janice Mae at the funeral, and I'm hoping we can talk."

On the fifth ring Sylvia's phone had shifted to voicemail.

"Please call me back at 248-997-4216."

Hopefully, she'll break her silence and return my call — and now the damn email. He bemoaned how the unmitigated volume of unimportant electronic letters burned up so much productive time. Like many others, Thompson was apprehensive about missing an important message. That sensibility drove the busy Chair each day to the laborious task of sifting through sometimes more than one hundred fifty messages to find the buried five that were important. He was ten minutes into his chore when his cell phone rang. He recognized the number.

"Hello, this is Dr. Thompson."

"Yes, Dr. Thompson, this is Sylvia Williams, Carla's mother."

"Thank you so much for calling me, Ms. Williams — I'm so sorry for your loss."

"I appreciate that, Dr. Thompson."

"The reason I called is because I'd like to meet with you, and whomever you want to come with you."

"Yes, my sister told me you wanted to speak with me."

"Ms. Williams, I'd like to go over, with you, some of the things that happened, and some that are happening." Thompson was gentle with his tone and careful not to be too specific.

"Yes, I'll come talk with you, and you don't mind if I bring my sister?"

"Not at all, I think having Ms. Sipple here will be a very good thing."

"When is a good time for you, Dr. Thompson?"

"Thursdays are usually good for me, what works for you?"

"Thursdays are fine."

"Then how about this Thursday in the afternoon?"

"What time?"

"Does two o'clock sound good?"

"We'll be there. Thank you."

"Ms. Williams, *thank you* and take care."

"Good-bye, Dr. Thompson."

"Bye bye, Ms. Williams." Thompson felt humbled when he interacted with people who treated him with such deference after he had personally failed them or others in medicine had fallen short of their expectations. These encounters were, for him, more evidence of the essential good that is most people.

***

On the appointed Thursday, Sylvia and Janis Mae walked with Thompson from the front door of his office building, where he met them, and took one of the elevators to the fourth floor. After entering his office, he closed the door and offered the women seats on his couches. The sisters sat on the larger of the two sofas and Thompson sat on the other. The seats were positioned at a ninety-degree angle to one another. Thompson and Sylvia sat at the two adjacent ends, and he felt awkward. The thought that perhaps he shouldn't have invited them sprinted across his brain, but he pushed to ignore it. Yes, he was uncomfortable, he had never been in a situation like this, but, he knew reaching out to Carla's family was his obligation, and his recurring thoughts about it pushed him to act on what he came to accept as his responsibility. The relatively new Chair was fully aware that his actions were not the norm, particularly not at Winslow.

"Thank you very much for coming to see me. I know this is difficult. I want you to know I'm very saddened by what happened to your daughter and niece. She was a young, apparently, very healthy woman, and at this point we don't know for sure why she died."

Thompson reached for the tissue box on his desk, pulled several out and handed them to Sylvia. She dabbed at her eyes.

"Go on, Dr. Thompson, I'm okay."

"Are you sure?"

"Yes, go ahead."

"I asked you to come see me because there are several things I want to discuss with you. We are conducting an investigation to find out exactly what happened to Carla. When the investigation is completed, I promise you I will sit down with you, and whomever you want with you, and I'll discuss the results and tell you what happened."

"Dr. Thompson, how long do you think it will take to finish the investigation," Janis Mae asked.

"No more than two months. That's Winslow's policy whenever something like this happens. It's very rare that the sixty-day deadline is not met. I also want you to know that I'm very aware that Carla left three young children behind, and I feel very bad about what the loss of their mother means for the rest of their lives. But, I also know that those babies have to be taken care of, and I want you to know that if it turns out that something we did was wrong, I will do everything in my power to make sure you get financial support."

Both sisters looked surprised by Thompson's words.

"I know that no amount of money can replace Carla, but if we did something to cause her death, we will step up to our responsibility to help your family."

"Well, Dr. Thompson, we'll wait," Sylvia said.

"I appreciate your patience. You have my cell number; please feel free to call me for anything I can do. Call me whether it's a Sunday or a Thursday or whether it's late at night or early in the morning – I mean that."

"Thank you so much, Dr. Thompson," Sylvia said. Janis nodded in agreement. "We'll wait for your call."

After escorting his guests to the lobby entrance, Thompson returned to his desk, leaned back in the swivel chair, and with both sets of fingers interlaced against the back of his head, he gently rocked. *This place is one crisis after another. 'Hang down your head doctor Tooley, hang down your head and cry.' What a mess he was, my first mess, and they've come one after another ever since. Don't you even think of complaining you motherfucker...remember during the interviews when I just had to have this job. Well now you got it so shut the fuck up and get on with it.*

Three months into his Chairmanship, Thompson was going through the papers in his desk-top in-box when he found an incident report and began reading. The incident occurred twelve days earlier which seemed odd to Thompson.

"Cathy," he spoke into the phone, "when did you receive this incident report I just read?"

"Pretty bad huh? It was in the interdepartmental mail that came yesterday afternoon, just before I left. Why do you ask?"

"Because the incident happened almost 2 weeks ago, it's serious, and I'm just now hearing about it? What the hell is that?"

"Just a minute, I'll be right in."

"Dr. Thompson, what do you expect," she said, after closing the door, "when for twenty years no doctor in this department was ever made to answer for anything they did? The nurses and everyone else just gave up 'cause they know nothing's gonna be done to any doctor around here."

He turned to gaze out the window briefly.

"Welcome to Winslow, Dr. Thompson", Weaver said just before slipping out of the office. These words, which she uttered whenever she witnessed Thompson awakening to another negative Winslow reality, in time, came to irritate him greatly.

Cultural malaise...

Cheryl Lawson, an O.R. supervisor, and author of the repot, was the circulating nurse during the incident. The surgery was performed by Dr. Brian Tooley. She described how Tooley was handed the instrument he requested twice, and each time he said it was not the retractor he asked for. The third time he was given exactly what he demanded, he became enraged, slammed the retractor down on the instrument table and struck the hand of the scrub tech who passed it to him. According to Lawson, Tooley yelled, "Next time I bet you'll give me what I ask for." Most of Halla Al-Hakim's face was not visible behind her surgical mask, but those in the room saw the surgical tech wince and squint after being hit. "Yes, Doctor," she said in an Egyptian accented voice faltering with humiliation and pain, but she stayed to finish the case. Later, in Winslow's Emergency Department, she was diagnosed with fractures of her left fourth and fifth metatarsals, the bones in the hand that run from the wrist to the first set of knuckles.

In her report, Nurse Lawson described Tooley as being "The most out of control doctor I've ever seen." After calling the author of the report, and speaking with two other O.R. personnel who were present during the incident, Thompson took a day to contemplate what he needed to do, and he made several outside phone calls to figure out how to do it. He phoned his boss, the man who hired him, Dr. Richard Caruthers, Winslow's Chief Medical Officer, the next day to let him know about the incident and what he intended to do. The CMO was thirty years out from his Canadian Football League days as a star quarterback. He decreased his very successful and busy private general surgery practice to part-time in order to take his current administrative position as Winslow's top doc. Caruthers maintained his superb athletic physique, now topped by a crop of thick gray hair, and his decisive attitude which matured on the gridiron and saved lives in the operating room. Thompson was not surprised by his boss's response. The CMO let out a long sigh and told his Ob/Gyn Chair,

"Do whatever you think is right, and I'll back you."

After talking with his boss, Thompson had Weaver, call Tooley. When she reached him, he told her he was not in the hospital. She informed him that he needed to be in Thompson's office within an hour.

"What's this all about?" Tooley demanded. Weaver had known the doctor for fifteen years and had never exchanged a cross word with him.

"Dr. Tooley," she said in a drawn out 'come on' kind of cadence, "Do you really think Dr. Thompson lets me in on any details like that?"

"Fine. I'll be there in 45 minutes."

The Administrative Assistant did know why the Chairman summoned Tooley. Thompson never confided to anyone connected to Winslow, but the more he got to know Weaver, the more he began to trust her loyalty. She was the only person in the hospital he felt at all comfortable sharing sensitive details with.

Thirty minutes later, Weaver ushered the gynecologic surgeon into her boss's inner office. Tooley was white with the skin tone of a tanning salon devotee. He was almost sixty, slightly overweight, and had black hair streaked with gray. He wore a medium gray sports coat, black slacks, a white dress shirt, and the ensemble was accented by a trendy black silk tie with a silver and light blue pattern. His generous use of cologne imparted a fragrant aura that preceded him and lingered in his absence. Thompson shook Tooley's hand, while motioning for him to have a seat. Tooley planted himself on an end of one of the couches, and Thompson sat on the other couch next to him,

"I called you in," Thompson told the surgeon, "because I read an incident report about a surgery you did two weeks ago. Is it true that you hit an O.R. tech's hand with a Richardson retractor?"

"Hey, she kept handing me the wrong god damn instruments, and I finally got fed up and slammed the fuckin' thing down on the instrument stand."

"Do you realize that Halla Al-Hakim suffered two broken bones in her left hand?"

"Who's that, the O.R. tech?"

Thompson nodded.

"No, I had no idea."

There was no remorse or concern in Tooley's words or intonation.

"There's no way I hit her hard enough to break her damn hand."

"Well, I'm not here to argue with you about that Dr. Tooley, but the hospital's by-laws are very clear about their prohibition against inappropriate physical contact between personnel. Your actions, in my view, constitute inappropriate physical contact. I also believe the evidence I've reviewed so far, raises a legitimate question of whether you're a danger to your patients or other personnel, and therefore, I'm suspending your clinical privileges, effective immediately, pending an investigation by the department's Quality Assessment Committee. If they find fault with your actions, I'll ask them to make specific recommendations on how to resolve this."

Tooley seemed genuinely incredulous when Thompson finished. He showed no other emotion, and he did not argue with Thompson. He slowly said, "Okay," and nodded his head in affirmation of what he heard.

Thompson said, "I'll call the committee together as soon as I can. We'll hear from the O.R. personnel who were present during the surgery. Once the committee has heard from those individuals, you'll be given an opportunity to address the committee and then answer any questions the members have. Is there anything you want to ask me?"

"Nah," Tooley said shaking his head. Both men rose. Thompson proffered his hand, but Tooley ignored it, and walked out.

That evening, with only a slight slur, after draining a second tumbler of straight vodka over chipped ice, Tooley told his wife,

"The idea that I've been suspended for demanding that my orders are taken seriously in the O.R., where I'm captain of the ship, is absolutely unfucking believable. When that high and mighty bastard suspended me, I felt like my insides suddenly dropped away from my belly, like you feel when you're in a roller coaster dive. And, this is what I get for admitting more patients to that fuckin' place than any other surgeon."

* * *

Thompson was heir to the legacy created by Dr. Samuel Reinhardt the previous Chair of Winslow's Obstetrics and Gynecology Department. Reinhardt and his younger sister were adopted by Al and Sharon Reinhardt - a couple with no other children. The family lived in Dempsey, North Dakota, a place known for its isolation and artic winter temperatures. The siblings grew up in the loving home of their attentive, hard working parents. Al was a plumber who owned his own business, while Sharon was a practical nurse who worked at the local hospital. In his adult years, Reinhardt was fond of telling people, "Growing up, I had everything I needed and enough of what I wanted."

In high school, Reinhardt, who was hopelessly uncoordinated, discovered debate and developed a passion for it. The miserable athlete became a splendid debater, and the debate team captain. His talent and dedication were central to bringing the state championship to Dempsey High School. Sharon and Al realized their son was exceptionally bright, but they were at a loss when they tried to figure out where his arrogance and sense of superiority came from.

Reinhardt left Dempsey for college when he was eighteen. He received a debate scholarship to the University of Minnesota in Minneapolis. In his freshman year, Sam chose medicine as a career. As in high school, his outstanding academic performance was over shadowed by core arrogance which impeded friendships and made his class room presence disdained by many teaching assistants and professors.

In his third year, Sam took a job he was not really suited for. He became a resident assistant in Buckley Hall, one of the largest dormitories on the Minneapolis campus. He dreaded the responsibility he signed up for — dealing with the troubles and infractions of the mostly underclassmen inhabitants, but the small amount of money he earned, along with the free room and board that came with the position, allowed him to pay all his expenses, not covered by his scholarship.

Illegal drinking was rampant in all of the dorms during Sam's RA tenure. Buckley Hall, in fact, was known among the students as "The Speakeasy" because so many illegal alcohol escapades got their start or finish in Sam's Dorm. Thursdays thru Saturdays were, without fail, bad. Patches of vomit colored the bathrooms and hallways, along with passed out kids in the same places. Sam would mete out harsh warnings usually via letters slipped under dorm room doors, but he took no definitive actions to stop the booze bonanzas for which his dorm was famous. And, in the mandatory monthly meetings that all RAs attended to discuss common problems and ideas for solutions, Reinhardt never volunteered the problems occurring in Buckley. Even when asked directly, his answer was always,

"Buckley's doing well, no real problems."

Michael Geffen walked into Reinhardt's life by way of the upperclassman's RA responsibilities. The sixteen-year-old was short, skinny and almost ghostly white. His black horn-rimmed spectacles completed his look which screamed "NERD!" This sandy haired freshman was a graduate of Strake Academy, Minnesota's most prestigious preparatory school. Geffen was a *bono fide* whiz kid and hopeless dweeb. Despite finishing at the top of his senior prep school class academically, the scholastic super star was a social misfit. He made acquaintances in the first weeks of his freshman year, friendship, however, did not become part of his collegiate life. His undergraduate social isolation was a mirror of his prep school experience. Geffen knocked on Sam's door several times during his first month of living in the dorm. The reasons for his visits were trivial, and Sam soon figured out that Geffen was lonely, and homesick, neither of which Sam wanted any part of. The RA was never verbally abusive to his freshman charge, but he was brusque, and Geffen's visits abruptly stopped. By his sixth week on campus, Geffen discovered alcohol for the first time, and it didn't take long until Sam discovered him passed out on the bathroom floor down the hall from his room. Looking at the pitiful skinny kid with caked vomit around his mouth and on the front of his shirt, Sam thought, 'Better here than at my god damn door.'

Partying on the first Friday and Saturday after Thanksgiving break was heavy. The problem of drunk, vomiting, passed out students peaked. The inebriants acted as if they had all survived a week of parents, along with forced sobriety. And, now, at last, they once again had free access to their elixir of life — alcohol, in all its varied and wonderful forms. By early Sunday morning, the raucous behavior, with its deafening musical sound track, and the near endless shrieks, were overtaken by an almost eerie silence. It wasn't until close to 7 p.m. that Reinhardt got the first knock of the day on his door. It was Bruce Weber, one of the freshmen. He was supposed to meet Geffen in the library for a tutoring session at 5. Over the last month, Geffen helped him with calculus he told his R.A.,

"...and he's never missed a session or even been late."

"I'm sure he's sleepin' it off somewhere, I wouldn't get too worked up about it."

'You know Mike's not a partyer."

He must keep his drinking pretty much to himself Sam thought, but said nothing.

"What should we do," Bruce said.

"We? We should do nothing right now, he'll turn up."

Weber had a disgusted look when he turned to leave.

By Monday afternoon, there was still no Geffen. Reinhardt was now concerned enough to dial the "in case of emergency" contact number the missing freshman listed. Reinhardt reached Geffen's father who spoke with a slight undercurrent of irritation.

"I'm sure it's one of his silly pranks," Mr. Geffen told Sam. I don't get that kid, for the life of me."

"Do you think Mrs. Geffen might know where he is," Sam asked gingerly.

"No, she's been in Europe for the last week, and I'm sure they haven't talked. I plan to speak with her this afternoon. I'll let you know if she's heard anything, but I'm sure he'll turn up eventually. Say, listen, I've gotta run to a meeting. What's your name again?"

"Sam Reinhardt."

"Right, I've got your number here, when you find him let me know, willya?"

"Yes, of course."

"Thanks."

Sam sat at his desk mulling over his options. He needed to get this over with, and get back to studying for the physical chemistry exam he would be taking the following morning. He decided to use his master key and go into Geffen's room. There was a policy that required him to notify campus security and wait for an officer to show-up, before entering a student's room uninvited, but he didn't have time for that nitpicky bullshit. He would just go in, look quick, and leave. He had to know for himself that the little bastard wasn't holed up in his room causing everyone all this grief.

When he opened the missing freshman's door, Reinhardt was completely unprepared for what he saw. Geffen's bed had been turned on one end and leaned against the far wall with a heavy desk wedging it in place. There was dried blood on the floor in two patches, each was located beneath one of Geffen's dangling arms. His body was suspended by a belt looped around his neck, the other end having been tied to one of the up-ended bed legs. There were several text books with blood stained covers scattered beneath the body. Geffen had probably stood on a stack of these books prior to kicking them away. As insurance that his suicide attempt would be successful, he slit both wrists before hanging himself. Reinhardt saw the razor blade on the floor under the limp body with its subtle sway.

The R.A. was shocked. "How could the little bastard have done it," he muttered to himself. "What a way for me to have to end the term." His mouth began filling with salty saliva, and he made a quick move for the bathroom two doors down. He made it to a toilet and wretched for almost five minutes. This reaction would have surprised anyone who knew Reinhardt, however, the anger that accompanied his physical response would have surprised no one. A couple dorm residents heard the sounds of his vomiting and came out of their rooms to see what was going on. Sam had the presence of mind to close the door to Geffen's room as he was heading to the toilet. When he came out of the restroom, he said nothing to the students who were looking at him.

Sam got back to his room and called the campus security office. "There's a real mess over here," Sam told the receptionist who answered his call, "you've gotta send somebody right away."

Sam never spent much time thinking about Michael Geffen's demise. In Sam's mind the dead freshman was, "...a little rich kid with big problems and parents who didn't really give a damn about him. There certainly wasn't anything I could have done to stop him." That was it for Sam Reinhardt. He moved on.

Chapter Nine

Thompson called an emergency meeting of the department's Gynecologic Quality Assessment Committee to review the facts of the Tooley incident and make recommendations. He didn't know if this was the proper venue to conduct an investigation and possibly decide on a course of action in this case, but Winslow had no guidelines or traditions for adjudicating situations like Tooley's. Thompson was, therefore, free to "make it up as he went along," and that's what he did. Early in his career, he became aware of an incident in which a physician was summarily suspended on very questionable grounds. The physician was never given an opportunity to speak on his own behalf. The hospital where the incident occurred had by-laws which supported the process. When Thompson reflected on how that investigation was conducted, he vowed if he was ever involved in a case of summary suspension, and if it was in his power, the accused would always be afforded the opportunity to present their version of what transpired. Having the QA Committee serve as the panel to hear facts and make recommendations seemed an appropriate, fair, and fast way to get the matter resolved. Although as Chair, Thompson had the authority to appoint all committee members, over 90 percent of the current participants were installed by his predecessor. Allowing the QA committee to sit in judgement of such cases insulated Thompson from accusations of favoritism or charges that he was carrying out a personal vendetta.

The QA Committee met two days later at 4:30 p.m. on a Wednesday. Dr. Earl Seavers called the meeting to order and invited the Department Chair to address the committee. Thompson thanked all the members for attending on short notice. He very briefly described the incident report that necessitated the current meeting. He told the QA members,

"I spoke with several people who were present in the operating room when the incident took place. After those conversations, I decided the behavior described in the report, and by others who were there, called into question whether Dr. Tooley poses a danger to patients and the people he works with. That is the standard called for by the hospital's by-laws before a summary suspension can be imposed."

Thompson then described how the proceeding would be ordered.

"After you've heard from all those involved, including Dr. Tooley, I will describe exactly what you are being asked to do, and I will leave the room in order for you to do your work. Any questions?"

There were none.

"I can't believe this whole thing has gone this far," Cheryl Lawson began, as the first witness to describe Tooley's behavior to the committee.

Her words spurred a wave of disgust that washed over Thompson. His emotion was inspired by Lawson's unwitting clear acknowledgement of what he inherited.

She went on to describe Dr. Tooley's anger at being handed, "...the instrument he kept asking for instead of the one he apparently wanted. He made a very sarcastic remark the first time it happened. As the case went on, Dr. Tooley seemed to get more angry at the slightest things."

"Can you give us an example," Dr. Seavers asked.

"We had trouble getting the suction machine to work properly, and he started cussing. Then he was having trouble getting his light adjusted, and he got even more upset and vulgar. Finally, when he called for a Richardson Retractor, and it was handed to him the third time, he went ballistic, started dropping f-bombs, and he screamed out at Halla Al-Hakim the O.R. tech, 'Can't you do a god damn thing right? You're as worthless as tits on a bull!' That's when he slammed the Richardson down, and it hit Halla's left hand."

There was no talking among the committee members for several seconds after Lawson finished. Seavers broke the silence.

"Do you believe Dr. Tooley meant to harm Ms. Al-Hakim?"

"No. I don't think he hit her on purpose. He was so out of control I don't think he even looked when he slammed that retractor down."

Dr. Phillip Jacobs, the senior partner in an eight-person Ob/Gyn practice, asked, "Did Dr. Tooley say anything when he realized the retractor hit Ms. Al-Hakim's hand?"

"Yes, he said, 'That'll teach you to pay more attention when you're in here with me.'"

Again, the members said nothing. Several were shifting around nervously in their seats, others were making quick repetitive movements with hands or feet, and many stared, out windows, at the floor, or at the ceiling. No one asked another question.

"Ms. Lawson, thank you for coming before the committee. I need for you to remain mindful of your obligation to keep these proceedings strictly confidential. Please tell no one what was said or what you observed with respect to this meeting or any other aspect of the committee's work."

Lawson nodded her appreciation of Seavers' words. "I won't say a word."

"Thank you, Ms. Lawson, you're excused."

Next to address the committee was Al-Hakim. She was accompanied from a small side room to her seat by Dr. Elaine Botsford, another private practice member of the committee. Al-Hakim looked small and frightened. She was nervously rubbing the outstretched fingers of her casted left hand, with the fingers of her right hand, and she was very pale.

Al-Hakim came to the United States from Egypt with her four young children in the late nineteen eighties shortly after her husband, Farouque, died. He was a private security guard who was killed during an anti-American protest while protecting a compound that housed U.S. workers in a Cairo suburb. When the expatriates discovered Farouque's wife and their children would be destitute, the group went to work. They petitioned the U.S. Embassy in Cairo and pushed their company to use its considerable influence. Within a month, Halla and the children were on a plane to the Detroit area where she had a sister.

The newly widowed immigrant did not speak English, and two weeks after her arrival, she enrolled in an English emersion course. Three months later she was hired as a housekeeper at Winslow. Five years into her house keeping career, Hallah enrolled in a surgical tech training program. She earned her certificate on time, and went to work in Winslow's O.R.. At the time of her injury, Al-Hakim was completing her seventh year as a surgical tech. Two of her children were in college and two were still at home. On their way to the Emergency Department, just after Tooley's rampage, she confided to Lawson her fears about being fired. She told the doctors treating her hand that the surgeon didn't realize her hand was in the path of the retractor when he hammered it down on the instrument stand.

Seavers' tone was gentle. "Ms. Al-Hakim, we all thank you for coming today. You don't have to be afraid of anything. No one here is going to be mean to you. You're not going to lose your job, and we all admire your courage for agreeing to talk to us, because we know this is difficult for you."

She began to cry, and Seavers called for a brief recess. Botsford went over to Al-Hakim, knelt by her chair and handed her several tissues she pulled from the box on the table. Botsford put her arm around the frightened witness, and told her in a whisper, over and over, "Don't worry. Everything's gonna be just fine."

All the physicians in the room had worked with Al-Hakim. They knew her to be quiet and respectful, as well as hard working and excellent at her job. They knew she always went out of her way to please the doctors she worked with. She stopped crying after several minutes, the committee members returned to their seats at Seavers' urging, and the meeting resumed.

"Let's come to order everyone."

The background din faded, and Seavers said, "Ms. Al-Hakim, will you please tell the committee what happened during the surgery with Dr. Tooley when your hand was injured."

In a voice halting from emotion and accented from her birthplace, Al-Hakim recited a story that was consistent with what the committee heard earlier. She did not think Tooley meant to hit her,

"...but, he was so mad, I don't think he looked at all to see where he was slamming down that retractor."

She paused, then continued.

"I really don't want anything bad to happen to Dr. Tooley. He made a mistake. I know he's one of the best gynecology doctors at our hospital, and his patients love him."

Ann Rutledge, Nursing Director of Obstetrics and Gynecology, and a voting member of the committee, spoke when Al-Hakim was done.

"Did Dr. Tooley apologize to you?"

"No, but, I haven't seen Dr. Tooley since this happened."

There were no further questions, and after thanking her and reminding Al-Hakim of the need for strict confidentiality, Seavers told her she could go. The committee heard from three additional O.R. personnel, all of whom were present during the incident, and none of their stories deviated in significant details from what the committee previously heard.

After the last O.R. witness finished answering questions, Seavers dismissed him, and announced the committee would now hear from Dr. Tooley. Tooley was escorted in from the hallway by Botsford. He took the seat previously occupied by the other witnesses.

Seavers turned to Tooley and said, "Dr. Tooley, on behalf of this committee, thank you for agreeing to meet with us. As you know, this committee was asked by Dr. Thompson to hear from hospital personnel who were present for one of your surgeries. Dr. Thompson was informed that during the case in question, you struck Ms. Halla Al-Hakim with a Richardson retractor. You understand that, right?"

Tooley spoke clearly and in a strong voice. "Yes, I understand."

"You are free to make a statement to the committee, and afterwards members may want to ask you questions. We would appreciate it if you would answer members' questions, but you are not required to do so. All proceedings of this committee are considered peer-review, and as such, are not discoverable in a court-of-law unless the confidentiality of the proceedings is breeched by you. Do you understand that?"

"I do."

"Do you wish to address the committee?"

"Yes."

"Go right ahead," Seavers said in a friendly tone.

"First of all, I did strike Ms. Al-Hakim with the Richardson. I didn't mean to do it, but I did, and I'm sorry about that. She kept passing me the wrong instruments. I told her several times that she needed to pay more attention to what she was doing, but she kept making mistakes to the point I just couldn't take it anymore, and I blew my stack the way I've seen a lot of other docs around here do when these O.R. techs can't do their simple jobs right. These kinds of incidents wouldn't happen if the hospital hired smarter people for these jobs. Maybe they should get paid more. Anyway, I'm sorry she got her hand banged up, and if I ever get mad like that again, I'll be a lot more careful if I slam an instrument down. I hope we can forget about this and move on."

Unease accompanied the lack of speech in the room. Finally, Dr. Marc Jansen, one of the department's fulltime employed physicians, asked, "Dr. Tooley, do you think there was anything wrong or inappropriate about your behavior during this incident?"

"Well, I think getting mad about being handed the wrong instrument multiple times at a critical point in the case when I'm trying to get better exposure is a natural reaction."

"But, your behavior, the anger and then slamming down the instrument — do you think those things were wrong or inappropriate?"

"If you're asking me if I regret that Halla got her hand banged up, of course I do. If you're asking me whether getting angry was inappropriate, I have to say no. If you're asking me about Halla's hand, it was an accident, and I'm sorry."

Botsford asked, "Dr. Tooley, did anyone mention to you that Ms. Al-Hakim handed you the instruments you actually asked for, and that you may have mistakenly asked for a Richardson when you meant something else?"

"That's a bunch of crap! I know damn well what I asked for, and no one's gonna tell me any different."

Botsford was undeterred by Tooley's angry words.

"Did you apologize to Ms. Al-Hakim?"

"No, not yet, but I have every intention of doing that next time I see her."

After a long pause, it was clear there were no other questions. Seavers turned to Tooley and said,

"On behalf of the committee, thank you for your time, your statement, and your answers to the members' questions. Please, be mindful to keep everything we discussed strictly confidential."

"You don't have to worry about that."

"Dr. Thompson will be in contact with you over the next several days."

"Okey, dokey," was Tooley's relaxed reply. He seemed to have ignored Thompson from the moment he entered the meeting. He rose from his chair and strode from the room.

With Tooley's departure, Thompson stood to address the committee.

"This is a new role for you as members of this committee. You've heard several accounts of the incident from people who were present when it happened. I'm now asking you to determine, amongst yourselves, what you believe happened. After making that determination, I want you to decide whether you believe Dr. Tooley's behavior violated this hospital's by-laws. If you as a group believe that no by-laws were breeched during this incident, then your work is finished. But, if your majority opinion is that by-laws were breeched, then I want you to consider a range of options for addressing Dr. Tooley's behavior and forwarding your recommendations to me. They can range from doing nothing and lifting Dr. Tooley's suspension to concluding that Dr. Tooley's clinical privileges at Winslow be permanently terminated. I will use your recommendations to guide me in my final disposition of this matter. Are there any questions?"

There were none, and Thompson left.

The committee deliberated for less than an hour. There was no disagreement over whether Tooley slammed the instrument down in anger. The committee also agreed he most likely had not intended to hit Al-Hakim's hand or cause her any physical harm. All agreed that he had little or no remorse over the incident, indeed, the consensus was that Tooley acted as if there was nothing wrong with his angry outburst.

Seavers put several motions to a vote. A clear majority agreed that the unrepentant surgeon had violated Winslow's by-laws, albeit unintentionally. Not one person voted that Tooley should regain his privileges without some sort of reprimand. About twenty percent thought Tooley should have his privileges terminated. In the end, the committee voted to recommend that Tooley be required to participate in an anger management intervention before the lifting of his suspension. The committee also recommended that Thompson require Tooley to formally apologize to Al-Hakim, both face-to-face, and in writing, as an additional condition of the reinstatement of his privileges.

Thompson received the committee's report shortly after it adjourned, and he met with Tooley the following afternoon. He told the well-dressed doctor that, based on the committee's suggestions, he identified a program in Nebraska called *Fresh Start for Professionals*.

"These folks do behavioral assessments and make recommendations for interventions along with treatment when it's indicated. Whatever *Fresh Start* recommends, that's what you're gonna do."

Talking to Tooley, who was 10 years his senior, in this forceful, direct, and directive, manner, pressed the Department Chair to overcome his upbringing which demanded respect and deference for one's elders — in all circumstances. Thompson disliked these situations but forced himself to put on his war face and be convincing. The metric of his believability success was that most who left these encounters described him as arrogant or they used a different descriptor that also begins with the letter "A."

Thompson was caught off guard by Tooley's lack of defiance or dismissiveness. He appeared somewhat docile when, without protest, he agreed to go to Nebraska for the evaluation.

Three weeks later, the results of *Fresh Start's* analyses found their way to the top of Thompson's inbox. The evaluation revealed no clear evidence of substance abuse or mental illness. The analysis did, however, uncover serious behavioral problems in Tooley's interpersonal interactions in both his family and professional relationships. *Fresh Start* recommended eight to twelve weeks of residential therapy, and Tooley was adamant in his refusal to participate in such a program. Submitting to that program, he argued, would cost him hundreds of thousands of dollars in lost income,

"Besides, they don't have a fucking clue, everyone they do their analysis on is all fucked up according to them. *Fresh Start* my ass — fresh way to make money is what they're about."

To everything Thompson said, Tooley repeated, some variation of, "No fucking way, it's not gonna happen..."

Thompson was equally unyielding and had no words of compromise.

"Dr. Tooley, there is no pathway for you to regain your privileges at this hospital that doesn't include eight to twelve weeks of residential therapy."

Tooley stood up, his face flush with anger, "We'll see about that, but in the meantime, you can shove that program up your ass."

Thompson shook his head and stood his ground,

"I won't support the lifting of your suspension until you complete the plan they've laid out."

Tooley screamed at Thompson as he stormed out of the office, "I'm not about to sacrifice my time and money or jeopardize my family because some know-it-all new kid on the block, who doesn't know his ass from his elbow, tells me to. You will regret this."

Tooley rushed to his office and called his golfing buddy Ron Blazer, Winslow's CEO. He told his friend about the predicament he was in.

"I'll look into it," the chief executive said, "Keep your cool, and I'll get back to you."

After speaking with Caruthers and concluding he was a brick wall, Blazer spoke to the Chair of Winslow's Board of Directors, Les Ryan. He also called several other board members. Blazer was surprised to learn that they all knew about the situation.

"They tell me the good Dr. Tooley is quite a piece of work," Ryan responded to Blazer. "It sounds like his behavior alone might cost us a pretty penny in law suits one day."

Blazer called Tooley late that evening and told him he had been out maneuvered.

"I'll try a few other things, but it doesn't look good."

As a last ditch attempt, Blazer picked up the phone and called the OB/Gyn Chair directly. After dispensing the requisite social niceties, the CEO told Thompson,

"I'm calling you about Brian Tooley. I know he's got some rough edges, but I've known him for almost 10 years, and I only know him to be a good human being. He's also a great doc. So, I'm asking, can you find any other way to get him some help that won't involve requiring him to go away for an extended period? You'd be doing me a tremendous personal favor, and I'd be in your debt for a long time."

Thompson did not reply for several long seconds. He was not considering what he believed amounted to an allurement and quid pro quo from Blazer, instead, he was contemplating how he would respond without revealing his rising, bilious disgust. He let out a long sigh with his hand over the telephone receiver.

"Mr. Blazer—"

"Call me Ron."

"Okay, Ron, I wish there was another way around this, but there isn't. Dr. Tooley, in a fit of rage, broke the hand of one of our employees, plus he has a long history of melt downs with staff when he gets angry. If I don't do this now, there's a big chance that he'll do something far worse one day, and we'll all lose in a huge way."

"But can't you consider something local that doesn't force him to stop his practice?"

"I sent him to the most experienced people I could find who work with behaviorally challenged professionals. They recommended residential therapy as about the only possibility for rehab. I really don't have a choice. And, as far as letting him do something local, there are only two programs like the one I chose in the country and neither one of them are in this area. I'm asking you, as his friend, please, try to convince him that this is for his own good."

"I don't agree with you, Harold, but it's your call, not mine. Thanks for your time."

It was a dismissal.

"Anytime."

Blazer hung up. Thompson sat in his chair. *That cost me.* Thompson's thoughts again drifted back to northern Vermont and its strenuous test of his young character.

Many of the "first timers," including Thompson, slept restlessly the night before their wilderness departure. Their unease was stoked by upper classman who loved telling horror stories about past expeditions. Tod Johnston, a senior classman, told a group of underclassman the story of Dennis Mueller.

"Yeah, 'ole Mueller was a sophomore, and he used to brag, to everyone who'd listen, about what a big drinker he was. So, he snuck a quart of Wild Turkey in his backpack, and he started hitin' it after dinner the first night out. An hour or so before everyone hit the sack, Mueller was soused, and he was real good too, because nobody, not even Steve Koegle his lean-to mate, knew he was dead drunk. That night he unzipped his sleeping bag, because it got too hot, and he jammed one of his bare feet into the snow at the rear end of the lean-to. By the time he woke up in the morning, that foot was so frost bitten and damaged, they had to take him out by snowmobile. When he finally got to the hospital in Montpelier, it was too late. They had to cut his foot off. Old Mueller never did come back to school. They say the only reason his parents didn't sue was because 'ole Headmaster Richardson went to visit them in Boston, and personally apologized for what happened. Supposedly, Mueller's folks were filthy rich any way, and they knew Dennis was a hopeless fuck-up."

Johnston neglected to tell his horrified audience of 14 and 15-year-olds that his story happened 2 years before he started Bermingham, and what he didn't know was that as he told his tale, Mueller was in Boston walking around on both the feet he was born with.

The story got to Thompson. He reasoned through Mueller being responsible for his own misfortune, but he was rattled by the five hours it took to get that boy to safety. For Thompson, the incident meant that if anything went wrong, even accidently, "Your ass was still in the sling," and this realization drove his fitful last night of sleep.

By 7:30 the next morning campers and equipment were rolling down a two-lane highway toward the starting point of their five mile hike into a northern Vermont first growth wilderness. They reached the staging area two hours later, and it took another hour to get backpacks matched to owners, and the teams configured and in formation. One of the unique features of this experience was each camper carried on his back all of the provisions he would eat and otherwise use for the four-day, three-night trip. They lined up by teams, and the column they formed stretched the length of a city block. Days earlier, Tim Bradley, an eleventh grader, volunteered to break trail. His backpack was snowmobiled into camp. The snow was three to four feet deep. Bradley wore Bear Paw snow shoes and the team directly behind him was rotated about every three quarters of a mile. The snow shoed trail breaker kept an incredible pace for the first four miles before he collapsed from exhaustion and was snowmobiled to the hospital. The rumor later circulated that he dropped two tabs of Dexedrine before leaving his dorm that morning.

By one o'clock, the group reached a large clearing in the forest. This place would become their camp, and for some, their crucible. Thompson was in a team of eight. He and Bill Scott were the best fire starters on their team, and therefore, they were assigned to work their conflagratory magic and bring three large cans full of water from the nearby stream to a boil. The other six boys were sent to scout places to build lean-tos on the clearing perimeter and collect the branches and pine boughs that would be their construction materials. Thompson and Scott used a collapsible shovel to dig out a small fire pit in the snow. They found a number of fallen tree branches and sawed them into ten three or four- inch diameter mini logs of about two feet in length. The little logs were positioned side-by-side to make a base. For tinder, they gathered tiny dry twigs and pieces of birch bark until their collection was about the size of a baseball. While on their knees, they placed the tinder on the base, and with cupped hands, frozen breath, luck, and skill, they turned their little baseball into flame on the third match they struck. They fed their little sphere of light and warmth with progressively larger pieces of wood until they had a very respectable blaze. An hour after arriving at the campsite, the two fire-starters had the cans full of the precious ingredient, boiling water, for their team's first day's lunch of dry packed instant chicken or beef noodle soup, hot chocolate and cheese chunks with cracker packs. Two of the other teams came over to use the fire because they were unable to get one started.

By the time everyone was finished eating, there was about an hour and a half left before sunset. The campers felt better after their hot meal, and they were ready to tackle their next task. Thompson and Scott banked the fire to preserve the coals, and joined the others in building their lean-to. They found two ideally positioned trees, with minimal snow around their bases, and using hemp twine, lashed each end of a single five-foot long, one to two-inch diameter branch to each tree about four feet above the ground. Each boy took a separate eight-foot long branch and lashed an end of it to the horizontal branch close to each tree. The free ends of these branches touched the forest floor and formed a right triangle with the tree and the ground. More branches were lashed together in a crisscross pattern to form a sturdy frame. Pine boughs were laid on the top and sides of the frame, and a 10 by 10 foot polyethylene sheet was draped over the top of the boughs. Snow was heaped on the top and sides of the plastic until it was covered completely. The snow cover was insulation. Thompson and Scott spread a light weight tarp on the ground inside, and put foam rubber pads and their sleeping bags on top. There was enough room for them and the gear they didn't want to leave outside. Their last tarp was used to cover the entrance.

It was just after sunset when the school assembled in the middle of their campsite. All lean-tos were built, sleeping bags were positioned, and other gear was put away. Headmaster Richardson gave a pep talk telling the boys how well they performed and how proud he was of the group. He encouraged them all to eat well and get some sleep. Thompson's team cooked their half chickens in foil along with their frozen vegetable packs and bread rolls. Desert was raisins and thick chocolate bars. The fire gradually sank deeper into the snow base until it reached the bare ground. They added large pieces of wood and the heat melted the snow walls back and formed a pit. The boys helped carve back the walls even more, and eventually there was enough space for the team to all sit around the fire pit which was almost four feet deep. It felt 5 or 10 degrees warmer in that pit, and it was late before the last pair of boys headed to bed. When Thompson and Scott got to their lean-to, they took turns slipping boots off, and banging them together several times to get as much snow and dirt off of them before placing them in the bottoms of the sleeping bags. This kept their footwear from freezing overnight. Both boys stripped off their parkas, flannel shirts, heavy wool pants and got down to their insulated underwear. With socks on, they got into their sleeping bags. They spoke briefly about the day's events, engaged in a farting contest, which Thompson lost, and both were dead asleep 15 minutes later. That first night's, temperature dropped to 20 degrees below zero.

From his childhood days to his current odyssey, as a Cub Scout and Boy Scout, Thompson romanticized accounts he read as well as TV shows and movies, that depicted people drinking water directly out of streams and lakes. This trip was the first time he was able to drink water in that way. Three hours after falling asleep, his new love for wilderness water conspired against him. He awoke and lay in his warm sleeping bag, the scent of the pine boughs in his nostrils, fighting the intense urge to urinate. He knew he would have to crawl out of his cozy cocoon and pee, but he fought the mounting pressure. The wind rattled bare tree limbs outside producing a sometimes rhythmic and quite uninviting sound.

He finally gave in, steeled himself, crawled out of the bag, fished his boots and wool pants out, and pulled them on in the cramped space — Scott didn't stir. After turning to lie on his stomach, with his feet sticking out under the tarp covered entrance, he rose to all fours, and inched himself backwards into the painful cold. He brushed snow off himself when he stood, and then hurriedly took four steps away from the lean-to and began relieving himself. His urine gave off steam as it exited his warm body toward the frozen ground. When he finished, he felt like he had given up a half gallon's worth. He got his boots and pants off, shoved them back in his sleeping bag and joined them. It took about ten minutes for him to feel warm, and he fell fast asleep. Unfortunately, he had to repeat this micturitional ritual three times. The last two times he didn't bother to pull on pants or boots. He stood in the dark woods freezing, peeing, and seriously wondering what the hell he had signed up for, "God please let this be over," was his quiet prayer.

The encampment started coming to life at about seven-thirty in the morning. Boys crawled out of their dwellings and dressed. Some got water from the stream for boiling and for brushing their teeth while others, like Thompson, worked on getting fires started. Many of the students were cold and visibly depressed. Gaiety in the group was absent. The low-keyed din of the camp was ruptured by Mr. Richardson as he yelled, "Is everybody happy?"

Some of the boys muttered, "Fuck you, Fatman." It was spoken so that only the boys closest to them could hear it. A few yelled back in monotone,

"Yeah, we're happy!"

Richardson tried several more times to raise an avalanche of enthusiasm by hollering out his question again. He stopped trying after his fourth yell. Thompson was not miserable, but he wasn't real happy either. He could see the misery many of his schoolmates were in. He respected Richardson too much to call him by his nick name — yet, his responses to the Headmaster's entreats were quiet and devoid of energy. Thompson knew Scott was cold, and he was concerned about him. He tried to get his shelter mate to laugh by telling him two of his best dirty jokes. Scott gave up a slight smile, but his grim face never really disappeared. Thompson started shadow boxing with his friend, and Scott responded. Thompson started mimicking one of his heroes, Muhammad Ali, "I am the greatest," he shouted while he rattled off more Ali quotes in his impersonation of his idol. Scott began smiling and dancing around as he and his lean-to mate threw mock punches toward each other. After about ten minutes his fellow fire starter was smiling, and Thompson thought his buddy was probably a lot warmer.

They made and devoured their breakfasts of hot instant oatmeal, hot drinks and fried Spam. They cleaned their utensils, the pots and pans they used, and generally neatened up their lean-tos. Richardson then led the group in calisthenics and a short hike. By lunch, the Headmaster and his staff knew they were facing a dangerous situation by keeping the boys in the woods with the sub, and near zero temperatures. The day time temperature reached only eight degrees. Mr. Shortman, one of the more unpopular instructors, had to be evacuated because he was hypothermic and had serious frostbite. Several of his staff urged Richardson to call off the trip and head back. He wouldn't hear of it. After much debate and some strongly voiced opinions, a compromise was agreed to. There was a logging camp and cabin two miles up the trail. It had a coal fired stove and fuel to fill it. They would offer the boys the option to stay there over the next two nights. Two thirds of the boys packed up their gear and hiked to the cabin. Thompson was not among them. He hated the idea of another long walk in the bitter cold. The option was out of the question for him. He decided to stay the night and make the most of it by himself. Scott decided to leave.

Thompson was careful to limit his water intake during his second day in the woods. He only got up once to urinate in the night, but otherwise he slept soundly in the minus eighteen-degree darkness. In the morning, after breakfast, Richardson assembled the remaining boys and announced they were all going to walk to the logging camp. They should bring their lunch and dinner provisions. They would cook and eat in the cabin, and those boys who opted to spend their last night in their lean-tos would hike back, just before sundown. The forty remaining boys packed up and moved out. They reached the camp in just under an hour. The cabin was a large structure of about fifty-five hundred square feet. The ceiling was eighteen-and-a-half feet high, and there was no upper floor or basement. The coal burning heater brought the inside temperature up to a balmy sixty degrees. Originally, benches lined the walls, but many were moved, and the campers sat in groups. They were now laughing, telling stories, and there was some trash talk going on. It was the first time in two days that their struggle against the cold was not their foremost thought. There was no recorded music or news from the outside world because bringing transistor radios or tape recorders was forbidden. Instead, they sang camp songs, and some of the boys played rock-paper-scissors. Their rules called for the loser to receive a two-finger slap by the winner across the inside forearm. Some pretty nasty welts were raised as a result of this game.

They cooked on several fires that were started outside and safely away from the cabin. Dinner consisted of an eight-once steak, instant macaroni and cheese, frozen vegies, and bread rolls, most of which were extremely misshaped from their back packed journey. The cooking skills of the boys varied widely as did the doneness of their steaks. A few of the diners appeared to be eating raw meat. They finished dinner with raisins and chocolate. When the latest arrivals packed up to leave, eleven of their ranks decided to stay. Thompson walked back with the others. The outside temperature which reached fifteen degrees above zero was now falling fast as daylight faded. The group sang on the way back. They started with the Mickey Mouse Club theme song, and then began a rendition of *A Hundred Bottles of Beer on the Wall* – "...you take one down and pass it around they'll be 99 bottles of beer on the wall..." The time walking passed quickly.

Back at his lean-to, Thompson arranged his belongings, urinated, striped down to his long Johns, stuffed his boots, along with his clothes, into his sleeping bag and got in. He lay there for a time thinking about why he hadn't been smarter like many of the other boys and admitted to himself, and anyone who cared, that he was miserable, scared, and not very tough. He was close to tears, but fell asleep before they could flow.

Chapter Ten

In the weeks following his meeting with Carla's mother and aunt, Thompson called Sylvia several times to ask if there was anything she needed and to reassure her that the hospital's investigation was ongoing. Without saying it directly, he also made the calls to let her know he had not forgotten his promise to her. He was surprised by how easily these conversations flowed and by Sylvia's openness. She told him that she appreciated all his effort, "...because a lotta folks in my family don't believe the hospital will ever tell us what really happened." He took her comments in without ever confessing that he shared some of these doubts. She told him that Xavier was having the hardest time adjusting, at least outwardly, to his mom's absence. "The only reason they haven't suspended him from school for some of his acting out is because they're making a real effort to be understanding."

During their third conversation, Thompson gingerly asked, "Are any of the children's fathers involved with them?"

"No, they aren't. I don't know where Christopher's daddy is. Xavier's father, who I knew the best, because he married Carla, died. Sam Brooks was a good man, and probably the only good man of the three. And, Elise's daddy I met several times, but I can't say I knew him at all. His name is Winston and he's doin' time in the Jackson State Prison if that tells you anything."

The more Thompson learned about Carla B. Williams the more his curiosity was piqued. He wondered how a well-educated physically attractive woman, who was so full of drive and ambition, wound up having deadbeats father two of her children. When his conversation with Sylvia ended, he knew that loose ends and half answers were the best he could hope for in his quest to understand

Carla's anima. To achieve the degree of insight into this remarkable individual that he desired would have required Thompson to get a woman named Joy Sanders to talk openly about her deceased friend, and there was no chance of this. The Department Chair and Carla's closest confident did not know of one another, and although Sylvia logically would have guessed at Joy's intimate knowledge of her daughter's personal life, the two were not close, and they never discussed this aspect of Carla.

Joy and Carla weathered years of one another's life struggles including their men storms. Their spiritual connection, and length of friendship, allowed Carla to be more open with Joy than with anyone. Joy could author the memoir *The Loves of Carla B. Williams*, with a richness of detail that would have astounded the chronicle's primary subject. Joy was with her best friend when Carla met Christopher's and Elise's fathers.

Both women were in their mid-twenties when they decided to meet after work at a popular downtown Detroit club called The High Water. It was a Friday, Carla was in her first year of full time teaching and trying to recover from a very tough five days during which one of her students was severely stabbed in an after school gang melee. Joy was finishing her second year at American Bank of Detroit and celebrating her first week after a promotion to Consumer Loan Officer. The newly empowered banker was festive and bubbly while Carla was uncharacteristically pensive. They were seated in a booth bordering a shiny black dance floor that, after about an hour, came alive with the reds and blues of sweeping strobe lights and the movement of what seemed like every foot in the place. Joy now had to almost shout above the loud noises of music, voices, and motion to describe how different her new job was. In turn, Carla hollered an occasional question but mostly sipped her frozen daiquiri. Its familiar icy strawberry sweetness combined with the rum base to blunt some of the raw edges she was carrying. Joy spoke, and Carla nodded or made nonverbal sounds of affirmation or sympathetic disapproval.

The high school teacher felt a sudden new presence and looked up to see a tall, slender, well-dressed black man, probably in his mid-twenties, standing at her side. Michael Watford's voice was just at the beginning of his hit *So Into You*. The stranger looked directly into Carla's eyes and with his hand extended to her said, "Can I get this dance?"

She smiled at him while she said, "No thanks. I really didn't come out to dance tonight."

When he was out of earshot, Joy said,

"*Excuse me*, but you musta had a *really* bad week to not wanna take the wrapper offa that piecea eye candy."

"You are *sooo* out there," Carla said, laughing for the first time that evening.

Unbeknownst to the booth mates, David Cardwell gave the DJ a twenty-dollar bill in exchange for playing Prince's song *I would die 4 U,* and allowing him to use the cordless microphone to karaoke. David had a rich tenor and sang with a natural vibrato that distinguished his effort. Carla noticed some commotion on the other side of the room, but didn't think much of it. She did think that whoever was singing sounded good. The singing got louder, and Carla looked up to notice David was again standing at their booth singing, "I would Die 4 U...Baby if you want me to..." The whole club was watching and many laughed and shouted their approval. David was now down on one knee and singing which drew even louder cheers. When he finished, he was kneeling at Carla's side as he spoke into the microphone,

"Now will you please have the next dance with me baby?" Carla had a big smile when she took the microphone from David and with her left arm outstretched, palm up, as if asking the audience, she said,

"How can I say no?"

The crowd went crazy with applause. David stood up, and reached out to her. Carla took his right hand, he helped her up, and they walked over to the DJ hand-in-hand. David returned the microphone and asked the DJ to play Whitney Houston's version of *I will Always Love You*. The new couple danced to the delight of both themselves and most of the other folks in attendance. The dance floor filled with couples enjoying the chance to dance close and slow with their partners.

Carla and David saw each other regularly that summer. He began calling her "Sun" like almost all of her close friends. She really liked David. He was a gentle man, who was well-mannered and had a wonderful subtle sense of humor, but he was not goal oriented. He didn't know what he wanted to do with his life when he graduated from high school and joined the army, more to fill time than anything else. David became an infantry soldier who did one tour of duty in the first Gulf War during which he participated in the 100-hour ground assault on Iraq. After six years of active duty he was honorably discharged, and when he got home, he told his mother, "I just wanna find a steady job and live with the fewest hassles possible."

David became a mail sorter for the Postal Service and was very content with his life of work and play.

By the second year of her full-time assignment at Wheatley, Carla had become a very popular teacher. Fair, caring, and tough was her "rep" with the kids. She was committed to helping struggling students which she did by staying after school to help with homework, and she sometimes met students on Saturday mornings at the Boys and Girls Club of West Detroit to tutor them in math and reading. She related to the high schoolers both on their level and as an adult authority figure. She accomplished this with her poise and approachability, which made the kids comfortable, however, she left just enough of her street life persona on the surface that the kids respected her in a way that was different from the respect they gave many of her colleagues. The 'word' on the Wheatley grapevine was, "If you mess with Miss Williams, you might could get hurt."

As a coach, Carla was known as a task master. She enforced discipline and respect for authority while demanding fitness and dedication to the concept of team. Her teenage basketball coach, Mr. Emanuel Brown, focused on, and demanded the same fundamentals. His influence pulled Carla away from the edge of a void of life long failure and misery.

The time Carla spent with her students fueled her growing desire to have children of her own. After two years of dating, she knew she did not want to marry David. They were very compatible on many levels. They could take vacations together for a week or two weeks and never once get on one another's nerves. She appreciated and respected David, but for Carla, liking David, having great times with David, appreciating and respecting David, did not equal loving David — at least not romantically. Carla had a primal longing for emotional intimacy. It was not something she was fully conscious of, she couldn't articulate this desperate necessity, but she craved it nonetheless. It was a need never fulfilled in her relationship with David.

On the subject of marriage, David never raised the idea. For Carla, although only 24, the specter of turning 30 without children was very much on her mind. Her urge to have a child over shadowed every other long-term aspiration she had. When she broached the idea with David, she sensed that he was not paying attention — it was as if he was having an absence seizure, or he was very non-committal and abruptly changed the subject. Yes, on the marriage component of family they were of similar mind, but on the question of having children they were polar opposites. David's seeming disinterest in parenthood did not dampen Carla's desire whatsoever, and for many reasons, she believed David was the ideal man to father the baby she was determined to birth.

Eight months after her 24th birthday, as self-assured as Carla was, her stomach was alive with the flutter of butterflies on a sunny Saturday afternoon in late May. She was seated next to David in his top down two-year-old convertible. They were on Belle Isle, the city's largest park which is an island about a half mile out from the Detroit

River shoreline. The temperature was in the high 70s, but the breeze coming off the water added a slight humid chill. The young couple watched a barge plod down the middle of the waterway. The craft's enormous size and slow speed gave it a surreal appearance. Carla was on the verge of telling David several times but couldn't make the words come out. She tried counting, starting at one, with the resolve to tell him immediately when she reached ten, but she got to ten at least six times, but her lips didn't move. A gust of the cool wind caught the wordless expectant mother off guard. A chill coursed through Carla. It focused and emboldened her. She shifted her body to the left and said, "David, you're gonna be a father." She braced for his angry response, but instead she got a big smile. "You're not mad?"

"No, I figured this was comin'. When do you wanna get married?"

"Not right now — I mean, David, you don't have to do anything for this kid. I'll raise it by myself. You can help only if you want to."

"And, why wouldn't I want to? This kid will be mine too you know."

Despite his lack of interest and lack of direct role models for being a father or a husband — David never knew his father and his mother was always single, he was attentive to the soon-to-be mother of his first child in every way he could be.

Carla had numerous bouts of intense morning sickness. When the nausea and vomiting came on, she couldn't keep any food or liquid down. She lost four pounds in the first twelve weeks of her pregnancy. Her vomiting became so severe that on 3 occasions she was admitted to Winslow for overnight stays and treated with intravenous glucose, electrolyte, and fluid replacement. David slept in her room on the uncomfortable cot the nurses provided, and when she was in her apartment, he laid next to Carla rubbing her back until they both fell asleep. Carla awoke suddenly one early morning. She jerked up with such force that David was jolted into consciousness. Carla took one look at him, threw her right hand over her mouth and made a hurried move to the toilet where she vomited for what seemed like an eternity. David often humorously told this story to their friends and family. He would end the tale by saying, "Man she's got me thinkin' I'm the ugliest fool on the planet."

Carla had some degree of *hyperemesis gravidarum* for her entire pregnancy. She got thru it by sucking on lots of hard candy, constant sips of ginger ale, and drinking ginger root tea when she could. These remedies were all prescribed by her most primary doctor, Sylvia.

The mother-to-be was determined to continue her work schedule until she went into labor. She missed a total of four days of school in spite of her hyperemesis and the attendant hospitalizations. She also kept up a regimen of light exercise because it was part of her, and she read that physically fit mothers, in general, had easier labors. She walked with her cousin Sheila Tate who was the daughter of one of Sylvia's older brothers, Thomas. The workout buddies grew up together, with Carla being older by three years. The two women looked like sisters. Sheila shared her cousin's caramel colored complexion, and she was only a half inch taller than Carla. Sheila's pretty facial features were reminiscent of Carla. The accounting department employee had no sisters and always felt a big sister kinship with her older cousin. Sheila was an avid runner, but Carla convinced Sheila to be her walking partner for a two-mile stroll four times a week. While they walked, the pair talked about everything from newborns to why men act so stupid. Sheila finished college with a degree in business administration, and she was working in the accounting department of a medium sized auto plant supplier. She had a boyfriend she planned to marry, and she was looking forward to getting some parenting experience by helping Carla care for her new arrival.

On a Monday morning, In the middle of her 9:30 Social studies class, Carla received a call on her classroom phone from the Principal's office. The secretary told Carla to call her mother immediately. Carla told her class she was leaving for a few minutes to get a message, and she headed to the teacher's lounge around the corner from her classroom. She turned on her cell phone and called her mother. Ten seconds into the call Carla's eyes and cheeks were dripping with tears. Sylvia told her that Sheila went out for a run earlier that morning and was the victim of a hit-and-run accident. She wasn't discovered for at least forty-five minutes, and when the ambulance arrived she was unconscious with a faint heartbeat and almost no blood pressure. The paramedics attempted to resuscitate Sheila, but she was pronounced dead on arrival at the Anthony University Medical Center.

Carla was an emotional wreck. Next to her mother, and Joy, there was no one she was closer to than Sheila. Carla sobbed over and over to Sylvia, "Why Sheila, why my baby sister?" Wheatley's principal was called to the lounge. She did not come close to consoling Carla, but in less than five minutes, told her beyond-distraught-faculty-member she had to go home for at least the rest of the day. She answered Carla's protests by telling her not to worry about teaching or coaching. "Other faculty members will pitch in." It was immediately clear to Sylvia that her daughter was in no condition to drive. She spoke to Principal Wadlow and asked her to tell Carla she was on her way to pick her up.

They drove to Sylvia's home. Carla stayed with her mother for two days before returning to her own apartment. David stayed with Carla when she returned home. He tried hard to make her life comfortable. He listened a lot and helped her bear her grief in the best ways he knew.

The funeral was held five days after Sheila's death. The three days Carla worked prior to bidding her beloved cousin her final good-bye were the most difficult in her teaching career.

The service was held on a cold sunshiny October Saturday morning. David, Sylvia, and Joy were Carla's strength that day. She cried almost non-stop throughout the service. Three hours after they returned home, David had to take Carla into the hospital for abdominal pains which turned out to be false labor. Carla eventually regained her calm and resigned herself to going on with life minus her dear "little sis."

* * *

Eleven weeks after losing Sheila, Carla's water broke while calling drill commands from the sidelines to her basketball players. One of her fellow teachers helped her out of the gym and into his car. He drove her to the hospital where Carla was admitted, and went into active labor within two hours. She delivered Christopher David Sterling Williams nine hours later. Carla was overjoyed as were David, Sylvia, and Joy who were at her side in the birthing room while she pushed her baby boy out and into the world. David was given quick instructions and a pair of sterile scissors which he used to cut Christopher's umbilical cord as Sylvia and Joy took lots of pictures.

Carla's hospital course was short. She elected to go home after twenty-four hours because she found the hospital noisy and a very difficult place to sleep. The new mother and Christopher stayed with Sylvia, the newly minted grandmother, for the first two weeks after the delivery. Months earlier, Sylvia planned time off work to help with Christopher, and her daughter was able to get a lot of rest. But, when Carla moved back to her apartment, for reasons she couldn't verbalize, she felt afraid to be alone with Christopher. She asked David to stay with her as much as he could, but this didn't seem to dissipate her fears. Carla wasn't sleeping well at all. She would wake up to feed her son, and toss and turn for hours after she finished nursing. She was often not able to fall back asleep. Carla became super irritable, and she angered easily at David. She cried often for no apparent reason, and she felt terrible. She talked to her mother about what was happening, and Sylvia told her she was having the "baby blues."

"Don't worry honey, I had them with you, and they passed after a few days."

Unfortunately, Carla sank into a deep blue funk that wouldn't lift. She told Joy, "I look out my window sometimes in the middle of the morning, it looks as dark as midnight and I feel like my body is dragged down with heavy weights."

She didn't feel like eating, and lost fifteen pounds in three weeks. David was the frequent object of Carla's angry rants, and several times he retreated hurriedly out the door of her apartment with Carla screaming curses at him. Finally, at her six-week check-up, Carla was diagnosed as having postpartum depression. She was given a prescription for anti-depressant medication which she didn't fill.

"I'm not crazy, mama, I don't want to take that stuff," she told Sylvia.

Several days later, after sobbing to her mother that she felt like she wanted to die, Sylvia came to Carla's apartment, convinced her to fill the prescription, and Carla began taking the medicine. Sylvia took more time off from her job and stayed with her daughter and grandson. She pressed her daughter to take the medicine over Carla's complaints that it wasn't working.

"Remember, Baby, the doctor said it will take some time for the drug to start working, please don't give up."

After a little more than two weeks, Carla began to feel better. She was able to return to Wheatley, although she continued to take the medication for two months. Unfortunately, her arguments with David were so vehement that there was no road to recovery for their relationship. Carla tried to make amends for her behavior and nasty degrading comments, but David was through. He didn't come back to see his son, and eventually he bid for a post office position in Atlanta. He got the position and left Detroit a month later. Several years after leaving Christopher and Carla, he married. Carla never heard from him again. She grieved and beat herself up over the loss of Christopher's father for many months.

"Joy, I own that I was an evil hateful bitch to David, but I was sick and didn't know it. I tried to explain to him how sorry I am, but he wouldn't hear it. I'd explain and apologize over and over and he'd just say, "I gotta go," and that would be it."

"Girl, you did everything you could do to try and make it right. I think he just didn't wanna stay, he probably never wanted to stay."

"That's what I'm startin' to think too, I feel real bad, but I can't change what happened. I gotta just go on and raise my son."

Chapter Eleven

Several days before the first meeting of Davidson's committee, Sedaris made an appointment to meet with Thompson. The two men shook hands as Sedaris walked into the office. Thompson knew his Chief of Gynecology would not have come for something trivial. But, he couldn't read through the former combat pilot's placid mien. It was this element of Sedaris's bearing that, not infrequently, led people who did not know him to severely underestimate the ferocity of purpose he was capable of bringing to any cause that incited his sense of right and wrong. His Air Force leadership position was not accidental. He had a reputation for intense loyalty to his comrades as well as to his mission, and this trait was at the core of his professional and personal relationships.

When they were seated on the couches, Thompson nodded toward Sedaris and said, "What's goin' on?"

Sedaris stared at Thompson for a moment before saying, "I'm very concerned by the tone of this review of the case of Chambers. It feels like Davidson's staff is being pointed in selected directions by some of his precious stakeholders."

"Can you give me specifics?"

"It seems that Anesthesia and Surgery are trying to position themselves as blameless guardian angels rather than the other angel they probably are."

"Which angel are you talking about?"

"The original highest one — Satan."

Thompson was so caught off guard by the remark, and its timing, that the laughter he couldn't contain was from his gut. Sedaris didn't crack a smile.

"What do you think I should do?"

"Nothing. I'm only here to let you know that if you begin to hear what a bad choice you made for this committee, you'll know it's because I'm digging."

* * *

The first Sentinel Event Committee meeting was held in the afternoon, on the third Wednesday after Carla's funeral. The Departments of Surgery and Anesthesiology were represented by their Chairs, Dr. Ross Hibbard and Dr. Jamie Rykowski, respectively. Nurse Christine Bowright, Director of O.R. Staffing, represented her division. The physician contingent on the panel completed with Drs. Sedaris and Patricia McHenry. The later was in the last year of her Ob/Gyn Residency and served as the Administrative Chief Resident.

Warren's description to Thompson, of the events that took place during and after Carla's surgeries, did not differ in any meaningful details from the timeline constructed by Davidson's staff. There were no challenges to the staff's events sequence from any of the committee's members. The staff presentation implied that Warren had all the information he needed, relatively early in Carla's post-op period, to take definitive action to save his patient's life. Instead, the staff's summary suggested, Warren was inept in his interpretation of his patient's vital signs and clinical condition, "...which," the report stated, "...led to a spiral of lethal procrastination."

The meeting was heading toward a non-contested rubber stamp of the findings and their interpretation by Davidson and his staff when Sedaris said, "Excuse me, but I have several questions about these findings."

"Please," Davidson said.

"When I went through this document, I became quite curious about two things. The first was the patient's vital signs. I was puzzled about why a woman who is bleeding to death, like this patient, never raises her pulse."

"You know that doesn't always happen when patients go into shock. What are you saying," Dr. Rykowski asked pointedly, before Sedaris could continue.

"I'm saying, for one thing, you are absolutely correct, and this case is a perfect example."

"Then, what's your point?" Rykowski said.

"My point is why, and my point became my question — why did this mismatch between pulse and blood pressure occur in this patient? I began to look closely at the intra-op and post-op portions of this report, and it turns out, this patient had two episodes of gross hypertension during her original surgery, while she was under general anesthesia, both were accompanied by high heart rates in the 120s to 130s. Her blood pressures were not mildly elevated, they became dangerously high. They were in the 220 over 140 range. She could have easily suffered a massive stroke. And, for the benefit of the non-medical people here today, some patients, for reasons that are unclear, respond to this kind of anesthesia with these very dangerous blood pressure spikes."

"Excuse me, Dr. Sedaris," Dr. Rykowski said in a voice dripping with irritation. "But, why does extreme hypertension, on the one hand, a phenomenon, which, as you pointed out, is known to occur sometimes with general anesthesia, and subsequent post-op *hypotension,* make you concerned or suspicious about the conclusions we heard here today?"

"The whole thing raises my curiosity because this patient's hypertensive-tachycardic episodes that happened during her surgery show us that her system had the capacity to respond to low blood pressures normally, by raising her pulse, yet an hour later she doesn't."

Dr. Hibbard spoke up,

"Dr. Sedaris, what are you proposing as an alternative explanation for why this patient died?"

"I'm not proposing a different conclusion right now — I haven't had access to the medical record yet. What I am saying is that when a set of circumstance like these present themselves, we owe it to our current and future patients, and ourselves, to dig deeper for causes than we've done here."

"Even if we find other factors that impacted this case, it is virtually impossible that they would explain away Chambers' bad judgement and procrastination."

"So, Dr. Rykowski, are you saying, with all that's at stake here, it's not worth a more in-depth look?"

Before Rykowski or anyone else could respond, Davidson said, "Doctor Sedaris, do you have any other concerns or questions about this preliminary report?"

"Actually, I do. I believe that in addition to a closer look at the records, before we finalize our conclusions, we need to thoroughly look into the current practice of closing the O.R.s on L&D when there are patients who are post-op from major surgeries in the recovery room there, and we need to look into why the main O.R. did not have a room staffed and ready for this patient when she arrived."

Boatwright who appeared to have been concentrating on Sedaris' comments said, "Dr. Sedaris, are you saying or implying that somehow the O.R. was at fault in this case?"

"No, I'm not, but we need to clarify why a room was not ready when Dr. Chambers and his team arrived with the patient. Apparently, nothing was prepared for immediate surgery. The O.R. may have never been contacted - there might be several reasons for what happened, but we need to find what those reasons are."

Davidson addressed the group.

"I invite anyone, over the next few days to forward to me any information they discover that may call into question or shed more light on what we've heard today. The patient's actual medical records will be made available for anyone here today to examine. In light of

Dr. Sedaris' comments, my staff and I will follow-up again with those who participated in this patient's care, and we will re-examine records with today's comments and questions in mind. We will confirm where we can, and amend our report if appropriate. In the meantime, I want the committee to proceed with creating an action plan to address the issues identified thus far, including those raised by Dr. Sedaris this afternoon."

"Help me understand this," said Rykowski. "You're asking us to create an action plan before we know if the things we heard today are relevant?"

"Yes..."

"That makes no sense."

"The logic is that even if we can't find evidence to support the concerns that were raised, at the very least, we've identified some serious potential problems."

There was no further opposition to Davidson's request for an action plan, and an energetic discussion began.

* * *

Davidson's staff re-questioned several O.R. and recovery room personal involved with Carla's care, and they interviewed all of the physicians involved. They also meticulously re-reviewed the entire medical record in light of what they heard during the committee meeting. The final report reflected these efforts. When Thompson was given a copy of the report, after the Board of Directors officially accepted it, he took the 45-page document home and read it while lying in his bed. The weary department head was intrigued, but not surprised by the findings and conclusions.

Thompson placed the report on his night stand when he finished reading it. He turned his reading lamp off and lay in the dark. It was almost midnight and he had to be in at 7:00 a.m., but sleep eluded him. Thompson jumped from one thought to another, but he kept returning to his impending battle royale with Winslow's administrators. He also thought about his promise to Sylvia and her sister to tell them the truth about what happened to their daughter and niece — the mother of three young children, the role model and mentor for hundreds of kids, the ambitious professional in the midst of increasing her skill set — god damn it! Why her? This was a part of being the Department's Chair that he could never have imagined, getting involved in sensitive, emotional patient problems he had no hand in creating. He acknowledged that he was the architect of a large portion of his anguish. Reinhardt hadn't handled the job this way and neither did Winslow's other department heads. Thompson knew he was alone on this quest of his choosing — alone and making it up as it came up.

Lying on his stomach in the dark, craving for sleep to overtake him, he kept thinking about the unhappiness that the fulfillment of his promise to Sylvia would cause her and her family, as well as the fear it might provoke in many of Winslow's medical and administrative leaders. The possibility of not making good on his pledge of openness did not occur in any of Thompson's cornucopia of thoughts which included, "Why don't I just go crazy — insane?" He asked this rhetorical question of himself sometimes when he felt overwhelmed. These self-doubts brought on a flood of childhood and young adult memories in the almost hour-and-a-half before unconsciousness finally, mercifully overtook him.

Chapter Twelve

Warren kept up a normal schedule of surgeries on both his private patients and the resident procedures he scrubbed on. He continued his private office hours as well as doing his time as a proctor in the resident clinics. The stew of angst about Carla's death, the impending sentinel event report, along with the tortured emotions he felt about the unhappy union he shared with Gina, all gave rise to a dour demeanor that was noticeable and quiet unusual for him. He walked through his days joyless. The maintenance of his air of self-confidence was for years a tremendous energy drain, and that persona was now barely perceptible. He sat in his Winslow office on a late Wednesday afternoon in front of his computer, pressing himself for the words to begin composing a recommendation he agreed to write for one of his medical students. Instead of working the keys to fashion the needed letter, his mind wondered back to junior year at his semi-rural Rutherford High School.

Warren was just past his 17th birthday on a cold Monday afternoon in late January. He was working with his team of three other students in their advanced biology class. He was engrossed in the dissection of the team's fetal pig cadaver. Brad Moore was acting as if he had no interest in the dissection, or the accompanying discussion. He was making one wise crack after another, including stories about the, "...poor little piggy's unlived childhood, snatched away by a cruel pig abortionist, and now *this* little piggy has none."

Warren smiled. He almost always found Brad's off the wall humor funny. Andrea Whitmore, who was working with Warren, also laughed, but she and Warren continued working in earnest. After ninety seconds of staring at the open animal carcass, with its accompanying formaldehyde odor, David Sheridan, the fourth team member, hurried out of the room with his hand covering his mouth. He made a run for the boy's restroom.

"Warren, the way you're moving through this pig's tummy, you must have been all over the books last night," Andrea said.

"Yeah, I really got into following the paths of the vessels and then the nerves."

Warren had steady quick hands. His dissection partner watched him easily, and accurately, separate and expose blood vessels and nerves from their surrounding tissue. He preserved the origins and branch points of the structures while minimally disrupting the neighboring anatomy.

"Does playing that saxophone of yours give you those flying fingers," Andrea asked. Warren smiled,

"I never thought of it like that before."

He occupied the first saxophone chair in the high school band, and he played with a rock group called the *Wild Walkers*. As they continued their dissection, Warren was able to explain a lot of the anatomy and the related physiology to his partners because he had studied so hard over the weekend. Brad got serious enough to start taking notes before the lab session ended. He promised his teammates he would make copies for them.

Five years later, Warren described that afternoon to a medical school admissions interviewer,

"I felt like a surgeon going through that dissection. I still get excited when I think about how I felt that day. That was the day I decided I wanted to be a doctor."

Winter Carnival at Rutherford High School was a weeklong celebration of frost and fun. The event was held in mid-February and included toboggan and cross-country skiing races, figure skating and hockey competitions, ice fishing derbies, as well as ice and snow sculpture contests. The week culminated with a semi-formal dinner and dance. During Warren's senior year, the banquet was held on the Saturday after Valentine's Day. The dance was to be the first big performance for the *Wild Walkers.*

The Saturday morning of the dance, Warren was eating breakfast with his three sisters. Two hours before his children were up, Max left to work at his car dealership which he started twenty years earlier by selling used cars from his front yard. After ten years of hard work, he managed to obtain a coveted Ford Motor Company Franchise, and his business was now thriving. His effort to become a franchisee was so difficult that he refused to observe the Michigan tradition of no weekend car sales. Claire was still in bed. It was not unusual for her to stay in bed for most of a weekend. Sitting at the table, the entire bottom of Warren's left foot was planted on the floor, but only the toes and balls of his right foot touched the linoleum beneath him. He was rapidly bouncing his right foot and knee up and down, while he took short sips of his orange juice, and used his fork to play with the cold scrambled eggs on his plate. Without looking at her, Warren told his older sister, "Cynthia, you're gonna have to take Mary and Barbara to their dance lessons today and pick them up."

His tone was sharp and edgy. "No, I don't, and no I won't."

Warren exploded. "You sit around all weekend and do nothing. I'm playing for the dance tonight, and I need every minute to practice."

"I need to praaactice, I need to praaactice," Cynthia mocked her younger brother in a high-pitched voice that made him even angrier.

Warren turned his head, thrust it toward Cynthia and said, "You either do this for me, or you won't have a friend left when I get through with you."

Cynthia's self-assured haughtiness collapsed. She said, almost tearfully, "You're not going to order me to do anything."

Cynthia was in her second year of community college, and although their circles of friends did not overlap, the town was small and friendship circles often touched. She knew her brother had stories that would make her a pariah.

"I didn't order you. Can you please take the girls to dance this morning?"

"I'll think about it," Cynthia said. Her voice was choked with emotion as she got up in an angry, upset huff and headed to her room.

Warren turned to Mary and Barbara. His two younger sisters were silent throughout Warren and Cynthia's exchange. He gently told them to rinse their plates in the sink and then get ready for dance. They responded to their big brother more like he was a father figure instead of a sibling. It was obvious to anyone who witnessed Warren's interaction with his little sisters that he doted on them. Their "okay" acknowledgements were pleasant and giggly as they headed off to get washed and dressed. They were oblivious to the undercurrents in motion around them.

Warren went to his room, closed the door and tried to start practicing. At first he was fidgeting, playing with things in his room. He leafed through his stamp collection. He also looked at some of his prize-winning bug collection catches before he finally got down to playing his saxophone. For hours he repetitively played numerous scales and all the songs in his group's repertoire. He interspersed songs with scales and scales with songs. Playing his horn made him feel good. The music took his mind in directions that distracted him from his fears and helped melt his tension. He played through his doubts about his abilities, and his worries about how the evening would turn out evaporated.

Over two hundred students attended the banquet. With the teachers and parents who were there, the total attendance topped two hundred fifty. By the time the awards and acknowledgements were made, it was eight thirty when The *Wild Walkers* took the stage. They were seven in all. Six boys played instruments, and they had a lead singer named Ken Baker. He was a handsome kid whose sharp facial features were accented by his clear white skin. He was five-nine, and with his shaggy deep brown hair, moved around on stage with a command that was inconsistent with his age. They began playing covers of Huey Lewis and the Newsboys, The Temptations, and they did Led Zeppelin's *Stairway to Heaven*. Many of the couples danced non-stop to one song after another. Forty-five minutes into their performance, Ken Baker took center stage. With microphone in hand, he began singing an A cappella blues line.

"Has anybody seen my baby...has anybody seen my girl."

He cried the words out as if he was suffering from excruciating heartache. At this point, Warren, who had donned a pair of black rimmed very dark tinted sunglasses and a stingy brimmed black hat, "duck walked" across the stage, crouched low with one knee bent, and the other leg stretched out in front of him while he moved across the stage playing his sax which was slung low on his audience side. Warren's antics screamed Chuck Berry. He sidled up to Ken and they did a call and response routine. Ken cried out, "Why would she do me that-a-way," and Warren mimicked Ken's voice on the saxophone. This went on for almost two minutes, while the kids responded with frenzied screams along with wild cheers and applause.

Many of the adults were cheering as well. Warren's stage persona was somewhat of a caricature of his everyday outward self. On stage he was the quiet unassuming hard working member of the band. But, underneath there was a spirit that could turn mischievous, and stir things up. The Call and Response led right into a ten-minute whole band blues rock rendition of, *Send My Baby Back to Me*. The tune brought almost everyone to the dance floor. The performance was high energy and the audience was using its feet to give the band a big thumb's up. The steep upward arc of the group's frenzied performance climaxed with this tune. The *Wild Walker's* ended their show with a slow dance version of Peter Frampton's song *Baby I Love Your Way*. The night ended for Warren with a feeling of relief and many compliments peppered by slaps on the back.

The reminiscence ended and Warren was staring at the blank document on his desktop screen. *Maybe I should have stuck with the music like Ken and become part of a premier rock band — the odds were only 1 in 45 hundred thousand that I would have made it. I could have avoided Gina...but I would have avoided my kids too and I wouldn't trade them for anything. I know you get to the other side and it's just a field of brown grass...I know that, but it's nice to dream 'cause the grass I'm in now sure ain't green.*

* * *

Thompson arrived for his usual Tuesday morning Labor and Delivery rounds with the resident/nursing team that worked the previous night, and the new team taking over for the day. He used his version of the Socratic Method to prod the residents into explaining and justifying their reasoning for the actions they took, or did not take, for every patient presented. Many of the trainees hated these sessions. They were forced to read beforehand and then reason in front of an audience of about thirty to forty which included medical, nursing, and allied health students who gathered to listen. There was great risk of public humiliation. Thompson tried not to press his questions to the point of overwhelming his resident presenters. However, that he had little time for lazy doctors or lazy thinking quickly became well known. For Thompson, behavior that appeared to emanate from an attitude of "I don't care" bordered on mortal sin. If he became convinced that a physician or nurse did not care about the patients they were responsible for, whenever possible, he took steps to separate that person from his department.

A few of the brightest doctors in training actually enjoyed the opportunity to go toe-to-toe with "The Big Man." It was known that, when he was wrong, Thompson would concede points and admit his errors. These moments were rare, but they were cherished by his residents. Those that were able to wrest a concession from Thompson garnered a great deal of respect from their colleagues, the nurses, and some attendings. Thompson never challenged the nurses in the way he challenged his residents, and in keeping with a centuries long history of doctor nurse rivalry, many of the nurses took great pleasure in watching some of the "know-it-all" residents squirm under Thompson's clinical interrogations.

"Doctor, you just admitted that Ms. Stevens, who is six hours postpartum, with blood pressures spiking to the two hundred over one twenty range and is making less than thirty ccs of urine an hour, is the sickest patient on your board, right," he asked during one rounding session.

"Yes," answered the third-year leader of the resident team.

"Then please explain to me why no doctor has been in to examine and assess this patient all night?"

"I have no excuse, Dr. Thompson," the resident was smart enough to answer. Thompson moved to question the group on what they needed to do for this patient going forward.

"You call me on my cell at ten this morning without fail, and tell me what's goin' on with this patient," he said to the third-year leader who was taking over. The demand for an update call was foreign to the residents. They became accustomed to this expectation and realized that their department Chair would ask for these calls on any patient he was concerned about whether the patient was from the resident clinic or a private practice.

The degree of Thompson's involvement with hands-on-patient care was disorienting for many of the physicians and nurses. They were quiet comfortable with Reinhardt's hands-off approach. Many of the L&D nurses openly admitted that they wouldn't be able to pick the former Chair out of a police line-up. Reinhardt once complained to his wife, Martha, that if he took call like "...the plain old staff docs," it would undermine my authority as Chair. People would look at me like I was nothing special." Reinhardt's most memorable involvement in L&D affairs had nothing to do with patient care, it became known, at least to Winslow's legal staff, as the "Claxton Coupon Caper."

Reinhardt's handling of department issues, particularly physician misbehavior, was woefully inadequate. His arrogance was reflected in both a lack of bedside manner and horrible people skills. He enjoyed "catching" doctors violating rules, and his preferred method of reprimand was a sarcastic threatening letter. However, the threats rarely resulted in disciplinary measures even for the most egregious offenses. The few times Reinhardt did take meaningful action occurred because he was pressured by administration. Several Chairs of the department's Quality Assessment Committee resigned because Reinhardt refused to follow unanimous recommendations to discipline physicians when their clearly negligent behavior resulted in patient injury. And, at interdepartmental Chair meetings, during discussions about specific problems faced by the hospital's different units, Reinhardt never acknowledged that his department had any problems. In this way, he believed he projected an image of superior leadership.

Ray Claxton was a bespectacled, pudgy, plain looking native of rural California and a third-year resident in Winslow's Ob/Gyn training program. He was book smart and socially inept. Seventeen years into his tenure as Chair, Reinhardt received a complaint about Dr. Claxton. Several nurses complained to L&D's nurse manager that they were tired of Dr. Claxton's lewd and suggestive comments, along with his "accidentally" brushing past them while making, what they believed, willful body contact with their breasts, behinds and legs. Eunice Slattery reported her nurses' complaints to Reinhardt. Slattery began working with the Ob/Gyn Chair when he first arrived at Winslow, and she was well aquatinted with his famous propensity to do nothing about physician work place problems, whether behavioral or practice related. She used a stern tone to tell Reinhardt he needed to do something about Dr. Claxton, "...before the situation blows up in everyone's face." Reinhardt told Martha that night he was not happy about the problem Slattery dumped in his lap or the directive tone she used. Nonetheless, four days later, the Chair pushed himself to call Claxton into his office. Without questions or the presumption of innocence, Reinhardt told the young doctor that he better, "...knock off the sex stuff with the nurses, *and you know damn well what I mean."*

Claxton appeared unnerved, scared, and surprised. He managed to tell his boss that he would cease and desist. And then, with a sickening mousy tone, Claxton asked,

"Sir, if I may, which nurse complained?"

"Do you think I'm a god damned idiot? Get the hell out of my sight while you still have a job, and if hear another word about this, you'll be gone that day!"

Three months later, Claxton popped up on Reinhardt's radar again. This time the complaint came from Amanda Lessum in the resident clinic. She told Reinhardt she received a call from one of the patients complaining that for two months she and Dr. Claxton were having phone sex several times a week. The young woman said she started feeling guilty and asked Dr. Claxton to quit, but he kept calling. Reinhardt was livid. The problem had to be contained before it engulfed his department, and the entire hospital. This time when the young doctor arrived at his office the Department Chair began shouting at him, "Are you out of your fucking mind? Phone sex with a patient?"

"No sir, I mean..."

"What?"

"...I'm sorry sir." Claxton was whimpering.

"You finally got one thing right."

"Sir?'"

"You are one sorry sack of shit!"

Without getting input from anyone, Reinhardt ordered Claxton to write the patient an apology letter.

"And, you god damn well better tell her you're sorry about having phone sex with her and you promise you'll never do it again or call her again, ever!"

"Yes sir, I will sir."

"If you ever call her again, for any reason, you're outta here!"

"Yes, sir."

"In fact, don't you ever call any patient or any nurse or any woman even remotely associated with this hospital. Do you understand me?"

"I do, sir

"And, if I find out that you ignored what I just told you, or I get another complaint about you and sex, you're history, and I will report you to the state Medical Board which means you won't be able to get a license to practice medicine anywhere in the country. Am I making myself clear?"

"Yes, Dr. Reinhardt."

"You're god damn right I am."

"Yes, sir.'

"Have a copy of that letter on my desk by 3 p.m. today. Now get outta here, you stink."

When a member of Winslow's legal team recounted the story of Reinhardt's "phone sex resident" to a colleague, she said, "It was like Reinhardt gave the patient a coupon when he forced the resident to send the patient an apology letter. The patient brought the 'coupon' to a lawyer who presented it to us, and with no defense, and essentially a signed confession, we promptly wrote out a check for $60,000. The pitiful thing was," she continued, "Reinhardt never believed he did anything wrong, and he had the nerve to argue about it!"

Reinhardt never realized that the coupon caper was the beginning of the end for his tenure at the helm of Winslow's OB/Gyn Department.

* * *

Warren was in-house with the residents the previous night, and as was his habit, he attended L&D rounds in the morning.

"Warren, do you have a little time this mornin?" Thompson asked when rounds ended.

"I have office at nine."

"How 'bout now?"

"Sure."

"Let's grab some coffee, and walk over to my office."

When they got to his office, Thompson sat behind his desk after positioning two coasters on its Mahogany top.

"I read the report last night."

"Really? I didn't know it was out."

"It cleared the Board of Directors late last week, and I got a copy yesterday afternoon."

"How bad was it?"

Thompson's response was reserved in its optimism.

"Not as bad for you as it could have been."

Thompson remained matter of fact.

"What does that mean 'not as bad as it could have been'," Warren asked with a tone that was beginning to clog with emotion.

"I'll make a copy of it so you can be the judge, but please, don't let anyone see it, and give it back to me when you finish."

Warren left and Thompson put his feet up on the wide black granite window sill behind his desk. He reared back in his swivel chair and sipped his large cup of black, very aromatic coffee. He savored his morning delight with its rich deep taste finished with just a twinge of bitter. The aroma wafting to his nostrils heightened his alertness and calmed his thought process. The blue morning sky filled his vision while he made a mental list of the people he would speak with about his plan to meet with Sylvia to inform her about all the findings in the report and its conclusions.

Thompson knew that the idea of making a "full Disclosure," as the process was referred to, of what happened to Carla was a new concept in hospital-patient relations. Full Disclosure was espoused by most professional organizations as part of the culture of safety. However, he also realized the process was far from universally accepted by the healthcare industry. Although it might be a tough sell to most of the medical and hospital administrators, at least he was sure Davidson would be on his side.

Chapter Thirteen

Thompson was stunned by Davidson's response. The Safety Officer launched into a long winded, harsh denunciation of the Full Disclosure concept.

"Full Disclosure is untested and unproven. We'd have ABHA and the Feds snooping around, and I don't know about you, but I don't want 'em here. Plus, on top of that, we'd needlessly open ourselves up to huge legal liability from the patients and families by just freely offering up our findings."

"But isn't Full Disclosure just an extension of the culture of safety — you know, exposing errors to the light of day to encourage more openness? As for the legal liability, I don't have to tell you, a couple studies documented less law suits, not more, when hospitals fully disclose."

"Those studies you're talking about are case reports, one offs, nothing more. Full Disclosure is a theoretical fantasy dreamed up by academics who are trying to publish rather than perish, and to hell with us in the real world if we perish trying to operationalize their misguided idealism about human nature."

"Are you telling me all this safety culture talk is garbage?"

"Quite the contrary. The culture of safety that I'm trying so hard to build is anchored in the real everyday world where mistakes happen, patients sue hospitals, and we have an obligation to protect both of them. And, I can tell you, the idiocy of Full Disclosure is not the way to go. Trust me Harold, you'll alienate a lot of big wigs around here if you push that idea. It'll make things much tougher for me. I promise you, if you go ahead with this wrongheaded plan of yours, I'll do everything I can to block it."

Thompson was down when he left Davidson's office. He was also incredulous. Truly, he had misread the man. However, his view was now much clearer about the ordeal he was embarking on. Not revealing to Sylvia all that he knew about Carla's death was never an option for Thompson. The conversation with the Chief Safety Officer did not change his thinking about the commitment he made to Carla's grieving mother. Instead, his encounter with Davidson steeled his resolve to keep his promise.

Strong though his determination was, Davidson's words got Thompson's adrenaline flowing. His feelings mimicked those of his childhood and teenage years when, during a confrontation with another boy, it became clear he was on the verge of a physical fight. Thompson was now very aware of his heart beating, and the surges of energy shooting along the lengths of his arms and legs. He didn't like these sensations, now or when he was younger, but he knew what they meant.

**

Cathy Weaver made an appointment for Thompson to meet with Bonnie Sepulveda, Winslow's Director of Legal Affairs. She was the second child of Mexican immigrants, Hernan and Rita Sepulveda, who began life in America on the lowest rung of a slaughter house workforce and then became migrant farm laborers. Sepulveda, along with her two closest-in-age siblings, was born in the state of Chiapas, Mexico. In 1962, Hernan began harvesting fruits and vegetables in the fields of the Midwest and Southern United States. It took him two years to return to his family with almost two hundred dollars in savings. For several months, he took temporary jobs, which included both construction labor and work as a farm hand, in the area surrounding his small village in western Chiapas. One morning in April of 1964, the Sepulveda family walked the ten miles to the closest town with bus service and purchased tickets to Juarez. They arrived, got off the bus, walked to the Rio Grande, and with their meager belongings in cloth sacks, crossed the river on foot to El Paso.

Hernan got the family as far as Austin, Minnesota. It was mid nineteen sixty-four and easy for migrants to find low paying jobs. The family moved into a cheap three-room apartment. Eleven-year-old Carlos was charged with the care of his two younger sisters while Hernan and Rita went to work as part of a clean-up crew in one of the local meat processing plants.

After a year and a half of hard work and frugality, the couple saved enough to purchase a five-year-old Plymouth Valiant. They joined a group of migrants and crisscrossed the Midwest and South in search of crops to pick. Five years of filthy accommodations, along with mean, sometimes violent and dishonest employers, convinced Rita and Hernan to make a permanent home for their family which had grown to seven. They chose to settle in the southwestern section of Detroit, Michigan. By the time the Sepulvedas moved into their new home, the influx of Mexican immigrants, as well as their first and second-generation offspring, was nearly thirty years along. "La Bagley" as the community was originally known, was later Christened "Mexicantown."

Automotive manufacturing in the early nineteen seventies was booming, and Hernan thought he may be able to get work in one of the auto plants. He was hired for an assembly line job that paid enough to allow Rita to stay at home. Four years later, the five Mexican born Sepulveda's became U.S. Citizens.

Bonnie lost two grade levels when she enrolled in public school. Her need for remediation was the legacy of five years of irregular class attendance. The young immigrant caught fire with the desire to excel, and her drive garnered the attention of several teachers who went out of their way to work with her. Bonnie became an academic prodigy, and beginning in her junior year of high school, several colleges and universities from across the country made contingent scholarship offers. She chose a small, but prestigious, liberal arts school called Trevor College in Milwaukee. She earned her honors program A.B. degree *magna cum laude* in four years.

Sepulveda entered law school at the University of Michigan with an energetic idealism. She was out to save the world and was not shy about voicing her altruistic based opinions. Criminal law attracted the young world saver before she started her legal training. During some of her late-night college discussions with activist friends, she would explain her goal of protecting the innocent from a justice system, rigged against them, by becoming the best criminal defense attorney in the country. In her second year of law school, Sepulveda did an elective in the Detroit Public Defenders office. She put her heart, and many hours, into the case of a defendant she believed was wrongly accused of raping and robbing an elderly woman. After a trial and acquittal, the newly freed defendant and his legal team were walking side by side out of the court house, when their exonerated client boasted to Sepulveda and the Public Defender, Alycia Dunbar, that he *had* committed the crime. He bragged about having out-witted the authorities "with the help of my brilliant legal representation." In an instant, Sepulveda stepped away from their client, dropped her briefcases, and with both hands on her hips, in a tone seething with venom, but perfectly controlled, she spoke in her first language, *"aaa hijo puta de mierda capullo gilipollass imbecil cacho cabron!"*

Sepulveda's Spanish vulgarities were uttered with perfection because Henan and Rita were among a minority of Chiapans who, in addition to their native Mayan dialect, also spoke Spanish. They made sure their children followed suit. The young law student felt nauseous, but she had no urge to vomit. Their client felt the wrath of the nascent lawyer, and the insults, though he probably didn't understand what was said. He spat forcefully at Sepulveda's feet and hurried away.

Several minutes later, sitting in the dejected Public Defender's closet sized office, Dunbar tried to console her disillusioned assistant by reassuring and reasoning with her.

"Bonnie, you didn't do anything wrong. I was as taken in by the bastard as you were. I know you feel terrible, but you did an excellent job. I know it's hollow to say it, but we get fooled sometimes."

"I helped that animal walk," Sepulveda said through clenched teeth. "He hurts that innocent sweet old lady, and I helped him so he can go out and do it again. I'm sick, right here," she pointed, "right here in my gut."

"Come on, Bonnie, I don't have to tell you that the presumption of innocence and every client's right to adequate legal representation are the foundations of the system, and with these two tenets as a foundation, we're going to wind up fighting for, and getting some guilty defendants off — it happens — the system's not perfect. And, trust me, it goes the other way too — some of the innocent clients we defend, wind up in prison, sometimes for many years, and that hurts just as bad, maybe worse."

"I've never had such a big success feel like, and be, such a huge personal failure. I know I can't do criminal law."

"You need to think it over for a while before you close the door."

"If I stay in the criminal defense business, I'll need your help."

"And, you know I'll support your career in any way I can."

"No, what I'll need from you is criminal defense, because if I do criminal work, I'll probably murder half of my own clients."

"Think it over, Bonnie."

That was the last time they saw each other for six years. They spoke briefly by telephone a week later. Sepulveda called to tell Dunbar she had not changed her mind. Eventually, she decided to use corporate law as her way to contribute to the common good. A law school elective introduced her to Healthcare Law, and she set about learning every aspect of it.

Sepulveda began her career working in the Claims Compliance Division of the largest health insurance company in Michigan. The idea of working for a health insurance company would have made Sepulveda laugh when she first entered law school. But, she was so disillusioned by her criminal defense experience, that when she was asked to consider an internship with the company, the opportunity aligned with the promise she made to herself to find a niche far away from criminal law, and she jumped in.

During her insurance industry tenure, Sepulveda worked in the legal divisions of almost every department in the company including Human Resources, Corporate Compliance, and Contracting. She confided to some law school classmates how amazed she was by the opportunities she found to help, "...make things better for people who can't advocate for themselves." Twelve years into her corporate insurance career, the Director of Legal Affairs position opened at Winslow. The hospital was looking for an outsider, and Sepulveda applied on the advice of a friend. She survived a prolonged interview process, and when she was offered the position she accepted with enthusiasm and minimal negotiation.

Sepulveda was intellectually nimble, straight-to-the-point, insightful, and very protective of Winslow. She saw her position as a tremendous opportunity to serve the underserved on many fronts that ranged from the obvious — healthcare — to employment and education.

When Sepulveda arrived, Winslow was the largest private hospital in the United States. Of all her many accomplishments, her appointment as Winslow's Director of Legal Affairs was the only one that impressed her children. "Gee mom, Winslow Hospital is like the best hospital in the whole state," was the response from Lucie her fifteen-year-old daughter.

The Director and the Chair were briefly introduced to one another at a hospital function. A short time later, Thompson took the Director up on her encouragement to, "Contact me if I can ever help you."

Thompson liked Sepulveda. He was attracted to her good looks and reserved yet friendly personality. The Legal Department Chief was not quite a head shorter than Thompson, and although she carried a few extra pounds, they did not detract from her appearance at all. She wore her plentiful coal black hair up in various styles. Sepulveda's intelligence was also a turn-on for Thompson. Although he interacted with a couple of the other attorneys in Legal Affairs on several occasions, Thompson went to Sepulveda whenever he needed help with hospital by-law interpretation, issues of Corporate Compliance, or any other matters with potential legal ramifications. She provided him uncomplicated answers to his questions with clear rationales. When she didn't know the answers, she found the information, and was always timely with her follow-up. Thompson was delighted when he discovered Sepulveda's sense of humor, at least she laughed heartily at his stupid jokes, he noted. He was intrigued when he discovered she was divorced. He thought of asking her out, but whenever he was close to doing so, he convinced himself not to complicate his professional and personal lives.

The Ob/Gyn Chair was again caught off guard by the intensity of Sepulveda's resistance to his proposal for Full Disclosure. She told him that if he revealed the contents of the Sentinel Event Committee Report, his actions could result in massive damage to the hospital.

"Disclosing that report to the family may very well expose the hospital to huge damages, horrible publicity, and it'll open the flood gates of patients claiming harm from our hospital and demanding money." She went on to tell him that his proposal would undermine public confidence in the high-quality medicine practiced at Winslow.

"We worked hard for years to build this image and it would come down on our heads in a flash. You need to have a long think about what you're proposing. Your idea could, in minutes, trash what's taken decades to create." She later confided to one of the attorneys in her department, "I've read about this idea of Full Disclosure, but the litigator in me throws up when I think about forking over big money to the plaintiff pig attorneys without a fight."

Before the meeting ended, although he knew it would sound naïve, Thompson asked, "But what about doing the right thing, you know, acknowledging what that report found and sharing it with the family to give them some closure."

"The right thing," Sepulveda replied, "is to survive in this universe of sharks and keep doing the enormous amount of good we do for the people of this community."

* * *

Dr. Richard Caruthers served as Winslow's Chief Medical Officer for eleven years. The position often demanded an intricate balancing act between interests of the board of directors, hospital administrators, and his physician constituency. In the period between his ninth and tenth years in the position, the hospital began to face challenges it had never experienced. Competing healthcare systems built hospital facilities within Winslow's "bread and butter" catchment area. This competition came at a time of contracting revenues caused by shrinking government and insurance reimbursement coupled with national and local economies on the verge of recession. The hospital was also over committed financially. During the previous several years, Winslow opened new outpatient facilities, with their hospital subsidized practices, in communities it never previously served. These expansions represented the hospital's strategy to raise revenues and fight its competitors. The business models for these ventures always projected two to three years of losses while they attracted adequate patient volumes to make the satellites income generators. When successful, the outposts fed large numbers of patients to the hospital for more complicated outpatient tests and procedures. These new offices also increased the hospital's inpatient volumes.

Whenever the hospital subsidized new practices, long standing resentments from many private, financially independent, physicians were reenergized. These grievances became loud and angry when the hospital-supported practices were located even remotely close to the offices of one of the independent practitioners.

Many of the resentful physicians suffered from selective memory loss when it came to their humble professional beginnings in Winslow subsidized practices. Caruthers was forced to defend these hospital business decisions which embroiled him in fights he had no passion for. His usual mediating manner began to leave him. He became newly outspoken and blunt with representatives of his three, increasingly unwanted, constituencies.

Not infrequently, he was downright crude, "Good morning asshole, what's on your alleged mind today," became his favorite salutation. Finally, though, he faced a reckoning for his insults and lack of collegial respect—his enemies swarmed him, and he was forced by the Board of Directors to "resign."

One faction active in the hunt for Caruthers' head was led by Dr. Michael Isaacs, an Internist and year's long Caruthers adversary. A decade earlier, during an open meeting, Caruthers made a remark that was not offensive, but the squat Internist, with his slicked back thick brown hair and exquisitely trimmed mustache, took the CMO's words as a personal insult. His eyes seared at Caruthers through his black owl rimmed spectacles. The extreme red flush of his face and hands was accented because his normal skin color was very close to the pale white of business stationary. He later vowed to friends, "I'm going to bring that sonaofabitch down if it takes me forever."

The aftermath of Reinhardt's blunder in the Claxton fiasco, coupled with increasing pressure from doctors in his department over his refusal to take meaningful action against errant physicians, forced Caruthers to finally acknowledge the evolving "palace revolt." The CMO demanded his, now, former friend's, resignation. Reinhardt and Isaacs, however, remained friends. The former Chair's ousting, earned Caruthers another demerit from the Internist. Thompson's coronation intensified Isaacs', Reinhardt influenced, resentment of the new Chair before the two met. Isaacs believed, as did Reinhardt, that the new Chair was illegitimate and "...has no business being at Winslow."

In the course of his years' long vendetta against Caruthers, Isaacs accumulated a considerable amount of political power among physicians, administrators, and most importantly, with members of the board. When the time came to appoint a new CMO, Isaacs had no credible opponents, and the sentiment for his appointment among the three constituent groups was overwhelmingly positive. He officially became the hospital's CMO five days after Caruthers' departure.

When he first met Isaacs shortly after his CMO appointment, Thompson easily picked up on Isaacs' disdainful, dismissive attitude. Martin Octavio was Thompson's closest confidant about Winslow matters. The two met twenty-five years earlier in medical school. They practiced the same subspecialty, but Octavio lived and worked in southern California. His area of expertise, and his distance from Winslow's politics, gave him an insight and objectivity that Thompson often called upon. Octavio was a best friend and harshest critic. Several days after his encounter with Isaacs, in the midst of one of their frequent phone conversations, Thompson told his friend, "He looked past me, and he only made eye contact once at the end. I'm sure that if he could get rid of me, it would be a damn good day for him."

When Thompson walked into Isaacs' office at the scheduled time, the new CMO, using his right hand, motioned, without speaking, for Thompson to take one of the chairs in front of his desk. It was easy for Thompson to see that a considerable amount of money was spent to redecorate Caruthers' former space. Several expensive looking paintings adorned the walls which were covered with new deep blue wallpaper with grey accented markings. The room was twice the size of Thompson's office. It now included a siting area with two couches facing one another across the width of a mahogany coffee table, and two elegant chairs faced across its length. The coffee table rested on an ornately patterned deep maroon Persian rug. Several stone and wood statuettes were displayed around the room. Once Thompson was seated, Isaacs said,

"I understand you want to talk about this Williams girl and her family — is that right?"

Thompson made his case for Full Disclosure to the Williams Family. He went over the facts of what happened and the results of the sentinel event review. He informed Isaacs about Carla's children now being raised by their grandmother. He spoke about the financial strain now faced by Sylvia and the children. Thompson also spoke about the obligation he believed Winslow had to fill in the family's financial gaps, especially given the report's findings. Isaacs held up his right hand and stopped Thompson mid-sentence. For the first time, he stared straight into Thompson's eyes and asked in an angry, but restrained voice, "What planet are you from?" After a silence during which their eyes were locked, Isaacs continued,

"Are you out of your damn mind?"

"What do you mean?"

"You're reckless and selfish is what I mean. You're perfectly willing to sacrifice the hospital and the hard-working physicians on our staff, to admit guilt, to some ghetto tramp's family? Hell, she probably doesn't have a clue who the bastards are who fathered her kids. And, you're willing to bring us all down for this?"

Thompson felt his face flush along with the energy surges. He strained to keep his composure and not plant his right fist squarely in the middle of Isaacs' well-groomed face as the CMO continued.

"The physicians in this hospital would feel like we were blaming a group of their own for incompetence and then throwing them under the bus to save face for the institution. The doctors would be in an up roar, our competitors would use the incident to ridicule us as a dangerous third-rate operation, and then they'd rush to recruit away some of the best physician talent we have. I'm telling you, stand down from your selfish stupid crusade, and get with reality or *I* will stand you down."

Thompson hadn't felt as low as he did now since his childhood when he endured his father's frequent and without-reason ridicule or his harsh physical chastisement which he dished out for minor infractions or simply in tandem with mood swings. His father's aspirations to be a successful water color artist got him no further than a career as a commercial sign painter. His father was angry at the world and impatient with his only son. Many times in his late childhood and adolescence, Thompson doubted that his father loved him. His response to these feelings was, as he sometimes told very close confidants, "My father is the only person I ever hated." As he got older, Thompson realized that his mother's love and understanding saved his life. Eventually, in his very late teens, he resolved his feelings for his father. He recognized Jessie was frustrated and handled poorly his unfulfilled aspirations, as well as his other grievances with life. In getting to the other side of his emotional tangle, Thompson survived a long angry, rebellious period that, for a time, seemed endless. During that part of his life, his automatic reaction was always to challenge authority, from school teachers to bosses at briefly held jobs. Slowly, he came to understand that his father loved him deeply, sacrificed mightily for his family, and wanted only the best for his son and four daughters. It was this reckoning that allowed Thompson the calm and confidence to endure his failures and challenges, control his emotions and persevere.

Chapter Fourteen

Thompson's meeting with Isaacs took place on a Thursday afternoon. The following Tuesday, Thompson was at his desk going through email. He opened a message with "CONFIDENTIAL" in the subject line. The email informed him he was the subject of an inquiry by the professional conduct committee of the Medical Executive Committee. The email's author was Dr. Celia Green, Chair of the committee. Green's committee was investigating an anonymous allegation that Thompson made "uncomplimentary remarks" about Winslow practitioners to a patient's family. "If true, this behavior violates hospital by-law 3.4.7 which defines such actions as unprofessional and subject to sanction by the hospital's Board of Directors. Her message quoted the by-law, "The Medical Executive Committee shall investigate all allegations of such behavior. If the allegations are found to be true, the MEC, at its discretion, may recommend sanctions against the involved individual(s) to the hospital's Board of Directors. These sanctions may range from no action to termination of all hospital privileges." Green closed by writing, "I will notify you shortly of when and where the committee would like you to appear for an explanation, to be followed by questions and answers."

So, it's come down to good old fashion mud wrestling.

Beginning early in his chairmanship, Thompson believed his tenure at Winslow would be short. He marveled that he was close to the end of his second year. He enjoyed his job immensely, but recognized, for a variety of reasons, he didn't fit the notion, held by many, of how a Winslow Department Chair should look and behave. In his mind, race was only one aspect of his failure to fit the Department Chair mold expected by many within the institution.

Although he was affable, and frequently humorous, he seemed never afraid to voice concerns, and when possible, take action to stop behaviors he believed were problematic. Thompson was also not shy about opposing policy proposals he viewed as ill conceived. He was, however, a reliable team player once plans were finalized.

Oh well, always better to die for a cause than to die 'because.'

Unbeknownst to Thompson, the day after his Isaacs meeting, an administrator from Winslow phoned Sylvia and arranged a meeting at her home which would include Janis Mae. The following Monday, Marshall Cummings was at Sylvia's home at 1:50 p.m. – ten minutes early. In their phone conversation, Cummings described himself as white, five feet eight inches tall, with partially graying blonde hair, clean shaven, and he added with a chuckle, "I've got a medium sized spare tire around my middle." When her doorbell rang, Sylvia looked through her front door's peep-hole, and the man she saw fit Cumming's description. She opened the door and invited the administrator in. When Sylvia received his phone call, the caller ID on her land line verified the Winslow origin of the call, and when they finished talking, she called the hospital operator to verify his name, position in the hospital, and the phone number he called from.

Despite the sudden unexpected addition of three youngsters, Sylvia's home, at least the portion visible to guests, was an immaculately kept three-bedroom, bath and a half bungalow. The house was sixty years old and very well maintained. The front entrance put the visitor directly in the living room. While the two stood, Sylvia offered her guest something to drink. He politely declined, and Sylvia ushered him to a seat in the parlor's single chair. She joined Janis Mae on the longer of the room's two sofas, and both women looked directly across at Cummings. He again introduced himself, and continued by giving the sisters his, and the hospital's, condolences. Cummings explained that he worked for Winslow's administration. The hospital, he explained, made most of its decisions and took most of its actions based on input from both medical people like Dr. Thompson, and from the administrative side which was composed of people like him.

"The hospital depends on both sides to gather information and add opinions because medical people and administrators sometimes look at things somewhat differently. "Although," he hastily added, "almost always, both sides are in complete agreement."

He asked the sisters to tell him about all of the events that occurred the day Carla died. Sylvia was slow to start talking. With the laced kerchief she pulled from the left sleeve of her blouse, Carla's mother patted at the tears in the corners of her eyes before she spoke. She described bringing Carla to the hospital that morning and what went on in the surgery registration area.

"After checking in and then going to a different floor, I waited while they took Carla back to get ready. Eventually, I was brought to her cubicle where we waited. I could see how nervous she was — scared really. We said a prayer together, and she told me she felt much better. Then Dr. Chambers and his team came in. He told us how things would go and answered all our questions. He told Carla he'd see her again in the actual operating room. When they took Carla, that was the last time I saw my baby alive. They took me to the area where the families wait, and I stayed there until Dr. Chambers found me." She paused for a moment.

"You okay, Sis?"

Sylvia let out a long sigh and said,

"I'm fine. Dr. Chambers said that everything with the surgery went very well. He told me he was pretty sure there was no cancer, but he'd know for sure in a week or so. Sylvia stopped again, and brought a hanky covered index finger to her eyes.

"He said it would be a couple hours until the anesthesia wore off, and then I could see my baby again."

"Did he mention any complications or problems that had happened during the surgery," Cummings asked.

"No, he said everything went very well."

"What happened next?"

"I guess about two hours later, one of the, I think they're called Patient Advocates, came to tell me there was a problem. She said, '...nothing to worry about,' but they were taking Carla back into surgery. When I asked why, the woman told me she didn't think it was serious, but the doctor would find me and explain everything when they finished."

"A little over an hour later, Dr. Chambers walked up to my seat in the waiting area. We went to one of the small rooms around there, and he told me my baby was gone." She stopped talking and her tears flowed. Janis Mae reached to hold Sylvia's left hand. After several seconds, the grieving mother found her voice again, and in soft tones with slow cadence she recounted the remainder of that day's events with only an infrequent crack in her speech. Several times, during Sylvia's telling of the story, Janis Mae reinforced her sister's recollections. Other times, she would add a small piece of information that was always complimentary to her sister's story.

When Sylvia finished, Cummings asked his hosts if they ever met with Dr. Thompson. When they told him yes, he asked them if they would share with him what was discussed.

Sylvia responded, "We came to his office—"

"How did you happen to go there," Cummings said.

"I met him at Carla's funeral," Janis Mae said. "He gave me his card and asked me to please have Sylvia call him."

"It was about a week after the funeral that he called me," Sylvia said. "He told me how sad he was for our loss, and asked me if I would meet him at the hospital."

"Did he say he wanted to meet with you alone?"

"No, he told me to bring who ever I felt comfortable bringing."

"When did you actually meet with him?"

"Two Thursdays ago."

"Where did you actually meet with him?"

"In his office which I believe is on the fourth floor."

"And, how did he start off — I mean, what did he say?"

"Well, he gave us his condolences, and told us he had met Carla several times. He said her death was very unexpected, and the hospital was looking into exactly what happened."

"Did Dr. Thompson make it seem like the doctors or the hospital did something wrong that caused Carla's death?"

Sylvia became suddenly tense and hesitant. Janis Mae also looked uncomfortable.

"Mr. Cummings, we were surprised when Dr. Thompson reached out to us. No one in my family had ever heard of a doctor doing such a thing in a situation like ours, and we appreciate him very much."

"But, when you spoke with him, did he sound like he thought it was someone's fault that your daughter passed away?"

"He made it seem like he didn't know what happened. From what he said, it seemed like they were trying to find out why."

"Did he mention the doctors or say the doctors or the hospital might have been the cause?"

"He only said that my baby's death was unexpected and that there could have been a medical problem that she had that the doctors didn't know about, or it could have been a problem with the hospital or with the doctors. He said, hopefully, the investigation would find the answers."

"Did he say he would meet with you again?"

"Yes, he said he would meet and tell us what the investigation finds."

Cummings voiced his, and the hospital's, condolences again, thanked the women for their time, and stood up to leave. The sisters led him to the front door, and they said their goodbyes. Cummings hurriedly stepped down the walkway and on to his car. The Chief Administrator of Physical Plant Operations drove straight back to his office. Fifteen minutes later he told his boss Ron Blazer, that he hadn't heard exactly what he wanted,

"...but I know I can make it work."

Thompson met with the Professional Conduct Committee the Monday afternoon following the email he received from the committee Chair.

* * *

Dr. Green was in her late 50s and a twenty-year member of Winslow Hospital's full-time staff. Her lithe physique was the giveaway to her continued passion for competitive distance running. She completed her Psychiatry Residency at Winslow which offered one of the two most competitive Adult Psychiatry Training programs in the country. Eleven months before she completed her residency, Dr. Ann Baisden, the Chair of the Psychiatry Department, offered Green a full-time staff position to begin as soon as she finished the program. Green told her she was flattered but her heart was in child psychiatry, and Baisden told her, "When you finish your Child Psych Fellowship, please consider coming back here. I'll do whatever I have to do to get you here, I mean it."

Green completed an extended four-year fellowship in Child and Adolescent Psychiatry at Columbia University in New York City. When she finished the fellowship, she could have joined almost any academic staff in the country. She was smart, affable, worked hard, and the young doctor was an acclaimed clinical and basic science researcher. Her easy smile sometimes obscured the intensity of her dedication to her career. By the end of her training, her first authored peer-reviewed publications numbered seven. All of these papers detailed original research she conducted. Dr. Ceilia Green was a superstar. She turned down several very appealing offers from some of the most outstanding academic centers in the country and returned to Winslow Hospital. Her sense of loyalty to Winslow was profound. Her husband John Wilson was an internationally renowned PhD Psychology Professor. He accepted the Chair position at Anthony University to help facilitate his wife's desire to return to Winslow.

Thompson's past interactions with Green were always pleasant. Their paths crossed most frequently in the course of their roles as members of the hospital's Human Investigation Committee. HICs review almost all proposed research projects, involving human subjects. The proposals are vetted for ethical and patient safety considerations as well as for their scientific soundness before the research can begin. These committees are mandated by federal statute. Thompson was always impressed with Green's knowledge, in depth analysis, and her willingness to listen to other points of view. Thompson knew Green to have very strong views about the ethical dimensions of research from the humanistic patient perspective. She was also adamant in her beliefs and stances when the subject involved the honesty and integrity of those doing the research and reporting the results. On these two issues, she sometimes took positions that Thompson felt teetered on being self-righteous.

Green's perspectives on these matters were strongly influenced by two experiences. Her father, Bob, was an electrical engineer. Her mother Rosalinda, was born in Spain, raised in Venezuela, and attended college in the United States. Green grew up in Westchester County, New York, but because her mother worked as a translator at the United Nations, she attended United Nations sponsored schools for all of her pre-college education. These schools were created for the children of U.N. diplomats and other personnel. The junior high school Celia attended was brutally competitive. Some of the students took "adjustment leaves" during the school year. In reality, during these absences, the kids were receiving psychological evaluation, counseling and therapy. Some enrolled in other less competitive schools and never returned, though this was uncommon. In the middle of her seventh-grade year, Ceilia approached her two closest friends, Olga Swenson and Amina Adeyemi with a plan for cheating on an upcoming chemistry exam. They would use hand signals to pass information. All of the trio members knew that cheating was rampant in their school, and Celia's two comrades agreed to join her plan. When test day came, 12-year-old Ceilia was caught by her teacher ten minutes into the exam, her friends were not. Instead of a routine three-day suspension with the attendant grade sanctions, Ceilia drew a two week suspension because she ignored demands from her parents and her principal to identify her co-conspirators. The two girls had several very anxious days worrying about whether their friend was going to "squeal." When Celia finally returned to class, the girls hugged and cried during their first morning recess back together. When the two asked their friend why she hadn't turned them in she said,

"It was my bright idea and there was no use in anyone else getting in trouble over it."

She went on to tell them her parents were disappointed, "especially my mom. I'm grounded for six weeks — no telephone, no TV, and no activities except for church." She never knew of her father's secret pride that his daughter protected her friends when he found out the whole idea was hers.

Celia declared to her friends, "I've had lots of time to think about things, and I'm done with cheating. It was wrong what I did, and I'm not doing it anymore. I'd rather flunk." She never wavered from this declaration.

The other experience that had an oversized influence on Green's ethical outlook occurred as part of an undergraduate research project she worked on during the summer between her second and third year of college. She was a bright eyed twenty-year-old who signed on as a summer research assistant for a study to document major influences on childhood speech development. Her passion for helping children started when she became the biggest UNCEF Halloween fund raiser in her grade school. It was nurtured by her years of volunteering at a local foster home during her high school years.

Dr. Beverly Meriman, Chair of Greyson College's Psychology Department, invited Celia to join her summer research staff. As a freshman student in Dr. Meriman's Intro to Psychology Course, Celia impressed her professor. The Westchester native spent the summer visiting state run foster care facilities throughout Massachusetts. Greyson was located near the center of the state which gave Celia relatively easy access to most of the facilities she visited. Onsite, she culled through records of all children who were in the facility over the previous twenty-five years and were two months of age or younger when they entered and stayed until they were at least two years old. She abstracted twenty-two pieces of data from each record. This information included demographic, developmental, and medical information. Massachusetts mandated standardized record forms in the nineteen fifties, and this made the kind of research Celia was doing possible.

As more of the project data was analyzed, several times the young researcher noticed that when she analyzed some of the data, a number of key correlations were non-significant. She was later puzzled when she received data analysis summaries from Dr. Meriman's office that indicated the data was reanalyzed and the same correlations *were* significant. At first Ceilia believed she must have made errors in her statistical runs. She went through her reports and completed point-by- point checks to make sure she had entered her raw numbers correctly. She then re-analyzed her data using the same computerized statistical program Dr. Meriman's office used. In all instances her findings did not change – the correlations were not significant. Ceilia approached Dr. Meriman's research coordinator, Dr. Marcy Spellman. Spellman was very warm and friendly. She thanked Ceilia for bringing the issue to her attention, and assured the young researcher she would look into the matter.

Two days later. Ceilia was summoned to Dr. Meriman's office. The department Chair was of modest height with closely cropped black hair. Her drab green kaki skirt was ankle length, and combined with her black linen button down blouse to give her a military bearing which matched her stern manner. Meriman told her young protégé that Dr. Spellman had informed her that she, Ceilia, was being disruptive to her research and refusing to be a team player. When Ceilia tried to explain, Meriman cut her off.

"Do you realize, Ms. Green, there are millions of dollars in research support at stake here. Careers are at stake here. Do you understand that what you're a part of is bigger than you, it's bigger than all of us.

"Ms. Green you have a choice here, a choice that will set the tone for the remainder of your professional life. You either decide to stop your meddling and disruptive behavior, or you will leave this project, and if you speak with anyone about this conversation, I will personally end your career before you start it. Is that clear?" Ceilia was in shock when she answered, "Yes ma'am."

Green withdrew from Greyson before becoming a junior. She took a full year off and then enrolled in another small liberal arts college in southern Ohio. She finished two years later, and became a first-year medical student at the University of Michigan where she graduated *Summa Cum Laude*.

* * *

Promptly at 4:30, Green called her committee to order. Thompson waited in a lounge area two doors away from the meeting room. Ten minutes after the session began, an Administrative Assistant told Thompson the committee was ready for him. He walked into the room and took the only available seat. He faced Green from across an empty space created by the four rectangular tables that were positioned to form a square circle. There were five members seated along the table to his left and four similarly seated to his right.

Green began by telling Thompson that the committee was asked by the Medical Executive Committee to investigate allegations that he had violated hospital by-law 3.4.7 which expressly prohibits "the utterance of unprofessional comments to anyone about the competence or quality of care rendered by another healthcare provider to any third party." She told Thompson that an anonymous complaint was filed with the MEC, and it was the committee's task to determine whether Thompson violated the by-law. She further explained the committee would hear from a number of witnesses over the next ten days. They were charged to report their findings to the MEC within fourteen days.

"And, as you can see Dr. Thompson, in keeping with the by-laws, we have a stenographer present who will record everything said during this meeting. Do you have any questions for me?"

"No, I don't," he replied in a friendly tone.

Green asked Thompson to explain his understanding of the events that occurred in connection with the Carla Williams case. Thompson answered with a statement that took him a little over ten minutes to complete. Green then asked Thompson whether he had interacted with Ms. Williamses' family. Thompson answered that he had. In response to another question from Green, Thompson explained his attendance at Ms. Williamses' funeral and the first contact he made with her aunt. He then told the panel how he arranged a meeting with Carla's mother and aunt. He described in detail, and with as much accuracy as he could recall, what he said at their meeting. The committee members then began their questioning.

What led him to attend the funeral as he didn't even know Carla Williams, asked Dr. Mike Stewart, a private practice vascular surgeon.

"I did know Carla Williams. I interacted with her several times when I proctored the resident clinic."

"So, you go to a funeral for a patient you've met two or three times? That doesn't seem normal."

"I went to support Dr. Chambers who was pretty upset by her death and because, as Chair, I thought it was the right thing to do."

"Was it your idea to go in the first place?"

"No, Dr. Chambers told me he was going, and I told him I'd go with him. He was hurting and the service was held in a predominately black church in a neighborhood that I know can be pretty rough. I thought that by going with him, I might make it a little easier for him."

"You went to protect him?"

"Protect him from what?" Thompson replied in a tone that let Stewart know he regarded the question as insulting.

"You know, from the people in the church."

"Are you asking if I feared for his safety in a church full of grieving friends and relatives?"

"Never mind," was Stewarts reply.

Thompson had remained very cool throughout Stewart's volley of inquiries.

Dr. Cynthia McMasters was the next questioner. McMasters was the Chair of the Pediatrics Department, and she began by apologizing to Thompson for their need to be in this session in the first place. Her kind face gave her apology a deep sincerity. She told Thompson that she believed him to be a man of high integrity, and that in her experience he had always demonstrated that aspect of his character. She asked him to explain why he felt the need to meet with the Williams family.

"I knew the Williams were emotionally distraught like any family would be in their situation. I had a deep sense of regret about the challenges facing Carla's sixty-one-year-old mother. At the time of Carla's death, her mother, Sylvia, was a year away from retirement, and suddenly she had to take on the care and nurturing of three young children."

"Will you describe for us your conversation with Ms. Williamses' mother and aunt?"

"I expressed my sympathy and deep regret for their loss. I told them that because Carla's death was unexpected, the hospital was conducting an investigation to find out exactly what happened."

"Did you say anything about negligence on the part of her treating physicians or the hospital?"

"No, I did not."

"Did you say anything or use the words poor care or substandard care?"

"I absolutely did not." His voice was calm and emphatic.

"Did you give them the impression that something improper had occurred?"

"Well, Dr. McMasters, I can't really tell you what their impressions were, but I can say that it wasn't my intention to convey an impression like that—"

"Like what?"

"You know, that something improper went on. I couldn't have said such a thing because the investigation hadn't been completed at the time I met with them."

"Did you tell them you would get back to them with the results of the investigation?"

"Yes, I did."

"Why did you tell them that?"

"Because we owe them a forthright explanation of the facts — we at least owe them that. That *is* what Full Disclosure is all about isn't it?"

McMasters looked at him for a few moments before answering. "You speak of Full Disclosure as if it's an accepted tenant of medical practice."

"It is."

"And how did you arrive at that understanding Dr. Thompson?" But, before he could answer she said, "I'm well aware of Josie King and all of the thinking coming out of that case about disclosing information to patients and families when bad outcomes occur. But, Harold, you know as well as I do, those are opinions and not evidence based on data. You will admit, won't you, Dr. Thompson, that those principles are not universally held by healthcare providers."

Thompson had to concede her point.

"In fact," McMasters continued, "those opinions are neither held nor practiced by the majority of healthcare providers in the country, isn't that the truth?"

"You're correct. But, our hospital, and the Board, pledged that our organization will investigate all sentinel events and make the findings known."

"Known to whom Dr. Thompson? Did they say anything about disclosing the information to patients and families?"

Again, Thompson had to concede McMaster's point.

"I have no further questions right now."

Dr. Maurice Paul, an interventional cardiologist, was the next questioner. Paul was a man of medium height with light brown hair subtly stranded with gray. His facial features were pointed, and he wore an expression that was earnestly serious. "Did you promise the Williams family any money from the hospital for the loss of Carla Williams?"

"No, I did not."

"Did you speak with them at all about any kind of financial remuneration because of Carla's death?"

"I told her, 'Ms. Williams,' and I was very precise in what I said, 'I understood the financial burden you're facing in having to raise three young children.' I told her when the investigation is complete, we will disclose all that we discover, and if it turns out that something we did was not right, we would be mindful of the financial needs of her grandchildren."

"So, in effect," asked Paul, "isn't it true that you essentially assured Ms. Williams that the hospital would give her a substantial amount of money to compensate her loss? And, by doing that you in effect told her our hospital and our doctors were at fault for her daughter's death?"

"How did you twist that from what I just told you? I said nothing of the kind. You've convoluted my conversation with this grieving family and distorted my attempt to have empathy for their unfortunate circumstances into something I didn't say, do, or even imply." Thompson had passion in his words, and there was silence in the room for a moment after he spoke.

"Nonetheless, Paul finally said, "You implied fault on the part of our hospital and our doctors."

"No, I did not, but if that's how you see it then you and I have a fundamental difference in our opinions, and probably in our outlook on life too."

"What do you mean by that?" Paul's tone was full of anger.

"What I mean is that you and I probably don't agree on fundamental questions of what's right and what's not."

Dr. Green spoke up, "Are there any other questions for Dr. Thompson?"

Dr. Richard Carpenter, a Physical Medicine and Rehabilitation specialist asked, "How do you feel overall about this entire incident, you know, the patient's death, your talking with the family, even this inquiry?" Carpenter was in his late forties. He had a mop of brown rather unkempt shaggy hair and a very New York City air.

"It feels like a very unfortunate incident that's turning into a nightmare."

"Would you do anything different if you had a do-over?"

"No."

Green invited more questions, but there were none. She turned to Thompson and thanked him for his time and his candor. She told him they would forward their findings and conclusions to the MEC which would notify him of any action they decided to take.

With briefcase in hand, Thompson left the building and walked to his car in the parking deck. He sat in his vehicle lost in thought for several minutes. He remembered awakening early on the last morning of his first time on the crucible of the wintery wilderness of norther Vermont.

It took him a few seconds to figure out where he was. He heard a few of the others moving around and talking. *Today we're walking out.* The thought energized him. He was up and dressed in seven minutes. He made a fire and Rick Harrison handed him a number ten can, with a handle fashioned from a clothes hanger, full of water. They made their oatmeal, cocoa, and coffee from the hot water. The two campers cut up and fried three cans of Spam over the fire and dished out the greasy, and salty, morning delight to themselves and their hungry comrades. After breakfast and clean-up, they set about taking the lean-tos apart and scattering the branches and boughs. They were careful to retrieve all of the twine used for lashing, and they collected all of the polyurethane sheets. The boys at the logging camp really lucked out Thompson thought as he worked to get his assigned campsites ready to pass inspection by the team leader and one of the staff members. Once all sites passed inspection, the boys lined up with their back packs ready for the hike out. The staff with the cabin group and the staff with the campers stayed in touch via walkie-talkies. The campers waited about ten minutes for the other group to hook up, and the trip back to comfort began.

Thompson's team was chosen to start out breaking trail. This was not difficult in the beginning. For the first half mile, they stayed on the same trail they used coming in. But, then they veered left because the pickup point changed due to road conditions and in an attempt to shorten the walk out. They were now walking in snow that came up above Thompson's knees. After three quarters of a mile he broke down and fell into the snow. He was crying.

"Just leave me, I can't do it anymore," he cried out through his sobs.

Mr. Lecolier, the French teacher who came to his aid, grabbed Thompson by the upper arm and reassured him in his heavy French accent. "Harold it will be good. Stand up and rest for a moment."

A group of boys gathered around. They looked scared. Even those who didn't like Thompson had frightened sympathetic looks in their eyes. Lecolier told another boy to take the lead. He brushed Thompson off and told him, "You will make it. You're tough!"

It took several minutes, but through the fog of his exhaustion and humiliation, Thompson knew he wasn't ready to die crying in a snow bank. He wiped his eyes and took the rear spot on his team. He walked on in silence.

The boys could hear the running engines of the buses before they could see them. As the tired campers rounded a bend, the exhaust vapors from each waiting vehicle became visible. Hot exhaust air from the buses created small white clouds that wafted up from the tail pipes. A cheer went up, they'd made it.

Tired campers, some with smiles, took their seats on the buses after loading their gear. Thompson was distant from the conversations and laughter coming from many of his bus mates. He sat alone by a window, staring at the moving landscape. As they traveled back toward the familiar and comfortable, Thompson was wrestling with the knowledge that he had been forced to look into the abyss of his core, and he was confronting the realization that without the support he received he may not have survived.

* * *

Four days after Green's committee interviewed Thompson, Marshall Cummings sat in the same waiting area Thompson occupied before his appearance before the same committee. Despite the no nonsense business-like demeanor Cummings was trying to portray, he twirled an ink pen through the fingers of his left hand and his left leg moved in a fast up and down motion propelled by his foot pumping on his toes and balls of his foot with the heel not touching the floor. He arrived 10 minutes early for his interview by the committee.

In the days after his meeting with Sylvia and Janis Mae, Cummings fashioned the story he planned to tell. He constructed, and reconstructed his planned comments at least a dozen times, and practiced by himself, telling the story out loud several times. During the rehearsals, inflections and the volume of his voice in different parts of the intended narrative were altered to maximize his dramatic effect with care not to be obvious with his performance.

Cummings became annoyed after 20 minutes when he hadn't been invited into the room. Finally, at 5 p.m., 30 minutes late, Dr. Green came to the door of the lounge and invited Cummings into the meeting room. She began by introducing Cummings and apologizing for the length of his wait. She explained to the panel members how Cummings was asked by Ron Blazer to speak with Ms. Sylvia Williams and her sister about their meeting with Dr. Thompson. Green then asked Cummings to give the panel a brief description of his background. He explained he had come to Winslow twenty-three years earlier. He told the committee members how he began his career at the hospital as a stock clerk in the surgical supply department. Cummings explained how he attended college with help from Winslow's tuition reimbursement program. He graduated and eventually worked his way up to his current position as the Chief Administrator of Physical Plant Operations.

When he finished his brief bio, Green asked, "Can you tell us how you came to meet with the Williams sisters?"

"I don't know Mr. Blazer very well, but he called me and asked me to try and arrange a meeting with the sisters, to find out what had been said when they met with Dr. Thompson. I was surprised that Mr. Blazer called me because the only times I ever met him were when he toured hospital plant facilities with a group of high-level administrators or board members, and then our interactions were just introductions or greetings or me answering questions. He said he called me because he wanted someone to meet with the Williams family who would be totally removed from the medical situation and because of that, he said, he thought I could be totally objective and fair. So, of course, I agreed to do it, and I called Sylvia Williams, and she agreed to meet with me at her house three days later."

He described his meeting with the sisters as cordial, and then outlined the explanation he gave them about point-of-view differences and similarities between doctors and hospital administrators.

"I told them this to overcome any suspicions they may have had about why I came to talk with them."

Cummings looked at the faces around the tables, as if he was searching for reassurance.

"Throughout the conversation, I got the impression the sisters were trying to say something without actually saying it. They stated emphatically that Thompson implied both the hospital and the doctors caring for Carla Williams had made numerous errors. The sisters said these errors, according to Thompson, led directly to Carla Williamses' death."

The faces in the room bore a range of expressions from disbelief to knowing smiles and blank stares.

"The sisters described for me how Dr. Thompson told them he would see that, 'Justice is done.' They both said he promised them the hospital would take care of them for the rest of their lives."

When Cummings finished, Green invited questions from the attendees.

"If the story you just told us is accurate," said Dr. Maurice Paul, "you just delivered a bombshell. Are you sure that what you just told this committee is true to the best of your knowledge."

"Trust me, sir, it was a bombshell to me, but I'm telling you as close to verbatim as I heard without the benefit of a recording of the meeting. I pulled my car around the corner from Sylvia's house as soon as I left, and I sat making notes for a good thirty minutes while the conversation was still fresh. This matter is far too serious for me to risk inaccuracy in my presenting of the facts to you."

There were no further questions from Committee members. After thanking him, Green excused Cummings, and the members began discussing what they heard from him.

Chapter Fifteen

Three days later, Warren met with Green's committee. He was the last to be interviewed. After explaining the purpose of the committee's inquiry, Green asked Warren to give a brief synopsis of what happened immediately preceding Carla's death. Following his portrayal of the critical events, the meeting was opened for questions.

"Why did you attend Carla's funeral," asked Michael Stewart.

"Because one other time in my career, I had a patient die, and I didn't attend her funeral. I thought about that for a long time, and I told myself if I ever again lost a patient, that I had an established relationship with, I would do what I came to believe is the decent thing to do and attend the funeral."

"Did you ask Dr. Thompson to attend?"

"No."

"So how did he happen to go with you?"

"I told him I was going, and he said he'd go with me."

"Did he tell you he had any reason for going?"

"I guess I don't really understand your question."

"I mean did he tell you he was going because the funeral was in a bad neighborhood, or because he thought it was the right thing to do, or maybe because he wanted to meet the family."

"He didn't say any of those things to me." Warren was beginning to feel warm. His palms were moist and he just wanted the meeting to be over.

"Did he ever mention to you that he thought you or anyone else did something to cause Carla's death?"

"No."

"Did he ever mention that he thought the hospital was at fault?"

"At fault how?"

"You know, untrained O.R. personnel, system failures, anything like that."

"After I told him what happened, he did mention that he thought there may be system issues that sounded like they needed to be looked into. He did not use the word 'failures.'"

"System issues like what?"

"Like emergency O.R. availability."

"What did he think was wrong with emergency O.R. availability?"

"He didn't say anything was wrong with it, he said it needed to be looked into."

"And, that conclusion was based on—"

"It was based on what I told you when we started this meeting — my troubles getting an O.R. crew when I needed to take Ms. Williams back to surgery."

"What about money for the family?"

"What about it?"

"OK...did he ever mention to you that he thought the hospital should give Ms. Williamses' family money?"

"For...," Warren drew the word out, making it into a question."

"To compensate them for their loss."

"Not to me he didn't."

"How about to anyone that you know of?"

"No. Not to anyone that I know of."

Maurice Paul asked Warren,

"Do you believe the hospital should pay the Williamses' family money?"

"I don't know. I haven't really thought about it."

"Well today as you sit here, what do think about the idea of the hospital paying your patient's survivors money?"

"I don't have an opinion."

"Do you think Dr. Thompson had an opinion?"

"I don't know. How would I know?"

"Were you there when he spoke with your patient's mother and aunt?"

"No, I was not."

"What do you—"

"I take that back. I was there when he introduced himself to Carla's aunt just before the funeral started."

"What did he say to her?"

"He introduced himself and said he was sorry for her loss. He gave her his card and asked if she would have Carla's mom call him."

"That's all?"

"Yes."

"What do you think he talked about when he met with them in his office?"

"I don't know."

"Well, let's see, you gotta figure he gave them his condolences right?"

"Yeah, I guess so."

"And, he probably asked how they were getting along with the three kids to look after right?"

"I don't know. I guess so."

"Well, from what you know of Dr. Thompson — and you've known him for a while right?"

"Yes."

"And, how long would that be?"

"For about seven years."

"About seven years. Right. He hired you here, didn't he?"

"Yes, he did."

"So, from what you know of him, it certainly would not be outside his character or outside the realm of reasonable possibility, that he might have at least mentioned the family's financial situation would it?"

"I suppose he might have mentioned it."

"Thank you."

There were no other questions.

Warren was depressed and remorseful driving home after the meeting. *Thompson's being hung out to dry, but there's nothing I can do about it. The hospital's turning on him and they're wrong.*

Gina greeted her husband with a smile and a friendly chide,

"Hello, Stranger. Me and the kids thought you might've forgotten where we live."

When Warren's only response was a nod and a sad look, Gina said, "What's the matter?"

She followed her husband into their den and closed the double accordion doors. Warren lowered himself onto the sofa and his wife sat next to him. He propped his right side against the arm rest as he leaned back with his left forearm and wrist resting on his head while his legs were outstretched on the floor and crossed, left over right, at the ankles.

"I just survived an hour of interrogation by a committee trying to nail Thompson for things they *think* he *might* have said to Carla Williamses' family. "

"The girl who died?"

"Yeah."

"What are they saying he said?"

"I think they're trying to say that he told her family that we screwed up."

"He said that about you?"

"I don't believe he said that about anybody."

"Well, what makes them think he did?"

"That I don't know. They also seem to think he promised them money."

"What's this all got to do with you?"

"You mean other than the fact I killed her."

"Don't say that!" Gina's utterance was without sympathy or compassion – it was an order.

"They know we're close, and they wanted to see what I knew."

"What did you tell 'em?"

"Not much, because I don't know what he said or didn't say. I didn't hear anything from him about it. But, I feel bad that I caused this problem, and they're going after him for it."

Gina stared for a moment, directly into Warren's eyes.

"Don't stick your neck out. Thompson's a big boy, he doesn't need you getting into it. Think about your family for once."

She left him there, closing the doors on her way out. Warren thought hard about what she said. And, then his thoughts drifted on to a lot of things, but particularly to Gina, and he didn't like where his thoughts were taking him.

Gina. What he originally perceived as her love was a relentless self-serving agenda disguised as romance and adulation. The beginning was so innocent and care free — being pulled by the hand to dance in the aisle by a beautiful young stranger who sat next to him at the start of a rock concert. And, over a short time, he decided she really cared for him.

Warren was coming to realize that from age 15 or 16, Gina was on a husband hunt to trap the quarry who would provide the existence she craved so intensely. She was determined to have the material life denied her by her loving electrician father, an excessive drinker and nominal worker, whose chronic lack of income condemned the family to a perpetual life at or near the poverty line. Gina was the youngest of five. Her birth, after four consecutive boys, disrupted her mother's parenting norm in a visceral way. Linda Schneider cared for her daughter's every physical need, but there was an emotional void that never resolved itself.

Early in their relationship, Warren was amazed at how obsessed and knowledgeable his future wife was about Hollywood's rich and famous. Did her core goal drive her celebrity fixation or did the fixation drive the goal, or maybe it was all just a cycle without a discernable beginning or end. She lucked-up on Warren and irreversibly hung on. As he thought more about it, he realized how calculating she was. Her original plan to become an interior designer was nothing more than a perceptive strategy to get close to wealth. What Warren, the single young pre-med and med student, mistook for devotion, during a tough period in his life, was Gina's determination to protect and ultimately claim the pot of gold, not at the end of a wonderful rainbow, but at the base of a powerful lightning strike.

A half hour later, he became aware of a soft knocking. He opened his eyes and for a brief instant couldn't figure out where he was. When he said come in, his six-year-old opened one of the doors, ran to him, climbed into his lap, and hugged her father. Warren's arms instinctively engulfed his daughter's small frame and she told him, in a happy song like cadence, "Mommy said to tell you it's time for dinner."

* * *

Green's committee began its deliberations about Thompson's case immediately after Warren left the room. The committee Chair began by asking the members if they felt they needed to hear from any other witnesses. They all agreed, since their instructions did not allow them to interview anyone not employed or privileged by the hospital, there were no other people they wished to hear from. Green, reading from notes she took during the meetings, summarized the committee's interviews with Dr. Thompson, Mr. Cummings, and Dr. Chambers. She then opened the floor for discussion.

Dr. Cynthia McMasters addressed the group. "We have a big problem. By his own account, Thompson admitted to planting the seed with the family that mistakes were made."

"How did you get to that conclusion," asked Michael Stewart.

"Come on, Mike. He told us he spoke to them about the investigation being conducted. If that's not a hint that somebody thinks something went wrong, I don't know what is. Then he tells the grandmother that he and the hospital will be mindful of the financial burdens she now faces. That's pretty clear messaging in my mind. He implied this to the family before the sentinel event investigation was completed. To make matters worse, he essentially promised them the hospital would give them money. Thompson was wrong."

"Hold on," Stewart said, holding up his right hand to emphasize his message. "He didn't do either of those things." These comments surprised the other committee members in light of the aggressive tough questions he put to the Ob/Gyn chair. "I buy Thompson's explanation. I believe he did have empathy for this suffering family. He's a good man who was trying to do the right thing. The fact that he didn't lose it when I pressed him hard about his motivations for what he did makes me believe, even more, that his intentions were pure. What was he supposed to say to the family, we know your daughter was young and healthy, but hell, shit happens?"

"Damn it, Mike," Paul said. "He had no business meeting with that family in the first place. It was none of his business."

"Are you saying that a Department Chair at this hospital has no business meeting with a grieving family to try and provide some comfort and possibly some truth?" Stewart asked.

"The investigation wasn't even finished, so what truth did he have to offer?"

"Maybe just the reassurance that we were honestly looking for the facts of what happened and that we recognized the truth about the consequences of her daughter's death."

Paul said nothing at first, but shook his head in disbelief. Finally he said, "Thompson had no investigation results and therefore no truth to give. What he did was imply blame and a promise of money."

McMasters said, "I've been involved in several sentinel events with grieving parents and unanswered questions about care that was rendered. I've had to console their families, and I've always managed to do it without blaming our hospital or promising money. And, then there's Mr. Cummings and his meeting with the family. Everyone in here heard him when he told us that the patient's mother and aunt told him...," she paused to remember the word, "emphatically is what he said — they said emphatically that Thompson implied to them that many errors were made by those caring for Ms. Williams, and these errors led to her death. Now Mike, how do you argue around that one?"

"I don't believe him."

"Based on what," Paul said.

"I don't know exactly. I guess based on the fact that his story sounded too perfect to me."

"And, what would be his motive to lie?"

"I can't say, but I don't believe him."

"You've gotta do better than that."

"Thompson clearly stepped over the line with this family," McMasters added.

"The fact that he impugned the reputations of the care givers involved, and gave our hospital a big black eye, bothers me — a lot," said Paul.

Dr. Richard Carpenter spoke up for the first time. "This whole thing is bad to me. I imagine that we're eventually going to have to vote on whether we believe Thompson violated the by-laws; is that right, Celia?"

"That's right."

After a moment, Green said, "Then I think we ought to discuss the pertinent by-laws before we vote on anything."

"Open your by-laws booklet, please, to page 32," she said. "Look at section 3.4.7. It states:

> Except in the context of a formal peer review processes, it is deemed unprofessional for a healthcare Provider to criticize, berate, or otherwise disparage another provider or the care rendered to a patient by another provider. Such unprofessional conduct may result in disciplinary action up to and including termination of employment and/or staff privileges.

Mike Stewart spoke up again, "I truly believe that Thompson did not do anything even close to violating this by-law."

"Mike, what are you talking about?" asked Paul. "You heard what came out of Thompson's own mouth and you heard what Cummings told us. If telling that family, 'an investigation is going on, and when it's finished I'll tell you everything that we uncovered and, oh, by the way, we recognize that you need money,' if that doesn't violate the spirit and the letter of this by-law, then nothing does."

"What about Full Disclosure," Stewart asked.

"What about it?"

"I thought we were supposed to be promoting a culture of safety around here. Isn't full disclosure supposed to be part of that concept?"

"A culture of safety doesn't include unprofessional behavior toward colleagues, placing blame for a bad outcome on an institution before the facts are known, and offering the hospital's — that is to say our money in many cases — to people just because you feel sorry for them." McMasters said.

"I'm ready to vote on this thing now," Paul said, his words were heavy with anger and determination.

Green asked if there were any objections to proceeding with a vote, and Stewart said, "I know you've all made up your minds, and I know I could talk 'til the cows come home and it wouldn't change your minds. So out of respect for all of you, I won't do that. But, I want you all to know, I believe you're making a *very big mistake.*"

Green nodded a thank you to Stewart and asked, "Will all those who agree that Dr. Thompson violated hospital by-law 3.4.7 please raise your hands."

Nine hands went up including Green's.

"All opposed?"

Stewart's hand was the only one raised. Green turned to the transcriptionist and said,

"Let the record reflect the vote was nine agreeing that Dr. Harold Thompson violated by-law 3.4.7, and one vote agreeing that he did not violate 3.4.7."

Winslow's MEC was composed of the Chairs of all of the medical and surgical departments in the hospital, Nursing leadership, and leaders from the hospital's Administration, including the CEO and President. Only the physician members could vote on any motions put before the committee. It was empowered by the Board of Directors to adjudicate medical matters, including physician behavior. This "Med Exec" would then pass its recommendations on to the Board which was free to accept or reject the recommendations it received.

The committee met to discuss the allegations against Thompson, and the findings from Green's committee, on May 3rd, seven weeks after Carla's death.

Dr. Michael Isaacs chaired the meeting. Twenty-nine of the thirty-five voting members were present, and this totaled more than the two-thirds attendance required by the by-laws to qualify as a quorum. The participants were seated at tables which formed a large sharp cornered "U." Ron Blazer, and the President of the hospital's medical staff, Dr. Gerald Holcomb, were seated at the head table with Isaacs, as was Lavern Watson, Vice President, Nursing Services. Their table was nearest the large room's front entrance, and it faced the open end of the "U" configuration. Several other key operations managers, along with Bertram Wexler, the in-house legal advisor permanently assigned to the committee, were also present. Wexler was in his early sixties, possessed a head of thick gray, well-trimmed hair, and was without beard or mustache. The pitch of his voice was neither deep nor high, but it sounded slightly strained and raspy. His gold wire rimmed glasses combined with his other features to give him a no-nonsense air that was appropriate for his role as final arbiter of the procedural rules delineated in Winslow's by-laws.

Isaacs called the meeting to order. After disposing of some minor preliminary business, including the approval of minutes from the committee's previous meeting, Isaacs introduced the meeting's primary agenda item which was to be a discussion and potential action on the allegations against Thompson.

"If this committee, indeed, finds that Dr. Thompson's conduct did violate Winslow's prohibition against such behavior, then we must decide on what if any action we recommend be taken. The by-laws specifically state that sanctions for such behavior may include termination of hospital privileges and or employment. Are there any questions?"

No questions came from the solemn attendees, and Isaacs continued.

"Dr. Ceilia Green's Professional Conduct Sub-Committee was charged by me with examining the allegations lodged against Dr. Thompson, and I will now have her describe her committee's work, their findings, and their recommendations. Dr. Green."

"Thank you, Dr. Isaacs. As you heard, our committee was asked to look into allegations that Dr. Harold Thompson engaged in activity contrary to Winslow's by-laws. Specifically, he was accused of criticizing the care received by a patient who died several hours after an elective surgery. Dr. Thompson was not directly involved in the case, but took it upon himself to contact the family in the days following the patient's demise. Our committee is only allowed to interview people who are Winslow employees or who have current staff privileges at our hospital. We met with Drs. Thompson and Chambers — Dr. Chambers was the surgeon of record, and Mr. Marshall Cummings, Chief Administrator of Physical Plant Operations.

Mr. Cummings was asked by Mr. Blazer to meet with the patient's mother and aunt to determine what Dr. Thompson said when he met with them.

During our meetings, we allowed each interviewee to tell us about the interactions they had with the patient's family or with anyone else concerning any aspects possibly pertinent to the allegations we were examining. After each statement, we had a free flow of questions by committee members and answers by the interviewees. At the end of the process, the overwhelming majority of us were convinced that all of the information we heard from the two doctors and Mr. Cummings was credible. By a vote of nine to one, the committee members believed that Dr. Thompson conveyed a strong message of criticism about the care received by the decedent. In doing so, he impugned the reputations of several care givers, and he denigrated the reputation of Winslow. Eight of the committee participants are here today, and all of us are happy to answer any questions."

"The floor is now open for questions," Isaacs announced.

A question was asked about who made the allegations. Green answered that they were anonymous. How did the committee confirm Thompson's alleged remarks? Green answered that Thompson confirmed some of them, and Cummings got more confirmation from the family members. When one questioner asked for an example of the offending remarks, Green answered,

"Dr. Thompson told the family that the patient's death was unexpected, and there were many unanswered questions. He revealed to them that an investigation was underway to get to the bottom of what happened. He also implied that the family would get money from the hospital to help with the financial burden that had been created now that the patient's three children had no parents." The questions ended after about twenty minutes.

"If no one has anything more to ask, then in keeping with our by-laws as well as our policy and procedure, Dr. Thompson, who has decided to exercise his option to make a statement and answer questions, will be given the floor."

Thompson was accompanied into the room by Wexler. He entered and walked to the podium at the right sided tip on the "U."

Thompson faced the head table at the other end of the room as he delivered his short statement. He told this room of colleagues that he believed he had done nothing wrong. He said he had reached out to a grieving family to let them know that Winslow was not indifferent to their loss or the burdens they faced.

"I told them that we realized the death of their daughter and niece was unexpected and that we were also shocked by it. I told them the hospital was looking into exactly what happened, and I told them when the inquiry was complete, I would share all of the findings with them. I explained that the patient may have had an underlying health problem that no one knew about and this could have been the reason for what happened. Lastly, I told them that we recognize the financial burden they now face, and that when all the facts are known, if it turns out we did something wrong, our hospital will be mindful of the financial challenges the family faces in raising the patient's three children."

The room was quiet for a moment when Thompson finished. Isaacs broke the silence by inviting questions for Thompson.

Dr. Owens Tabor, Chair of Otolaryngology said, "In my forty years of practice I've twice lost a patient who wasn't supposed to die, and I promise you I never had a meeting with the family other than to give them the news and answer a few questions. What made you contact these people two weeks after the fact and then sit down with them?"

Thompson explained the Culture of Safety mindset that was being widely embraced by healthcare institutions all over the country. He also talked about the philosophy and use of Full Disclosure when things go in unexpected directions with patient care.

"I was practicing those concepts."

"In this medicolegal environment," Tabor asked.

"Actually, several studies have documented less litigation and less money paid out by institutions when Full Disclosure was practiced."

"I don't care what some pie-in-the-sky ivory tower eggheads who haven't practiced real medicine in years have to say. We all live in the real world and this idea of admitting guilt to patients is nuts. It fuels the fire and, at least in this state, it helps us get what little ass we have left sued off." Tabor's remarks drew many affirmative nods and some genuine laughter. He had a long-standing reputation for saying what was on his mind, no punches pulled.

Several other questioners asked Thompson if he directly referenced specific physicians or hospital personnel when he spoke about the investigation while it was in progress.

"Absolutely not."

"Do you consider your references to the family's financial burden an offer or promise of money from the hospital," asked Dr. Alyce Guzman, Chair of Ambulatory Services.

"No, I do not. I assure you I made no promise of money or financial support of any kind."

"Then why did you bring it up?"

"Part of the Full Disclosure philosophy is that physicians must make a specific recognition of all the consequences of the bad outcome they're speaking to the family about. To gain trust in these very difficult situations, one must get the family to understand that the hospital, and its care givers, have more than mere sympathy for the predicament the patient, if still alive, and the family, is left to face. It's confidence building, and it enhances the chances for potential resolution without litigation."

Isaac signaled the end of the questions by thanking Thompson for his appearance.

"Thank you, Dr. Isaacs, and all of you, for hearing me out."

With Thompson no longer present, Isaacs said, "The floor is now open for discussion."

Tabor spoke. "I think the good Dr. Thompson is self-righteous, destructive to himself and our hospital — and I think he's nuts. Hell yes he criticized the doctors and nurses taking care of that patient, and hell yes he needs to go."

"With all due respect, Dr. Tabor, I can't disagree with you more," said Guzman. "Many of us who've worked with Dr. Harold Thompson think he's exactly what this place needs: New ideas and the energy and tenacity to swim upstream to implement them. He's trying to nudge us into the twenty-first century, and it's uncomfortable at times. He worked tirelessly to make our obstetrical unit safer, he is passionate about teaching our residents and medical students, and he's dedicated to trying to do the right thing in this case, for the patient and this hospital. If he's nuts, I want us all to be nuts like him."

The give and take of points made with emotion, followed by spirited rebuttals went on for over an hour. Finally, when the discussion died down to quiet talk and whispers, for and against what had been openly discussed, Isaacs ended the discussion period by asking if there was a motion to proceed to a vote. Tabor spoke up.

"I make a motion that the clinical privileges of Harold Thompson be terminated."

"Is there a second," Isaacs asked.

"I second the motion," was repeated by two or three doctors.

"Very well, there is a motion on the floor, is there any discussion?" There was a brief pause. "Hearing none," Isaacs continued, please fill out the ballots Yvonne passed out.

Almost all Med Exec votes were taken by a show of hands. But, in matters that involved potential physician disciplinary action, votes were done by confidential paper ballot. When all twenty-nine ballots were turned in, a buzz of anxious conversation permeated the room while Yvonne and Wexler tallied the vote.

"Attention please," Isaacs' voice boomed out several minutes after the counting started. The vote is fourteen yes votes, eleven no votes and four abstentions. The motion carries."

Tabor wore a broad smile, while many of Thompson's supporters looked sad and sat quietly.

"I know this vote represents strong views on both sides—"

"Excuse me Dr. Isaacs." The words rang out in an Irish brogue familiar to everyone in the room. "If I may?" The request came from Dr. Marcus Quigley, Chair of Radiation Oncology.

"Yes, Dr. Quigley," Isaacs replied.

"Sir, my reading of our by-laws indicates that a vote on a motion to terminate clinical privileges must have a two-thirds majority of the quorum of voting members in order to pass. Unfortunately, Dr. Isaacs, we have no such majority of votes here."

Isaacs looked stunned. As his ears began to redden, he turned to Wexler who was holding an open copy of the by-laws in his left hand.

"Bertram what's your *official* opinion on Dr. Quigley's point?" He spoke these words as if they were a rebuke to Quigley.

"He's correct," Wexler answered after a moment of what appeared to be intense reading. There was a tinge of embarrassment in his tone. "The by-laws specifically demand quote "a two-thirds majority of a quorum of voting members present shall be required in order for any motion concerning physician discipline to pass.,"" he said.

The hour was now late and Isaacs appeared to be at a loss as to how to proceed.

Isaacs asked the group, "If we have another ballot, is there anyone present who believes they might be inclined to change their vote?"

This was a clumsy strategy at best. If anyone answered Isaacs' question in the affirmative, and if the result of a second vote changed by one, the identity of the doctor who changed his or her vote would be known to the other participants. No one answered Isaacs' question.

May I make a suggestion Dr. Isaacs," Green asked.

"Please."

"Given the lateness of the hour, I suggest that we table this matter and revisit it at our next meeting. In the meantime because of some of the things that were said about Dr. Thompson during our discussion, I suggest that you require him to have both a complete physical exam, with drug testing, and a psychiatric evaluation before we meet again. The results of those examinations should be shared with this body before we take another vote.

"Is that a motion Dr. Green?"

"Yes sir, it is."

"Is there a second?"

"Second," called out Quigley.

"Is there any discussion?"

No one spoke.

"Hearing none, all in favor, raise your hands.

Twenty hands went up.

"Those opposed."

Five hands rose.

"Are there any Abstentions?"

Four hands waved.

"The motion carries. I'll now entertain a motion to adjourn.

The meeting ended two and a half hours after it started. It was one of the longest meetings of the Med Exec, and its primary agenda item had escaped closure.

Chapter Sixteen

"There seems something amiss to me as well." Dr. Marcus Quigley spoke these words to his friend Michael Stewart who called the morning after the Med Exec meeting in which Thompson's troubles were debated. Quigley reared back in his office desk chair and swiveled slightly from side to side with the phone receiver cradled on his left shoulder. The radiation oncologist's outsized personality obscured his short thin stature. His full head of white hair and mustache-goatee were close cropped. The facial lines in Quigley's pale skin were not deep, and the Irish native's blue eyes twinkled with his frequent humor.

"The whole thing keeps nagging at me," Stewart said. "I just don't believe Cummings' story. It's too perfect. It screams "contrived" to me."

"How do you suppose we can hang a lantern on this fella and his merry tale?"

"I don't know."

"Aye, Michael, I'll tell you, I would be quite surprised if Messieurs Blazer and Isaacs aren't in this thing deeper than whale shit." Stewart responded with a hearty laugh. He was a man who usually laughed easily, but his mirth had become scarce over the previous several days.

"Where in god's name do you get these expressions of yours?"

"Well, you'd need to spend time in County Donegal where I grew up for the answer to that one."

"I've actually thought about hiring a private eye."

"That's not a bad idea. I'll gladly put my hand in my pocket for half the bill. But, I must ask, what's your interest here?"

"I just can't stand the thought that Thompson is getting screwed, and most of our leaders around here are ambling along like a herd of sheep."

"I'm with you on that one, but you do realize, that what you're seeing is the natural order of things throughout the civilized world. How many examples are there of supposedly good people, who allowed evil to go unchallenged because they wouldn't stand up?"

* * *

Stewart was a Vermont farm boy raised by two former hippies. He had four younger siblings. His mom and dad, Louise and Raymond adopted Stewart's younger brother. The elder Stewarts were young white college kids who met while they were preparing to go to Mississippi for nineteen sixty-four's Freedom Summer. After several weeks at a northern liberal arts college learning the principles and tactics of nonviolent social change they were assigned to work at a Freedom School in Natchez, Mississippi. By day they taught black children to read, write about their life experiences, and participate in discussions about citizenship. Their nights were taken up with efforts to get the parents of their students, along with other members of the black community, registered to vote. The couple became disillusioned with the pervasive intimidation they felt and witnessed every day, along with the frequent violence that erupted from the seemingly bottomless pit of white racism. They both decided to take a year off from college, and explore life in San Francisco. Their career as farmers began when Raymond's elderly uncle Horace essentially gave them his farm. He had no heirs and wanted to leave the place in family hands. The two young idealists, both from affluent families, decided to permanently forgo college and "get back to the land."

Growing up on a farm surrounded by animals, domestic and wild, along with the natural fauna and the crops his family cultivated, inspired Stewart's fascination with biology. It was this aspect of his childhood and adolescence that sparked his desire to become a physician. His closest, and lifelong, friendship was forged in the sixth grade when he rescued the only boy in his school with cerebral palsy from an older and bigger bully.

Maturity was forced on Stewart at age seventeen. Raymond was severely injured in a late night car accident on a freezing windy night. In the first days after the accident, his doctors were not sure Raymond would live. When they realized he would survive, they doubted he would walk again. The family's finances over the previous several years were marginal at best, and Raymond's condition threatened to bankrupt his family. Against the protests of a distraught Louise, and her barely-able-to-speak husband, Stewart dropped out of eleventh grade to work full-time on the farm. His father's recovery took two years, but thanks to the hard work of Stewart and Louise, along with help from the other kids and some neighbors, the Stewart's had their best two harvests in five years. The finances of their operation became viable again. Despite huge odds against him, as well as the culture of rural Vermont in the mid nineteen-eighties, at age nineteen, Stewart returned to his high school, graduated, and attended college in Middlebury, Vermont. During college, he met his future wife. A career in medicine was his clear goal, while his girlfriend, Madeline Worthington, aspired to become an economist. Stewart received acceptance letters from each of the seven schools he applied to, and just before graduation, he decided to attend Anthony University's Medical School in Detroit because Madeline was accepted to the University of Michigan's graduate program in economics. They married four years later after Madeline earned a PhD in economics, and Stewart finished Medical School. They exchanged vows in early June three weeks before Stewart started his general surgery residency at Creason. The couple, both of whom were white, adopted a five-year-old black orphan who Stewart helped care for during his last year of med school. The boy and his twenty-one year old mother were living in an abandoned house in which a fire was deliberately started a few minutes after 2 a.m. on a mid-February morning. His mother died of smoke inhalation and burns while Vashawn suffered severe burns, seven crushed ribs, multiple lung punctures, and smoke inhalation. It took three months before he was healthy enough to be discharged. The boy had no father or other family who were willing to claim him. To prevent his former patient from becoming a permanent ward of the state, Stewart became his foster father. Vashawn was the ring bearer in the wedding of his soon to be parents. Fifteen months after their wedding, Stewart and Madeline followed Louise and Raymond's example and legally adopted Vashawn.

During his residency and cardiovascular surgery fellowship, Stewart befriended a number of Detroit police officers most of whom he met in Creason's Emergency Department. On several occasions, he worked tirelessly to save the lives of some of his Detroit's Finest friends and acquaintances. Others he stitched up or spoke with for long periods while they waited for their prisoners to receive care. He knew a former detective on the force named Marchelle Dunlap. She retired after twenty years and started a private investigations business.

"Hi, Marchelle," Stewart said when Dunlap answered on the fourth ring. "It's Mike Stewart, from Creason's ER, do you remember me?"

"Dr. Stewart, of course I remember you." She sounded happy to hear his voice.

They exchanged pleasantries and caught up on each other's lives for several minutes before Stewart said,

"Marchelle, I've got a little problem I think you might be able to help me with."

Over the next half-hour he explained the Thompson situation to his friend, including many of its nuances. He described Cummings, Blazer, and Isaacs.

"You know Marchelle, I think Isaacs wants to get rid of Thompson. But, unlike a doctor friend of mine, I don't believe he's involved in anything underhanded. I can't say that about the other two - Cummings because his story stinks and Blazer because he's always come off to me as a slicked up corporate guy who's got no loyalty to anybody but himself."

"Is Thompson a friend of yours?"

"Not really."

"Then why do you care?"

"I guess because I like him. He shocked me when I first met him. You know I grew up in Vermont. I was having lunch in the doctor's dining room one afternoon, and I overheard Thompson talking to another doc about maple sugaring in Vermont."

"What?"

"You know, collecting maple tree sap and turning it into syrup and sugar. I grew up sugaring on our farm, and I was especially shocked to hear this black doc talking about it so knowledgeably. I don't think I saw three African Americans in Vermont until I started college. Anyway, I introduced myself, and he told me about his three years of boarding school in the state. I was really surprised. He was genuine and friendly. We didn't really get to be friends, but I just like the guy, and it pisses me off to think he's getting screwed."

"I can't make you any promises, but I work with a pretty smart cyber sleuth. I'll see what he can dig up, and I'll get back to you within the next two days"

They ended their phone call, and Stewart went to work seeing the forty patients he had on his schedule for the day.

* * *

When he awoke the morning after his Med Exec appearance, Thompson lay in bed thinking with certainty that his remaining time at Winslow would be short. His conviction that he acted in the Williamses' best interests, as well as Winslow's, was so strong that he refused to canvass the other Chairs to plead for their support, and by doing so, turn the process, that now entrapped him, into a political circus. Several times during his career he encountered medical students or doctors accused of academic or professional impropriety.

A number of these alleged wrong doers became obsessed with the cases against them, and whenever they were with people they knew, and many times people they did not know, they launched into lengthy monologues detailing the falsity of the allegations against them along with complex theories about the conspiracies that fueled their persecution. The atmosphere they created became increasingly unbearable, and these impassioned diatribes often ended with the aggrieved occupying the center of a widening empty circle. Many of these "defendants" drank too much, smoked too much, and generally engaged in activities that were harmful to themselves.

When he first learned he was the target of a Med Exec investigation, Thompson promised himself he would not obsess about his predicament nor engage in self-destructive behaviors. Instead, he continued his workout routine of thirty-five minutes of cardio and light weightlifting four times a week. He knew his way of defining right and wrong was the primary driver of the problems he faced, and at times he felt overwhelmed by the whirl of controversy whistling around him. It was again one of those times in his life when he asked himself, *Why don't I go crazy?* He imagined himself again facing the almost unbearable cold of his first wilderness experience in Vermont, however, this time he would stay in his lean-to, not because it was the path of least resistance, but because he decided that in this death struggle for his professional life, he would have to be beaten completely. There would be no terrible anguish punctuated by pleas to be left for dead on a seemingly impossible frozen battleground. This time he would focus his stare straight into probable defeat with no flinching, no whimpers, and not a single regret.

He got up, showered, dressed, and went to L&D to make rounds with the residents and nurses. Thompson did not brook a single blemish in his façade of confidence and authority.

***

Several days later, Cathy Weaver picked up the receiver of her desk phone as it rang. Before she could identify her office and herself, she heard the voice,

"Hello, Cathy, this is Mike Stewart, how are you?"

Several years earlier, Stewart performed a four-vessel coronary bypass procedure on Weaver's father. Her family still spoke of Stewart as the nicest doctor they ever met. The Weavers were amazed at her father's speedy recovery which they attributed to Stewart's skill.

"Hi, Dr. Stewart, long time no hear from."

"How's your dad, Cathy?'

"Still as sassy and hard to deal with as ever, and it's all your fault." They both laughed.

"What can I do for you Dr. Stewart?"

"I need some information, and I need you to keep this conversation between just us."

"Sure. What's up?"

I need to get the phone number for the mother of Carla Williams. Do you know who I'm talking about?"

"Sure, but what do you need that for?"

"Are you aware that your boss is being investigated by the Med Exec?"

"How could I not, it's the hottest gossip in this place."

"I don't want to say anything more about it, but trust me, I'm trying to save your boss's bacon."

"Give me a few minutes, and I'll call you back."

Less than a half hour later Weaver called back with Sylvia's number. She kept her word and said nothing to anyone about their conversation.

Sylvia didn't recognize Stewart's number when he called, and she pressed the ignore icon on her phone. She listened to his voicemail and returned his call about an hour later. After introducing himself and expressing his condolences he said, "Ms. Williams, a tremendous controversy has come up about the way Dr. Thompson handled his conversations with your family. I'm a member of the committee that was asked to look into it."

"Asked by whom?"

"By the higher ups at Winslow — the Chief Medical Officer to be exact."

"I don't know. This thing is starting to feel uncomfortable to me."

"You could be very helpful in clearing up some questions that have come up, Ms. Williams."

"What questions?"

"Questions about the things you discussed with Dr. Thompson and Mr. Cummings."

There was a brief pause in the conversation and then Sylvia said, "Do you want to meet?"

"I'd sure appreciate it if we can."

"Well, when would you want to meet?"

"I can come by tomorrow morning."

"I'll talk to my sister Mae, and I'll call you back."

When Sylvia called Stewart later that afternoon, she told him she and her sister would instead be willing to come to his office.

"That'll be fine," Stewart said. "And, Ms. Williams, I need you and your sister to please keep this conversation and our meeting confidential, at least for the time being. My office is located about six miles from the hospital, and I doubt any of the people I'm concerned about will know we're meeting."

The sisters were sitting in Stewart's office waiting room the next morning, a few minutes before ten o'clock. After giving her name, Sylvia asked the receptionist,

"Can you please let Dr. Stewart know we're here?"

Almost before the receptionist replaced the phone receiver in its cradle, Stewart bounded out of the door on the left side of the patient check-in desk. His was six feet, three inches tall, trim, and had a full head of sandy brown hair. He stuck his right hand out toward Janis Mae and said,

"I'm so glad to meet you, Ms. Williams."

Janis Mae wore a slight, probably embarrassed, grin when she said, "No, Dr. Stewart, I'm Janis Mae Sipple, and this is my sister Sylvia Williams."

"I apologize, Ms. Sipple." And, after shaking her hand he turned to Sylvia and greeted her correctly.

In his office, the sisters took seats in front of Stewart's desk. He offered them refreshments, but they demurred. At the beginning of their conversation, Sylvia appeared tense, and she was frugal with her words. She confirmed that Thompson met Janis Mae at Carla's funeral, and asked her to, "please have her call me. I didn't call him. I guess because I just wasn't up to it. He called me about a week and a half after the funeral."

Sylvia went on to describe how Thompson did tell them Carla's death was unexpected, and because of this, the hospital was looking into what happened.

"Did Dr. Thompson make it seem like it was the hospital's or the doctors' fault for what happened to your daughter, Ms. Williams?"

"No, he didn't. He didn't imply that at all. He said they really didn't know why Carla died. He said it could have been that she had some medical condition that no one knew about that could have caused her death, but he emphasized that they didn't know, and they were investigating to find out for sure if possible."

"What do you mean 'if possible'?"

"That's what Dr. Thompson said. He told us that even though they were looking into what happened, they might never find a satisfactory answer."

Janis Mae subtly nodded in agreement.

"Did Dr. Thompson talk to you about the hospital giving you money?"

The sisters turned to one another with bewildered looks, and Sylvia said, "Money? That's what that Mr. Cummings kept asking us about. He kept asking the same questions in different ways, almost like he was trying to get us to answer him with the words *he* wanted. We told him no, Dr. Thompson never promised or implied that the hospital would give us money. I don't know how or where all this money talk is coming from."

"So, he didn't mention the hospital giving you money to compensate you for your daughter's death, and to help you take care of your grandchildren."

"The only mention he made about that was when he told us the hospital recognized that one of the consequences of Carla's passing is the financial burdens I now face."

"What did you think he meant by that phrase 'financial burdens'? Didn't you think he meant the hospital should give you money to help ease those burdens?"

"That never crossed my mind, Dr. Stewart."

"Why do you think he brought it up?"

"I didn't really know at the time. A few days later, when Mae and I talked, we thought it was probably just his way of telling us he felt bad for our situation with the babies and all. When we talked again, we thought maybe Dr. Thompson meant that he and the hospital might try to raise money to help take care of the children. That's all we thought of it."

"That's all I wanted to ask," Stewart said. "Thank you both so much for coming by. It may come up that I need you to repeat what you told me to some of the Winslow higher ups, but I'll call you if I need you. I hope that's okay."

Both women wore expressions of suspicion, but they asked nothing.

"I promise I'll tell you everything you're probably wondering about when this controversy has been straightened out. And, once again, for now, please keep this meeting and what we talked about to yourselves."

They nodded agreement, and after exchanging handshakes and good-byes, they left.

Stewart did not sleep well that evening. He lay next to Madeline wide awake while she slept soundly. It took him three hours to fall asleep, and he was awake two hours later. He moved and fidgeted to the point that Madeline woke up.

"What's the matter, Michael?"

"The Thompson thing"

"What about it?"

"I just can't stop thinking about how this guy is getting framed for doing what's right."

They were lying on their sides facing one another. Madeline put her arms around her husband's neck and head and gently pulled him close. She kissed his forehead and kept him close until she again fell asleep. Several minutes later, he deftly freed himself and got up. Leaving their bedroom softly, he walked down stairs to the kitchen. After taking two large swallows from a glass of tap water, Stewart sat down in the breakfast nook. It was a few minutes before 4 o'clock. He peered through the nook's small window into the back yard which was still enveloped by the darkness. A half hour into some weighty thoughts, he picked up his cell phone, and touched the screen. The synthetic voice demanded "Command please." Stewart spoke "Winslow" into his device. His call was picked up on the second ring.

"Winslow operator" the male voice said clearly.

"Hi. This is Dr. Michael Stewart."

"How can I help you, Dr. Stewart?"

"I need to speak with Dr. Harold Thompson, Chair of Ob/Gyn. Will you please connect me directly to his home number?"

"Certainly, I will Dr. Stewart. For Identification purposes, I will need to get your physician ID number."

"7557."

"Thank you, and I'm connecting your call right now."

Thompson answered on the fourth ring.

"Hello," he said in a hoarse, sleep ladened voice.

"Harold, this is Mike Stewart."

"Why in god's name are you calling me at 4:30 in the morning?"

"I've got a question for you that's been keeping me awake for three days."

"And, what, you want me to keep you company?"

Stewart chuckled, "You're damn fast for a guy just waking up from a dead sleep."

"You poor thing, what could possibly be keeping you awake?" Thompson asked with exaggerated mock sympathy.

"Is protecting white people a learned behavior?"

"No, it's actually a real bad habit."

Through his laughter Stewart said, "Sorry about that. I was just trying to understand what you did, that's all."

"Well, now that I've helped your learning curve along, if it's all the same to you, I'll go back to what I was doing when you woke me up," Thompson managed to get out just ahead of a yawn.

"Tell me, Harold, did you ever have a run-in of any kind with Ron Blazer or Marshall Cummings?"

"Why do you ask?"

"Look, you really have no reason in the world to trust me, but without going into detail, I think I may be on to something that may help your situation."

"And why on god's green earth would you concern yourself with my problems?"

"It's a long story, but bottom line, you answering my question isn't gonna hurt you anymore or cause you any more problems than you already have, right"

Thompson was silent for such a long time that Stewart finally asked, "Are you still there?"

"Yes," Thompson finally answered. During his silence he decided Stewart was right - answering the question really couldn't make his situation worse.

"I've never met or spoken to Marshall Cummings that I know of. As for Ron Blazer, do you ever remember hearing all the talk around the hospital about Brian Tooley?"

"Yeah."

"Well, despite some of the gossip going around, Brian was not terminated or forced off the staff. I told him he needed to get a behavioral assessment after the incident in the O.R. when he broke the tech's hand by slamming down the retractor when he got angry with her. He went off to Nebraska, and got the evaluation. The program out there recommended 8 to 12 weeks of residential therapy. Brian refused. I got a call from Ron Blazer. He asked me to find an alternative to Brian having to leave his practice for a few months. I told him I wasn't willing to do that. He wasn't too happy about my decision, but I never heard from him again. Caruthers backed me up on that one, and I think he did some heavy politicking that prevented Ron from undoing my decision. I believe, in the end, it cost Caruthers his job. Now Mike, what I just told you is very confidential, so if it gets back to anyone that I told you this stuff, I'm a goner."

"Scouts honor, this conversation never happened."

"Were you ever in the Boy Scouts?"

"No." Stewart laughed, "but, trust me, I'm a Scout at heart."

* * *

The day after his conversation with Stewart, Thompson signed the check-in book in Dr. Scott Meyer's office. His appointment for the mandated physical exam was 2 weeks before the next Med Exec meeting. After completing the exam, Meyers sent a report of his findings and conclusions to Isaacs. The report contained the specifics of the exam Meyers performed as well as the results of the laboratory tests he ordered. He concluded his report by writing, "Dr. Thompson is in very good physical health. His current weight is 218 pounds, and I advised him to lose twenty-one pounds which would decrease his body mass index from twenty-six and a half to twenty-four point zero. This amount of weight reduction would bring Thompson from the "overweight" category to within the "normal" category. Also of note, Thompson's urine drug screen was negative for any illicit drugs, prescription drugs of abuse, or alcohol."

Thompson left Meyers' office at 11:30 which gave him an hour and a half to get to his psychiatric evaluation appointment. He was 12 hours into the fast he did in preparation for his lab draws at Meyers' office, and his hunger was raging. He drove to his favorite Deli which was a half mile from his appointment. It was a carry-out only business, and his call-in order of turkey pastrami on rye with tomatoes lettuce and spicy mustard, along with his order of chicken noodle soup, was ready when he arrived. The famished doctor-turned-patient added a bag of pretzels and a diet cola at the counter when he picked up his food. Seated in his midsize SUV, he listened to the Miles Davis recording *Kind of Blue*. It was one of several albums he previously downloaded to the small hard drive that was a part of his vehicle's sound system. The mellowness of the music complemented his melancholia as he munched his lunch and thought about what lay ahead. His thoughts darted back and forth as he contemplated finding another job and how far he was willing to carry his fight with Winslow's administrators. He didn't have a definitive answer to that question.

He arrived at Dr. Jeffery Sims' office 10 minutes before his appointment time. The waiting room was small and empty. The soft lighting complimented the room's pastel color scheme, while the generous padding on the seats all combined to provide an atmosphere of low stress and cheerfulness. He took a seat, leaned back while stretching out his legs, and felt his weariness descend on him.

Ten minutes later when the receptionist called for him to come back to one of the rooms, he was midway between wakefulness and sleep. He almost jumped at the sound of his name, but he managed to rise slowly and follow the receptionist/medical assistant to a small room with a desk.

"Dr. Sims would like you to take a personality inventory test."

"Okaay." Thompson's drawing out of the word bespoke of his apprehension.

"Are you familiar with this kind of testing?"

"I am."

"Well this one should take you no more than forty-five minutes."

She left Thompson to answer the test questions by darkening the appropriate small ovals on the computerized answer sheet. Although this would be the 3rd or 4th personality assessment exam of his career, Thompson was somewhat anxious now about whether the interpretation of his answers would be to his detriment.

He finished in the predicted time, and waited another quarter of an hour before he was invited into Dr. Sims' office. Thompson recognized Sims as someone he encountered several times around the hospital, but never spoke to. The psychiatrist, a head and a half shorter than Thompson, was in his early forties, and his thick black hair matched his very dark eyes. He sported a full well trimmed beard which harbored no gray. Sim's was trim and appeared to be in excellent physical condition with a manner that was not warm, but was affable.

"Dr. Thompson, I'm Jeff Sims," said the psychiatrist. He offered Thompson his hand and they shook. "May I call you Harold?"

"Sure."

"Please call me Jeff, turnabout is fair play after all."

Thompson smiled and he wondered if Sims had any idea about the high anxiety he was fighting not to show.

"Harold please relax. This isn't the Inquisition." Sims paused for two beats and said, "It's merely *an* Inquisition." Both men shared in the joke and Thompson's laugh was hardy and ironic.

Sims explained that his goal was to assess Thompson's mental state and personality traits. He would report his findings and interpretations to Dr. Isaacs. He asked Thompson many questions starting with his understanding of the accusations against him that the Med Exec was investigating. He wanted to know why Thompson thought they were investigating him, and what he thought about the process of the investigation. The psychiatrist delved into Thompson's sleeping patterns, his childhood, and his sex life. Sims was particularly interested in whether Thompson thought of himself as being depressed, and what kinds of plans, if any, he had made for the future. Their conversation took about ninety minutes.

"Well, Harold, it was good to meet you at last. I wish you the very best, and Isaacs should have my report in about three days."

Thompson walked across the parking lot, glad to be finished with Sims, and at a loss about what the psychoanalyst thought of him. He opened his driver's side door, slid behind the steering wheel and realized there was nothing to worry about because there wasn't a damn thing he could do about what Sims' impressions were or what he would report to Isaacs.

* * *

It took Marcelle Dunlap three days to get back to Stewart. It was almost seven in the evening, and Stewart was finished with his last patient phone call during which he delivered good news to a man who was worried that he would have to undergo a second vessel graft procedure. The patient was ecstatic about his test results, and profusely thanked Stewart. After hanging up the phone, Stewart grabbed his sports coat and turned to leave just as his cell phone rang.

"Dr. Stewart," he said, interrupting the first chime to speak. He rarely looked at the caller ID before answering.

"Hi, Dr. Stewart, it's Marchelle Dunlap. Is this an okay time for you?"

"Perfect," Stewart answered while he made his way out of the building toward his vehicle.

"Marchelle, can you hang on for two seconds while I Bluetooth you? And, please, call me Mike. I didn't see it was you before I answered."

"Not a problem, Mike."

"Whatdaya got for me?" he asked after his ear piece engaged and he got into his massive four-wheel drive, six passenger pick-up truck.

"I apologize that it took me so long to get back to you, but I think you'll be very interested in what we found."

"I'm all ears."

"As it turns out, Marshall Cummings is Ron Blazer's brother-in-law. Mr. Cummings was quite a hellion as a teenager. By the time he was seventeen he had racked up an impressive rap sheet with Juvenile Court convictions for burglary, auto theft, and shoplifting, not to mention the numerous MIPs."

"For Christ's sake, what is an MIP?"

"Forgive me for the jargon. It means minor in possession."

"Possession of what?

"Alcohol."

"Gottcha."

"He served a couple stretches in two different juvenile facilities here in Michigan. He was away for six months when he was thirteen, and he did another nine months that started when he was fifteen. He must have graduated from Thieves Academy with honors the second time around because, although he was suspected in a number of break-ins and car thefts, there wasn't enough evidence to charge him again for almost two years. When he was seventeen though, it all came crashing down on him.

"I'm just blown away that you found all this. I thought juvenile records were sealed."

"Well they are, but it's amazing what you can find these days." There was a smile in her voice.

"How?"

"I'll just say tricks of the trade and leave it right there."

"Yes ma'am, I got it – please forgive me, I'm going back to all ears now." She laughed,

"Mike, you're still the humorist. Anyway, three months shy of his eighteenth birthday, Cummings was arrested with two other men. One accomplice was twenty-nine and the other was thirty-five. They were charged with an armed robbery in which the young manager of a convenience store was severely beaten. The charges also included assault with a deadly weapon, intent to do great bodily harm, firearms possession violations, and possession of an ounce of crystal methamphetamine. The prosecutor had every intention of charging Cummings as an adult. According to notes from the prosecutor's office, Blazer told the lawyer who would eventually represent Cummings that his wife, Sarah, begged him to do something for her baby brother. Blazer told him he couldn't stand his brother-in-law, who he always referred to as "my wife's punk brother," but he said Sarah was losing her mind over the whole thing and pleaded with him to do something to save her little brother, who was facing a possible 60 years in prison if convicted on all counts.

Ron Blazer was a rising star at Hunt, Griffin, and Collier, a prominent regional accounting and wealth management company. He was a health care industry financial analyst. Despite his disdain for his brother-in-law, he needed peace at home. Blazer used his contacts to hire one of the area's most successful criminal defense attorneys, Wallace B. Liggett. Liggett spent fifteen years as a prosecutor, before jumping to the other side to defend the kind of people he had become an expert at convicting. Part of his prodigious success at preserving his clients' liberty was tied to his web of connections in prosecutor's offices all over the state. He maintained the willingness of many of his prosecutorial connections to cooperate with him by occasionally feeding them useful information about some of their targets. The currency he used to get his way never involved his clients or those of his partners.

Liggett worked his magic for Cummings, and all of the charges except the drug possession, were dropped against his client. He did not represent the other two defendants. The deal Liggett worked out prevented Cummings from having to testify against his hardened criminal confederates. Instead of jail time, he received five years' probation, and he committed to three months of residential treatment for substance abuse. He also committed to continuing outpatient therapy for at least five years. After five years the drug possession charge would be expunged from Cumming's record if he kept his nose clean — pun intended — sorry Mike, I couldn't help that one, and remained drug free and on the right side of the law."

Stewart was laughing when he said, "Good one!"

"It seems like a light went on in Mr. Cummings after this ordeal. He's never had another encounter with law enforcement or the criminal justice system — not even a speeding ticket."

"That explains a lot," Stewart said after a short pause. "Cummings is probably willing to die for Blazer if Blazer told him to do it."

"I certainly agree with you on that one."

"Thanks a bunch, Marchelle, and please send me your regular bill — no professional courtesy. This is one debt I'm going to be thrilled to pay."

Chapter Seventeen

Warren did not look good when he showed up to begin seeing patients in his private practice office. It was Monday morning, three days before the Med Exec was to meet for a second discussion and vote on Thompson's fate. Warren was usually neatly dressed in a shirt with a tie, dress slacks, and a sports coat whenever he came into the patient office on a day he did not have surgical cases. On this morning, his shoes were scuffed, his shirt was tucked in carelessly, and he was sporting two days' worth of hair growth on his normally clean-shaven face. When the receptionist greeted him a pleasant toned, "Good Morning Dr. Chambers," his response was grunted back as he moved down the hallway toward his office.

Jan Thornquist was a patient who began her care with Warren five years earlier. He delivered her two sons and a year after the second birth, performed her urgent D&C when she suddenly began hemorrhaging from her uterus.

"How's my favorite doctor," she said to Warren as he stepped into her exam room. She wore a bright smile.

"Hi, Jan," he said clearly. She was his first patient of the morning, and he willed himself through the encounter. He left the room after performing the yearly gyn physical exam, while his patient got dressed. He returned several minutes later, and with Jan sitting on the end of the exam table he sat beneath her on a stool, and went over the results of her lab tests which were performed a week earlier.

His tone was uncharacteristically flat when he said, "You're doing great. Your blood counts are completely normal, so it looks like the iron you're taking is working, because you're not even close to being anemic anymore." As he flipped to the next page he said, "Your triglycerides and cholesterol are outstanding too." He finished by telling her that the results of her mammogram were completely normal. He stood up and proffered his slightly moist right hand.

As she shook it, she looked into Warren's eyes and said, "Dr. Chambers, you look like you haven't slept in days and you look very troubled."

"It's nothing Jan." He only called patients by their first names when they insisted. "I've just had one too many nights on call."

"Well, you take care of yourself, because I don't know what I'd do without you for my doctor."

He managed to get through the remainder of his thirty-four patients that day without too many verbalized concerns about his depressed, exhausted affect. Usually he was excellent at masking his emotions when he interacted with patients. As he told residents and medical students many times, "Leave all bad attitudes and negativity at the door before you walk in to see the patient. They deserve our best face every single time."

Warren's compliance with his own best advice was marginal.

That evening, driving home, he was lost in thought. He had to slam on his brakes one time to avoid rear ending a car stopped at a red light. The adrenaline rush focused him on the road for the remainder of his drive. About a mile from home he turned into The Sullivan Nature Reserve, and found a parking spot overlooking the valley one hundred feet below. It was quiet. He turned the engine off, let his windows down and deeply inhaled the cool outside air. This nature preserve was his favorite spot when he needed to be alone.

Why am I, what am I, afraid of? This guy was there for me when those bastards tried to crucify me at Creason, and now this. I caused this shit and they wanna destroy him instead. I get up so much piss and fight, and then when it's time to dance, it all just drains out of me...I hate it...why can't I...How did David do it with just a sling and a smooth stone...guts and a steady fucking hand that's how...nerve goddam it!...where's mine?...NERVE, NERVE, RIGHT HERE, I'M RIGHT FUCKING HERE!...Ah hell, what's the point?...Gina's right, my family comes first not some boss that I really don't even know...but he doesn't know me either, does he? It's like me and Max...sorry excuse of a father...I couldn't call him out then or now, and NO I'm not going back over that, not right now.

Early the next morning as he looked in the mirror just after his shower, Warren knew he'd have to get some drops for his red stinging eyes before he got to Winslow.

***

At seven-thirty a.m. on the same Monday, Isaacs would again try to put an end to the Thompson case. He sat at his hospital office desk and closed the cover of the file folder marked "Harold D. Thompson, M.D." Medical reports from Drs. Meyers and Sims were the latest additions to Thompson's relatively small dossier. Isaacs picked up his desk phone and dialed Ron Blazer's inner office phone directly.

"Hi, Mike, hang on just a second, while I finish up with Alyce for two seconds." Alice Haynes was Blazer's Administrative Assistant. A minute later Blazer said, "Sorry about that Mike."

"No problem, I know how it is. I've got some news that should make you very happy..."

"You found a fifty-million dollar donor?"

"No, this should make you even happier — I got the medical and psych reports back on Thompson. He's as normal as they come according to both reports."

"And, why am I supposed to be so happy about that. That really pours cold water on us doesn't it?"

"'Oh ye of little faith,' quite the contrary, it strengthens our hand. Look, if they found that Thompson was seriously ill, or he was nuts, he'd have a right to claim disability and we might be stuck with him for years. These reports say he's well and we say he was willful." There was a grin in Isaacs' voice.

"You sure seem happy."

"You know how I feel about Thompson - he doesn't belong here. He should join that misfit Caruthers and go away — far away."

"Yeah, I *know* how you feel about 'em and pretty soon they'll both be fading pictures in our rearview mirror."

"I hope it goes that easy. From the beginning I've been worried about whether this thing will work. When you first told me about what he had done, I never thought we'd be able to prove it. Then when Cummings told us what those women told him, I started to believe that we might really be able to push Thompson out. But, our last Med Exec meeting made me realize what a bunch of do-gooder idealists we have on this staff, and I won't really relax until Thompson's gone."

They ended by wishing each other encouragement, and both hurried off to different meetings.

* * *

When Warren finished making walk rounds with the Gyn residents, during which they discussed and saw all of their hospitalized patients, he took the elevator down three floors. He got out and walked a few steps across the hall to the doctor's cafeteria. It was mid-morning and the only other people seated were a team of internal medicine residents with their attending physician. They were making "talk" rounds over breakfast. Warren got a cup of coffee which he generously sugared and creamed. He walked to a table across the room and around a corner from the talking doctors and sat down. He was alone, and it was quiet. The front section of the morning's *Detroit Herald*, which looked untouched was lying on the table, having been separated from the sports and business sections which were nowhere in sight. He glanced at the front-page story headlines with no intention of reading any of them in depth until he came to the headline, "Woman Severely Wounded While Saving Seniors." He picked up the paper and read on. The story told of a gun fight that erupted on Stenson Street between rival neighborhood gang members on Detroit's Eastside. The violence occurred in front of a senior assisted living home. Three of the facility's residents were sitting on the porch — two were in wheel chairs. Paula Burnett, a forty-year-old mother of three, who lived next door, ran to the porch and began pushing the seniors through the front door. As she pushed the third senior through the entrance, Ms. Burnett was struck by two bullets. Warren did not take another sip of coffee until he finished the story. Burnett was taken to Creason Medical Center where she survived an eight-hour surgery and was now in critical condition. Warren put the paper down and stared out the window at cars pulling in and out of the hospital's five story parking deck. He remained almost motionless for at least two minutes, and did not hear the cafeteria waitress walk up behind him.

"Dr. Chambers, is coffee all you're having?"

Warren jumped so violently that the waitress let out a short fearful scream.

"Oh, I'm so sorry, but I didn't hear you walk up. Are you okay? I must have been day dreaming."

"I'm okay, Dr. Chambers, you just startled me, that's all."

One of the other waitresses who was working just around the corner came quickly to her co-worker's aid. When Warren and Ms. Bruce explained what happened, the two women laughed heartily. Warren joined them, but his laughter was anxious and devoid of mirth. He apologized to the women and hurriedly left.

Warren went to his academic office, closed the door, and flopped into the chair behind his desk. It was five minutes after eleven. His afternoon was free from clinical duties, as it was every Monday, which allowed him time for academic and administrative work. He was hoping he could make it through the next fifty-five minutes without a call from one of the residents about a patient he'd have to accompany them to see. He tried going thru his email, but he found himself reading the same sentences three and four times. He stopped. He set his watch to alarm at noon, and then leaned back in his chair and closed his eyes.

***

Stewart picked up the phone on his office desk a few minutes after eight on that same Monday morning, and called the office of Winslow's CEO.

"Good Morning, Mr. Blazer's office, Alice speaking, how can I help you?"

"Hi, Alice, Mike Stewart here."

"Hi, Dr. Stewart, how can I help you?"

"I need an appointment with Ron, and I need to see him no later than tomorrow morning. If there's a problem tell him it's urgent."

"Hang on just a minute please."

She placed Stewart on hold. It took two minutes before she broke the boredom of the piped in telephone music the surgeon was listening to while he waited.

"Dr. Stewart, he said he's really booked up until Friday, can it possibly wait until then."

"No, tell him this is one of those things he'll probably kick himself a million times for, if he makes me wait until Friday."

She put Stewart back on hold. She was back in about three minutes.

"He said he can meet with you briefly at six-forty-five tomorrow morning?"

"I'll be there. Thanks, Alyce."

Stewart arrived at Blazer's office ten minutes ahead of schedule the following morning. Blazer was already in his inner office with the door open. He saw Stewart as soon as he walked into the suite. Blazer stood up, moved out of his office, and greeted Stewart with his outstretched right hand. They shook.

"Hey, Mike, how are ya?"

"Good Morning, Ron."

With an open-handed sweep of his right arm, Blazer motioned Stewart to precede him into his inner office. Alyce Haynes had not yet arrived, and the two men had the office suite to themselves.

"What can I do for you," Blazer said in a friendly tone. The men sat across the CEO's desk from one another.

"I've got some unpleasantries to talk about."

"Go ahead."

"It's about this whole mess with Thompson and the Williams girl who died in surgery."

"I thought all that was being handled by the Med Exec."

"Of course, we both know it is, but there's some pieces of it that don't make sense."

"How are you involved?"

"I was part of the committee headed by Celia Green. As you know we were asked by Isaacs to look into the allegations against Thompson. We were told to figure out whether he told the patient's family the hospital screwed up. Thompson was also accused of having offered the family money on behalf of the hospital, and we were told to look into that too."

"It was everybody's understanding on Med Exec that your committee all agreed that Thompson was guilty."

"Oh we did—"

"Then case closed, right?"

"Except for one vote, but the whole thing just doesn't work for me."

"Why not?" There was demand and irritation in Blazer's tone.

"Because your brother-in-law's story, at least the story he told us, didn't make sense."

Blazer jerked his head about fifteen degrees to his left, and he was now looking directly into Stewart's eyes.

"What are you talkin' about?"

"You know your own brother-in-law, right?"

"Fuck you!"

Blazer's face was flushed and ugly as Stewart stood up to leave.

"I was hoping we could settle things quietly. Obviously, we can't so I guess I'll go tell my story to people who want to hear it."

As Stewart rose and turned to leave, Blazer mumbled, "I'm sorry Mike. I wanna hear the rest of what you have to say."

Stewart turned his head toward Blazer who looked pitiful.

"*I'm* sorry, I didn't catch what you said."

"I said I'm sorry, and I want to hear the rest of your story." Stewart sat down.

"Your 'punk brother-in-law', as you liked to call him, told the committee about his conversation with Carla Williamses' mother and her aunt. The problem is, when I spoke with them, they told a very different story. According to the sisters, Thompson never said the hospital screwed up, he never promised them any money, and he never implicated any physicians in any wrong doing or negligence. And, if I ask, they'll come and tell their story to anyone who wants to hear it."

Blazer's face was anguished.

"As, for the convenience store stick-up man..."

Blazer's eyebrows rose.

"...turned hospital administrator, that's a tough one. I certainly understood his loyalty to you, after you saved him from hard prison time, but I couldn't understand what your motive might be for trying to get rid of Thompson. And, then I remembered what absolutely good friends you and Brian Tooley are. I also remembered how "fit-to-be-tied" angry you were with Thompson when he put an end to Tooley's reign of terror in the operating room and tried to get him some help.

Old "Brirate" would have lost a big chunka change going off to Nebraska for help, and you got pissed when Thompson stood his ground."

Blazer was silent. He stared through Stewart as if he was looking into a parallel world. Finally, he focused on his tormentor and said, "What do you plan to do about this?"

"Well the only things I really care about out of all of this are that Thompson gets exonerated, so he can tell the Williams family what happened to the mother of the three children they're now raising, and that the hospital steps up and provides financial support to help them do it."

Blazer offered no alternative lies to explain away the scenario the vascular surgeon presented, nor did he utter any threats. What made Stewart's position unassailable was that he didn't have to prove his tale of conspiracy in a court of law. He only had to convince members of the Winslow community — a community that sustained itself on gossip and had evidentiary standards that were nearly nonexistent. It was obvious that the story Carla's mother and aunt could tell would torpedo Cummings' story, and the circumstantial facts that Stewart uncovered would make believers out of an overwhelming majority of physicians, administrators, and board members.

"How do you suggest we end this," Blazer asked.

"Let Cummings take the fall. Have him go to Celia Green and tell her that he believes he overstated his case. Have him tell her he loves Winslow and he thought what he did was the way to protect the hospital. He should tell her he's been guilt ridden for the last two weeks, and finally decided to fess up. Celia will do the rest."

"You're giving me a total pass on this one?" Blazer asked.

"No, I just offered you one idea of how to end things quietly," Stewart said as he stood to leave. "You have to decide how you want to play it, just like I have, and I hope my idea helps you get to a soft end-point, because if it doesn't get you there, some of my other ideas are a lot messier."

Blazer stood and proffered his hand to shake. Stewart ignored it, and said, "It's seven-twenty, and I'm late for the O.R.." He quickly turned and walked out. Blazer walked over to close his office door. He returned to the chair behind his desk and sat down. He stared at his closed door for several moments, before he reached for the telephone receiver and dialed Cummings' cell phone number.

When Warren walked into the resident clinic Tuesday morning he was smiling as he managed the two large boxes of fresh donuts and bagels, the bag of cream cheese containers and plastic utensils, along with his briefcase. He was cleanly shaven, neatly dressed, and had a buoyant demeanor that his coworkers hadn't experienced in weeks. Instead of brooding in the back office reserved for the staff attending of the day, he stayed in the resident area, joking with them, seeing patients, and complimenting everyone on the good work they were doing.

"Dr. Chambers, you act like you got a good night's sleep for the first time in six months," said Amanda Lessum.

"Yeah, that's part of it," Warren said. "I feel better than I've felt in a long time."

Looking into his bathroom mirror earlier that morning, before and after shaving, it was the first time he witnessed his own smile in a very long time.

Blazer's instructions to his brother-in-law were terse.

"Ron, are you sure this is what you want?"

"You're goddamn right I'm sure. Now just get it done today. You realize that your idyllic little life could come to an end overnight if I wanted to hurt you with this, don't you?"

"Yes, yes I do."

"Then do it ASAP."

Blazer slammed the phone down, but before he could make his next call his phone rang. He picked up and said,

"It's Ron."

"Ron, it's Mike Isaacs. Are you alone so you can talk freely?"

"I'm alone with my door closed, so talk to me."

"That little bastard Warren Chambers called me after eleven last night. I'd been asleep over an hour when he called. He sounded like he'd been drinking, but he was sober *enough*. He told me that if we didn't lay off Thompson, and step up with money to help the Williams family, he'd tell the family everything himself."

"Do you think he's serious?"

"You know, in all my limited interactions with him, I always thought he was a gutless little divot, but he had a ferocity in his voice that scared me. Yeah — yeah, I think he'll do it."

"What are you gonna do?"

"I thought about going to the police."

"For what?"

"For black mail and extortion that's what."

"For threatening the truth?"

"Yeah, I thought about that, and you're right, it's the truth of the thing that makes it tough for us."

"But, even if he tells the family, it's just his word against the hospitals, right?"

"No, not right on two scores. First, if the thing goes to court, he'd devastate any defense we'd put up, and second, he claims he has a copy of the Sentinel Event Report."

"He's bluffing."

"That's what I thought at first, but then, thru his slur, he started reading me parts of the report. I pulled my copy this morning, and it read word for word what I remember him saying."

"I think we ought to drop this whole thing then, before it blows up in our faces."

Isaacs sighed and said,

"We were so damn close, but I guess I have to agree."

"Have you thought about how you can get it over with?"

"I thought about Cummings, and maybe we could ask him to change his story."

"But, if we do that, he'd have something on us, and I don't know him that well, do you?"

"No, I don't, and you're right. I don't know, I'll think up some story for Ceilia Green about new evidence uncovered, and blah, blah, blah. As much as she prizes integrity, I won't have to do anything else."

"Think about this real hard before you talk to her. She's a sharp cookie, and if your story doesn't hang exactly right, she'll know something stinks."

"I'll keep that in mind."

Blazer pushed the receiver button down briefly with his right index finger and then dialed Cummings' cell phone. His call went to voicemail.

"Marshal, call me back immediately, there's been a change of plans."

Blazer would not find out for an hour that his call was too late. Marshall paged Ceilia Green as soon as his earlier call with Blazer ended. She was in early and agreed to meet with him. He was sitting in her office fifteen minutes later, repeating the story he was ordered to tell. Cummings had always been a good actor and a convincing liar. When he left Green's office, she instructed her assistant to call an emergency meeting of her committee.

After speaking with his brother-in-law who called him while he walked to his office after meeting with Green, Blazer was able to quickly reach Isaacs.

"I don't know why he chose to lie and then picked now to recant, but it sure takes me off the hot seat," Isaacs replied to his CEO."

"You let me know when Ceilia calls you, and then I'll pass the word to Sepulveda and Wexler about what to do to head off Chambers."

"Ron have one of them talk to Chambers today, before he shoots off his big mouth." There was deep concern in Isaacs' voice.

* * *

Later that afternoon, Cummings repeated his story of deceit born of his overwhelming concern for Winslow's wellbeing. The committee obviously believed the story and his fabricated contrition because the members voted unanimously in support of Thompson. Green quickly transmitted the new circumstances and the results of the latest vote to Isaacs. He made no comments or gave any other signs that might convey his feelings about the change in Thompson's fortunes.

Chapter Eighteen

Thompson sat behind his office desk trying to concentrate on an internal review of his department's residency program. The evaluation was performed by Henry Davidson's department in advance of the mandatory external review which would be carried out by the Accreditation Council for Graduate Medical Education. The Council's site visit would occur in 14 months, and their findings would determine whether the program maintained its accreditation. It was 5:15 Thursday afternoon, 2 days after the flurry of conversations, and meetings, during which Thompson's fate was discussed and debated prior to the Med Exec meeting. Remarkably, these conversations remained confidential, and Thompson had no knowledge of them.

He did know the Med Exec meeting was underway, and he struggled in vain to digest the report in front of him. His thoughts were about his decision to avoid an active role in trying to persuade committee members, and others, that his actions were in Winslow's best interest. Thompson knew he couldn't stomach the indignity of, in effect, groveling for support. He knew what he did was ethical, and most important to him, moral. By confining himself to passivity, in his calculus, he was making a statement about his unwillingness to remain at Winslow if the arbiters of his outcome differed with him on the profound, yet simple, distinction of right versus wrong.

He sat staring at the report while he pondered his decisions, his inaction, and his what-was-to-come. Earlier in the day, he asked Isaacs' administrative assistant to let her boss know he would be in his office until late evening. Isaacs, he told her, could meet with, or call him there, after the meeting.

Just before six p.m., Thompson picked the receiver of his ringing desk telephone.

"Thompson."

"Dr. Thompson, this is Dr. Isaacs."

"Hi, Dr. Isaacs, I was hoping to hear from you."

"Yes, well I'm calling you in my capacity as Chairman of the Medical Executive Committee."

Thompson's stomach was a jostle of angst.

"As you know, we've been looking into accusations that you violated Winslow's by-laws, with respect to professional conduct, in your handling of the Carla Williams case."

"Of course, I'm very aware of that."

"After lengthy discussions that continued over two meetings, this evening by an almost unanimous vote, the members of the Medical Executive Committee decided that you did not violate any of Winslow's by-laws. This means the investigation into these accusations has concluded, and you remain a member in good standing with all of your rights and privileges intact."

"Thank you so much, that's great news..."

"You'll receive this notification from me in writing within three days.

"...I don't know what to say."

"Good night, Dr. Thompson."

"Good night." As he hung up, Thompson wasn't surprised by Isaacs' distant affect and unwillingness to engage.

At ten thirty, when Thompson got into his bed, he thought he'd fall asleep immediately. Calling Marty Octavio to share his news crossed his mind, but he lacked the energy for talk; he was drained. The rest he craved eluded him as he tossed and fidgeted for almost two hours before drifting off.

He awoke a few minutes after 6 a.m. Once oriented, he thought for a moment about all the things he had to do.

When Thompson finished rounding with his residents he walked over to his office. His ringing desk phone greeted him before he could push open his door. He grabbed the receiver.

"Hello."

"Hi, Harold, it's me, Bonnie."

"Hi."

"You sound winded."

"The phone started ringing before I got through the door, so I came through in a hurry to grab it."

"Do you have some time to talk?"

"Yeah, sure."

"Okay, I'll be right down."

When Sepulveda arrived, Harold motioned for her to sit on the couch closet to the door, while he sat on the small couch near the corner closest to his desk.

"Harold I've had a series of conversations with corporate and medical leadership, members of my department, outside counsel, representatives of the Board of Director's and our insurer about the Carla Williams case. We're all in agreement now, that you should go ahead with your plan to talk with the family."

"You realize that I told the family I would go through the results of the Sentinel Event review with them?"

"Yeah, I remember you telling me that's what you wanted to do when we talked about it the first time, the whole Full Disclosure thing you mentioned."

"Are you telling me that after all this, the powers that be did an about face?"

"Don't be a sore winner. You jumped ahead of where our collective mindset is around here. Be happy that we're trying to change, and let us catch up." She smiled after these words.

Thompson's voice cracked a bit when he said, "I'll keep that in mind."

"What I suggest is, you tell Ms. Williamses' mother, her name is Sylvia right?"

"That's right."

"Tell her she should find a lawyer to represent the family in our negotiations with them."

"You mean this is going to be a protracted back-and-forth, tit-for-tat contest to figure out how much money to offer them."

"Don't be naïve, Harold. We really want to do the right thing here too. But, this is reality, this whole Full Disclosure philosophy is mostly theory, and we also have an obligation, all of us, including you, to protect this hospital."

"So how long do you think the negotiations will take?"

"That depends on how reasonable the Williams and their attorney want to be."

"Oh Lord."

"What?"

"All right, any other suggestions?"

"Yes. I think you should schedule a meeting, have Dr. Chambers there, and advise Ms. Williams to bring whomever she feels comfortable bringing, and lay out all the report's findings. I'll attend along with Bertram, and have the Williams bring their attorney."

Thompson spoke with Sylvia two hours later, and it took her three days to get back to him with a suitable time.

Eleven days later, Sylvia Williams, along with Janis Mae, two other family members, and their lawyer, walked into the Henry Winslow Chairman's Library in the main Administration building. The room was a library only in the sense that it housed a collection of mostly leather-bound books shelved in a continuous line of walnut wood bookcases along one of its two longer walls. The shelves were enclosed by doors inlaid with small prism edged glass windows. Two large windows, in the wall opposite the bookshelves, were filled with a view of the south side of the hospital. The remaining wall space was mahogany paneled. A large portrait of Henry Winslow, the hospital's original benefactor, hung on the end wall farthest from the room's entrance. His eyes seemed to gaze into the distance and he wore a slight smile. Dr. Ignaz Philipp Semmelweis's portrait face was solemn as he stared down at the room from the opposite end wall. Semmelweis was a 19th century physician who studied and then advocated the midwifery practice of handwashing to prevent the spread of infectious disease. These ideas were derided and dismissed in the era of rampant communicable diseases, scant understanding of germ theory, and no antibiotics. In the years after his death, his work was of pivotal importance in decreasing the number of patients who died during hospital stays.

A long dark mahogany table that seated ten people on each side filled the room's center. Thompson rose to greet the Williams family and their counsel when they were escorted into the room by Cathy Weaver. Bonnie Sepulveda, Bertram Wexler, Warren and Sally Woodson rose also.

After greetings and handshakes, the Williamses' took seats next to Sally and Warren who were on Thompson's left. He sat directly beneath Winslow's portrait. Irving Lee, the family's lawyer, sat at the other end with Sepulveda immediately to his left and Wexler sitting on Sepulveda's left side. Lee wasn't quite medium height. He wore a solemn face and looked to be in his sixties. Sparse wisps of hair topped his rather large head and his watery gray eyes were outlined by brown and marron glasses frames the bows of which were slanted upward which perched his angled lens on the tip of his nose. Although his speckled maroon tie with white shirt combination didn't clash with his brown tweed sports coat and dark slacks, they didn't make a stylish match either.

This seating arrangement for Sepulveda and Lee was ironic. The history of their interactions always placed them on opposite sides of the negotiating table. Winslow had a reputation among the plaintiff's bar for refusing to settle out of court on almost every malpractice lawsuit ever filed against it. The hospital's mantra was "The care was excellent." Six times over the previous 15 years, Lee faced Winslow attorneys in court mandated case mediation sessions. Sepulveda was his adversary and nemesis in half of those cases. In past cases, Lee represented patients with cases most hospitals would have been eager to settle out of court, but Winslow, as was its standard practice, insisted on jury trials, and it prevailed six out of the six times. Winslow was advantaged by the politically conservative jury pools its trial courts drew from, and from its role as the largest employer in the county. When Lee first met the Williams family, they told him Dr. Thompson suggested they get a lawyer.

"I questioned them hard about this," he told his law partner Stu Richmond, because I thought it must have been a misunderstanding on their part. But, they stuck to their story. I was really dumbfounded, when Bonnie Sepulveda called me to say Winslow wanted to talk about settling the case before I even filed. I thought I might be hearing voices. I guess my dear old mom was right, "You live long enough, you see everything.' I really wonder what the hell they're up to."

When all were seated, Thompson began by thanking the family for attending, and he expressed his sorrow about the circumstances that made the meeting necessary.

"I profoundly regret the loss of Ms. Carla Williams, your daughter Ms. Williams and your niece Ms. Sipple and Mr. and Mrs. Tate. I knew her only briefly, but she was a bright light with an enthusiastic spirit who was obviously cherished by her children, all of you, and she was loved and admired by her students and colleagues. As I told you, Ms. Williams and Ms. Sipple when we first met in my office, the hospital would conduct an investigation of what happened because Carla's death was so unexpected. As I promised you, once the investigation was completed, I would share its findings and conclusions with you, and that is what I'm going to do today. Are there any questions?"

"How do we know you're going to share the real details with us," asked Johnny Tate.

Sylvia fidgeted in her seat, and with her hands, after her brother's question.

"I think you should hear me out and then decide whether you believe I've given you the true facts of the report and whether you believe the investigation was in-depth and unbiased. And, if you're still in doubt, I can let you read the copy I have here. I can't let you take it, but I'll let you read as much as you'd like."

"Go on," Tate said.

"The first part of the investigation examined the indications for the surgery. What that means is, the Sentinel Event committee investigators looked into whether the surgery should have been done in the first place. They concluded the surgery was proper for three reasons. The first was because the results of the biopsy of the lining of Ms. Williamses' womb showed a precancerous condition. They decided the second reason the surgery was reasonable was because Ms. Williams had first received non-surgical treatment with hormone medication, and the treatment failed. And third, Ms. Williams was adamant that she did not want to have any more children."

Before Thompson could continue, Tate interrupted,

"Is this what we have to sit through, a half hour of how everything that was done was proper?"

"Mr. Tate please, let me get through this before you come to any conclusions."

Tate continued his straight posture, but pushed back from the table slightly and waved his right hand in a hostile motion to proceed.

The room felt tense to Thompson as he continued his difficult self-assignment.

"Next the investigators meticulously examined the records of the procedures and of Ms. Williamses' time in the recovery room. They also interviewed everyone who participated in Ms. Williamses' care. They discovered a major breakdown in communication between the anesthesiology team and the surgeons. They deemed this communication failure as a major contributing factor in Ms. Williamses' death. During the surgery, Carla's blood pressure spiked dangerously high twice. Each time, she was given a medicine called a beta blocker to bring her pressure down. The fact that she was given this medication was never communicated to Dr. Chambers or his team. The beta blocker drug relaxes the blood vessels causing them to open up," Thompson demonstrated by widening a circle he formed with the thumb and fingers of his left hand. "The drug also causes the heart to beat slower, and both of these changes cause the patient's blood pressure to go down. The drug keeps working in the system for hours after it is given. After the surgery, when Ms. Williams began to bleed, it was very difficult to tell—"

"Couldn't they see she was bleeding," Tate asked angrily.

"No, they couldn't, Mr. Tate. Unfortunately, Ms. Williamses' was bleeding on the inside, internally. And, one of the body's natural first responses that should occur when someone is bleeding is that the beating of their heart should speed up. It's usually one of the earliest signals that something is wrong. Ms. Williamses' heart couldn't react this way because of the drug she had been given. If Dr. Chambers had known about the drug, he probably would have been able to figure out much quicker that Carla was bleeding internally and in trouble."

The room was almost quiet now as Sylvia and Sally both dabbed at their eyes with tissues pulled from a box being passed back and forth. Thompson continued.

"Ms. Williamses' surgery was not performed in our hospital's main operating room suite. Instead, it was done in an operating room in our Labor and Delivery area on the sixth floor. Many of our gynecologic surgeries are performed in this suite. Patients who have their procedures done in one of these two rooms are taken to a recovery room in the same area when their surgeries are completed. The last cases for each day, in these rooms, are scheduled to finish by three-thirty in the afternoon. The operating rooms are closed and without staff by four o'clock.

"Once Dr. Chambers and the team realized Ms. Williams was in trouble, he asked for one of the L&D operating rooms to be opened immediately. Dr. Chambers tried to get the nurse in charge at the flow control desk in the main operating room suite to send a nurse and two surgery techs to the L&D area to prepare and staff one of the operating rooms. His plan was to open Ms. Williamses' abdomen, find exactly where her bleeding was coming from and stop it. The nurse was resistant and convinced Dr. Chambers it would be quicker for him to bring Ms. Williams down four floors in an elevator, wheel her gurney across the hospital, and go up one floor to the main O.R.s. She assured him a room would be staffed and ready when he arrived. The investigators concluded the lack of emergency O.R. availability on L&D, as long as any post-operative patients are in the L&D recovery room, creates an unacceptably high risk to patient safety. They designated this safety breech as the second major contributing factor to Ms. Williamses' death."

By now Thompson had a line of teary red eyes on his left side that included Warren, Sally, and Carla's female relatives. He struggled to control his own composure as he continued. He had to clear his throat several times before saying,

"The last major contributing factor the committee discovered was a breakdown in communication between the nurse in charge of flow control in the main O.R. suite and the nurse responsible for executing the order to emergently open and fully staff an O.R. *before* Dr. Chambers arrived with Ms. Williams. The nurse who received the flow control order never understood the urgency of the order to operationalize a room prior to Ms. Williamses' arrival. When Dr. Chambers' team entered the O.R. suite, they were told no room was ready. Dr. Chambers immediately directed those who accompanied him to bring Ms. Williams into the empty O.R. ten feet in front of them. He began preparing the room as best he could. A full O.R.

team, including an anesthesiology doctor arrived in three minutes and the surgery began.

"A blood transfusion was started immediately by the anesthesia team, as Dr. Chambers opened Ms. William's abdomen. While he was in the midst of looking for the source of her bleeding, Ms. Williamses' heart stopped beating. The anesthesia team immediately began CPR, and they gave drugs to help restart her heart. After twelve minutes of resuscitation attempts with no success, the surgical trauma team was called. They tried everything possible to restart Ms. Williamses' heart, and after twenty additional minutes without success Ms. Williams was pronounced dead.

"We believe all of the delays and communication failures uncovered by the investigators are inexcusable and can't be allowed to happen again. In this spirit, we have developed an action plan that will put new procedures and requirements in place that we believe will prevent another tragedy like this."

By now, the soft sounds of crying were constant. Noses were being blown, and stuffed nasal passages became apparent when whispered words were spoken.

"Dr. Thompson, what is being done to make sure each problem really gets fixed," Sylvia Williams asked. Her words were stuffy and her voice was scratchy. "I know you can't bring my baby back, but I want to know that no other patient or family will go through this for the same reasons." Her tone was kind and increased Thompson's respect for her.

"Ms. Williams, the board of directors of this hospital mandates that when an action plan is formulated to eliminate problems that contributed to an unexpected death like your daughter's, all of the plan's elements must be implemented within sixty days."

"Yeah, but how do we know it's really being put in place," asked Lee.

Thompson restrained himself after hearing Lee's question. It grated on him. *What right does he have to say anything while we're trying to disclose the truth and apologize to this grieving family? How dare him!*

"You can be sure, Mr. Lee, because it's my top priority, and what propels that priority is not only my deeply felt regret over the loss of Ms. Williams and her family's pain, but implementing that action plan is also in the interest of future patients and this hospital.

"Ms. Williams, Winslow is very aware of the financial challenges you face because of the loss of your daughter, and because you are now raising her three young children. We realize no amount of money can replace your daughter, we know that. But, in recognition of our role in the hardships you face, we intend to give you financial support to help ease your challenges. Over the next few days, our chief legal counsel, Ms. Bonnie Sepulveda, who is sitting next to your lawyer, will meet with Mr. Lee to work out the details. Does anyone have questions?"

Thompson was relieved when the room was without spoken words for fifteen seconds.

"Well, I believe we're done." The tall department Chair stood and walked over to Sylvia who reached out her arms and hugged him. In a whisper she said, "I appreciate you, I truly do."

"I appreciate you too, Ms. Williams. This is one of the best days of my life."

Thompson hugged Janis Mae and shook hands with a now less reluctant Johnny Tate and his wife.

"I'm not a believer yet, Dr. Thompson, but you have surprised me."

"You'll see, Mr. Tate," Thompson replied with a broad smile, "you'll see."

Warren and Sally were crying in silence, without pause, and wiping away their tears with wads of soggy tissue.

"It's gonna be all right, Dr. Chambers," Sylvia said in a strong voice as she hugged him. "You kept your word and more, and that means the world to me."

"Thanks," was all Warren could get out.

Sylvia hugged Sally as well.

"I'm so, so sorry, Ms. Williams."

"It's okay, Dr. Woodson; you did everything you could do to help my baby."

Sylvia took Sally's hands in hers and said, as she looked into the young doctor's eyes,

"You have to go on now, train these hands of yours to be the best they can be, remember all this, but don't you let it hold you back. You're young and you have lots of good to do in this world, so you go do it."

As Warren shook hands with Janis Mae and the Tates, across the room Lee, Sepulveda, and Wexler were speaking in near whispers.

"Let's meet on Monday, Irving. Will that work for you," Sepulveda asked.

"Yeah, I'm actually open all morning."

"How about we meet at your office at ten-thirty?"

"Perfect."

"Irving, make us a reasonable offer," Sepulveda said quietly, as the three lawyers huddled. If you do that, we can settle this quickly."

***

"Harold, it's Bonnie."

It was eight days after Thompson made the emotionally draining full disclosure to Sylvia and her family. Although the ordeal was not always on the front burner of his mind, it was never far from his conscious thought. Still, this call from Sepulveda caught him a bit off balance.

"Hi, Bonnie, what's going on?"

"I called to let you know we finished up our settlement with Sylvia Williams."

"Really? I'm surprised. After our conversation before the big meeting, I was sure that the whole thing would drag on for weeks. What happened?"

"Well, I asked Lee to come back to us with a reasonable offer, and to our absolute shock he did. We accepted, and things wrapped up quickly."

"How much did we give her?"

'I can't disclose exact figures. But, I will tell you it was a little north of seven figures."

"Huh, I gotta ask you, did Lee take a third?"

"Yes, he did, that's standard."

"Jesus! For what? He couldn't have put more than twenty hours into this case."

"You're right, but we don't make the rules about what these guys charge."

"Is that a third of the "north of 7 figures, or is Sylvia left with north of seven."

"No, she she's left with a third less than we settled for."

"Is there any way to get to justice and decency in this world?"

"Harold, the bottom line is there is enough money to raise the kids in a comfortable environment, we stipulated trust funds be created for all of them so there'll be enough money for them to attend college, and we got Sylvia to agree to take a short money management course that's sponsored by the wealth management division of the hospital's accounting firm — that way there's no hungry stock brokers involved."

I guess that's all good, but Lee should be ashamed of himself." *I'll tell the bastard that someday.*

"Harold, I'm proud of all this. It really turned out very positively. You need to believe you did a good thing because you did. And, you also need to know that you've made some enemies through all this."

"Yeah, I'm very aware of that."

"Well, watch yourself friend, I'm here if you need me. I really hope you're around here for a long, long time.

"Bonnie, that's the kindest thing I've heard in a long while. Thanks. I just might come calling more often than you'd like."

Epilogue

Warren's mood was often pensive during the days immediately after the meeting with the Williams family and the attorneys. His affect was not foul or abrasive, but neither was it bright or mirthful as he often was. Thoughts of what he could have, or should have, done differently when he operated on Carla plagued him. He couldn't shake the second guessing. Other memories flooded in as well. He stood on the paved edge of the Sullivan Nature Reserve's parking lot looking out over the flat land below one early evening, and remembered his phone call to Isaacs and its aftermath.

People who knew Warren would not describe him as even a light drinker, but he dumped two quarter filled glass tumblers of a single malt scotch, a gift from a patient two years earlier, before he called Isaacs. His anxiety was tormenting him and the whiskey calmed and focused him into action. He smiled several times thinking about the conversation with the Chief Medical Officer in which he stood up for the man he finally accepted was his friend. After ending the call, he walked upstairs and trundled into bed with Gina who was awakened by his lumbering movements.

"Warren! You smell like a still, what's the matter with you?"

"Really? This from the vineyard who downs more than a half a bottle of wine every night with dinner?"

"Why the fuck did you wake me up?"

"I just got off the phone with Winslow's CMO."

"Why would he call at this time of night?"

"He didn't, I called him?"

"For what?"

"To tell him that if he didn't lay off Thompson, I'd tell the family everything I know about what happened to Carla."

"Oh my God, what kind of a fucking idiot are you, do you realize..."

Her harangue went on loudly and emotionally for almost a half hour. Unlike so many times in the past, as his wife ranted on, his usual angst was replaced by calm. He remembered feeling like the invisible electronic neck collar that shackled him, from his adolescence on, to a force field he could not penetrate, vanished. Instead of fear about his life, he felt free and positive. His constant feeling of being inconsequential was gone, and he realized that anyone who treated him that way again would do it at their peril.

Warren was seeing patients with the residents when he got a page from Thompson's office.

"Ob/Gyn, Dr. Thompson's office, Cathy Weaver speaking."

"Hi, Cathy, it's Dr. Chambers."

"Hi, Dr. Chambers, one minute and I'll put him on."

"Warren, how are you?"

"I'm okay, what's up?"

"I'm just calling to let you know, Winslow reached a settlement with the Williams family. I don't know the exact amount, but it's enough to let them live comfortably, and the kids will have enough money to attend college."

"Amazing huh? This place actually did the right thing."

"I think they got pushed from a lot of sides."

"What makes you say that?"

"I don't know, I guess just the way it all fell into place so quickly at the end. The powers that be suddenly wanted to dance to a new beat. I'm sure it will all come out some day."

"Yeah, I'm sure it will. For now, we can just be happy it happened."

"You're right. Well, I gotta get runnin'."

"Hey, Dr. Thompson?"

"Yeah?"

There was a pause.

"Thanks."
"For what?"
"Everything."

* * *

Thompson announced his resignation two years later. As he confided to Marty Octavio, "I've gotta find a place where my ideas and what I do don't keep a bull's-eye on my back."

Three months later, after a well-deserved rest, the former Ob/Gyn Chair took a position with a national patient safety think tank and consulting group called Safety Circle. He travels to hospitals around the country and the world promoting and helping to implement Ob/Gyn safety strategies.

Mike Stewart was not loud, but he was relentless in telling the tale of Ron Blazer and Marshall Cummings to Winslow's managers, directors, grass roots physicians, and some benefactors. His respect among his peers, and the veracity of his story, allowed him to achieve his goal. Four months after the hospital came to an agreement with Sylvia Williams, Blazer took a job with a large health insurance company and moved to Connecticut. He found his brother-in-law a position, and they started over, together.

Winslow's embrace of full disclosure ended before Thompson's departure. The hospital came under pressure from the defense firms it used. By communicating with contacts on Winslow's Board of Directors, several law firm principals convinced board members, they would save them large sums of money by returning to the old scorched earth mentality underlying the mantra, "The care was excellent." Although Sepulveda believed in the efficacy of what was achieved in the Williamses' case, she didn't protest because she didn't have passion for Thompson's process.

Irving Lee was also no fan of full disclosure. After Sid Richmond debriefed him about his experience in the Williams matter, Lee told his partner, "Not a bad way to make a buck I guess. But, looking back at it, Winslow was so wrong and so exposed in that case, I probably could have doubled what we got if we did it the old fashion way."

Warren and Gina separated just before Thompson's departure. Warren filed divorce papers several weeks after the private detective he hired delivered unshakeable evidence of Gina's ongoing extra-marital affair with a man she met through an online dating service. Warren also handed his lawyer evidence of Gina's eighteen-month old cocaine addiction. He couldn't believe he missed it. These facts were enough for a judge to award him full custody of their two children. A year later, he gave up his dream of an academic faculty position, and rejoined his former private practice. His feelings about the death of Carla and the circumstances of her children, now without their mother, or a father, motivated him to initiate the ongoing "big brother" relationship he developed and maintained with them.

CPSIA information can be obtained
at www.ICGtesting.com
Printed in the USA
BVHW031104260921
617565BV00015B/313